ON
SCIMITARS
AND
SCALPELS

Printed in Australia
Cover and internal design by Shawline Publishing Group Pty Ltd
First Printing: August 2023

Shawline Publishing Group Pty Ltd
www.shawlinepublishing.com.au

Paperback ISBN 978-1-9229-9368-7
Ebook ISBN 978-1-9229-9379-3

Distributed by Shawline Distribution and Lightningsource Global

A catalogue record for this work is available from the National Library of Australia

More great Shawline titles can be found by scanning the QR code below.
New titles also available through Books@Home Pty Ltd.
Subscribe today at www.booksathome.com.au or scan the QR code below.

ON
SCIMITARS
AND
SCALPELS

TIMOTHY GERRARD

ON SCIMITARS AND SCALPELS

TIMOTHY GERARD

*Dedicated to James "Steve" Thorpe, my good friend,
I miss the laughter.*

The first people to suggest that I might become an author one day were my mother, Margaret "Peg" Gerrard, and my Form Four English teacher, Mr Green. You both planted the seed. Further thanks go to friends for their editing and reading; Graeme Fletcher (aka the comma Nazi), Bill Legge, Vicki Smith, Ryan Popolier, Georgie Swanson, Garry Baker, Debbie Pearson, Andrew Powell, Kate Legge and Janet Gerrard. A special note of thanks to my pharmacist Raj Gupta who provided me with much useful information on India and Hinduism as well as my medications. My thanks to Tom Flood for your manuscript appraisals and ongoing support. Finally, I would like to thank Brad Shaw and the team at Shawline Publishing for the support and guidance given to me on my journey into the world of publishing.

1

I was only thirteen the day I killed my first man. It was both an accidental and intentional act. I was on my own, travelling, what I thought, far, far away from the warm comforts of home and family. I was not used to the rigours of caravan travelling: the constant dust and grit in my eyes, nose and mouth. The disgusting smell of the camels. Sleeping on the unforgiving shale of the semi-desert. Food that would never have made the table at home, and constantly sore back, bottom and thighs from riding my ill-mannered pony all day.

Our caravan was travelling from my hometown of Acre, on the coast of Outremer, to Jerusalem. There I was to enter into an apprenticeship with a well-renowned physician named Hadar. My merchant father had arranged the apprenticeship after considering my temperament, talents and aspirations. My father had business dealings with Hadar, mostly supplying the medical goods and equipment he required, but also in the reciprocal trade of the kinds of religious relics that were becoming very sought after in Europe.

Our small party consisted of sixteen pilgrims, three of whom were women. They were all on foot and carried staves or walking sticks to aid their passage. The six of us on horse or camelback were either merchants or bona-fide travellers. Accompanying us was a train of twelve pack animals, mostly camels, all roped together in a line, carrying merchandise and belongings.

Despite the truce between King Baldwin of Jerusalem and the Emir Saladin, no one travelled the roads of Outremer without an armed escort due to the prevalence of raiding bandits and Bedouin tribesmen. It was for this reason that our caravan was escorted by a small troop of Knights Hospitaller. There were three knights all mounted on fierce and warlike destriers, two sergeants and a young squire mounted on the smaller and gentler palfreys.

'Ippolito. Why so glum?' asked Raymond, the young Occitan squire from the south of France, as he pulled his chestnut palfrey up beside me. As usual, his still puppy fat and freckled face was smiling beneath its shock of strawberry blonde hair inherited from some distant Viking ancestor.

'I am not used to this. I suppose I am missing home, and a comfortable bed and seat,' I replied, giving emphasis to the latter.

'I suspected as much. You don't seem your bright and alert self. Cheer up. Tomorrow we should reach Montjoie, The Mount of Joy, and the very well-appointed monastery of Saint Samuel. I can assure you that you will feel very much better when we get there,' he replied with some enthusiasm.

I was about to ask what made Saint Samuel's so appealing when suddenly wild ululation and yelling broke out from the heights of a rise to our left. Almost immediately more than two dozen riders on horses and camels appeared from over the top of the rise. They were around four hundred paces away but were charging rapidly down the slope. All were waving swords or short spears in the air.

'Circle the pack animals,' came the bellowing command of Sir Giles above the noise of the attackers. 'Pilgrims and others either in the middle or prepare to defend yourselves.'

Raymond had quickly turned and galloped off to assist with circling the pack animals. This was quickly done as they were all roped together. Most of the pilgrims quickly rushed to within the circle. A small few of the men, with staves for walking, stood bravely around the circle to help defend it.

'Knights and sergeants on me to the left,' thundered the voice of Sir Giles as the Hospitallers raced to join him, drawing their long broadswords. One of the sergeants, Edward, was waving a vicious-looking chained mace above his head. None were heavily armoured, but neither were those attacking us. They bravely formed their small group into a line, with just enough space between each other to wield their weapons without endangering those beside them and charged at the oncoming marauders, yelling, 'St Jean, St Jean and Jerusalem.'

I saw Raymond standing with the few pilgrims willing to fight. I drew the slim but deadly stiletto my father had given me and ran over to join him. Raymond's blade was a short falchion. We were both still too small to carry or wield the great long swords the knights used.

'At least we have weapons and not staves,' said Raymond, trying to swallow. 'I pity those with only staves. They will break at the first blow of a sword or scimitar.'

We watched as the two charging parties came together with a great clash of metal. Sergeant Edward's mace was the first to make a kill as its spiked head smashed into the jaw, mouth and nose of a bandit, leaving a bloody, pulverised mess resting upon dead shoulders. Sir Giles removed the head of another rider with a great, swinging blow that continued to follow through and took the nose off a second rider beside his headless comrade. Within moments, the five knights and sergeants were locked into a whirling melee of flashing swords and spears, screaming horses, curses, dust and blood as they battled twice their number.

'Oh, Sacred Father,' gasped Raymond, 'the rest of them are coming for us.'

About another dozen bandits were charging directly toward our small band of barely defended individuals. Their cries and yells sent a chill through my mind and body, to say nothing of the small, wet discharge that squeezed through my nether end.

As the bandits drew closer, I noticed one of the pilgrims step forward from our line. He was tall, more powerfully built than the other pilgrims and had a much heavier and longer stave than his fellows. Grasping the stave at its narrow end, thereby giving him the length to stay out of sword reach, he swung the stave at the legs of the leading camel, bringing the rider down in front of our group. Immediately three of the pilgrims fell on the unseated rider with their staves, beating him about the head and quickly rendering him unconscious and bloodied.

The four pilgrims were joined by some others from both outside and within the circle, and they set about to repeat the strategy in two separate groups facing the hostile on-comers.

'We have a better chance if we work together as well,' said Raymond.

We moved together, drew and pointed our weapons. Unfortunately, the pilgrims had brought down a number of riders but not all had been subdued, continuing to fight with swords on the ground. The slaughter they wreaked among the pilgrims saw most of them fall. I watched as the tall pilgrim was felled by a slashing cut across his abdomen, spilling his bowels, their contents and his blood onto the desert shale.

Suddenly Raymond and I were faced by a wickedly grinning bandit with great gaps between his few blackened teeth, raising his sword ready for a swipe at one or both of us. He appeared to laugh at our much smaller blades and raised his sword higher for the kill.

'Now!' yelled Raymond.

We ran simultaneously at him, blades raised, which put him off guard for a second, allowing both of us to barrel into him and bowl him over along with Raymond and myself. I felt the stiletto rip from my hand as I rolled away from the bandit and jumped to my feet. Raymond was on his feet as well, an unbloodied falchion still in his hand. The bandit lay on his back, gripping the handle of my stiletto buried to its hilt in the soft part of his body immediately below the sternum and rib cage. The bandit was grimacing and staring down in shock at the handle. His legs suddenly kicked and jerked, his eyes rolled back in their sockets as blood flowed from his mouth and nose, and then he lay still.

Raymond and I were both stunned and did not notice the remaining raiders had penetrated our perimeter and were breaking into the circle of pack animals. They were busy leading them away from the fracas by the conveniently tied ropes. One of the raiders had a struggling female pilgrim slung across his saddle and with his free hand was beating her into subjugation about the head and shoulders.

I looked again at the dead bandit, his face frozen in its rictus of agony and death, my blade still inside him, the blood slowly spilling from his mouth and suddenly, I vomited all over the corpse.

'Nice touch.' Raymond laughed.

2

There was no point in pursuing the bandits as they herded our pack animals away, whooping and yelling with delight over their captured bounty. We were simply too few to even contemplate such a rash action. Of our original party of twenty-eight, only sixteen still stood upright. Eight pilgrims lay dead on the bloody ground, some still grasping the staves with which they had bravely defended themselves and the group. Of the Hospitallers, two, a knight and a sergeant, lay dead. The other three, one of them very pale and only semi-conscious, all carried wounds of varying severity. Their horses were not unscathed either. Of those who had taken refuge within the pack animals, the only victims were the kidnapped woman and a merchant who died defending his pack camel from abduction.

Of the bandits, sixteen lay dead, eight around the skirmish with the knights and eight around the pilgrim perimeter. We had taken a heavy toll on the bandits, just as they had on us. The big difference was they had our pack animals, belongings, shelter, food and water.

Sir Giles did not waste any time in assessing the situation, and while Raymond was still bandaging a long but shallow gash to his left forearm, he called us all together.

'We have all lost friends and comrades here today but there is no time to grieve if we are to stay alive. It is over a day and a half of arduous uphill travel to Montjoie, the nearest refuge to our current location. We have no food or shelter and only the limited water left in our personal skins remain to us. We do have six serviceable horses that are unscathed and can be ridden on rotation every hour to ensure we all get some rest in the journey that waits ahead of us. Be aware we must walk through the rest of this day, through the night and into late tomorrow before we can have any real rest or sustenance. We do not have the time, or the body fluids, to bury our dead in this heat. All of you gather what you still have and be ready to move on in fifteen minutes.'

We all had misgivings about leaving our dead unburied but Sir Giles had been correct about there not being the body fluids in all of us to bury eleven men in the desert scree and make the journey as well. We were already thirsty from the heat of battle as well as the heat of the day. I checked my water skin and found it only half full. I imagined it was probably the same for the other travellers. Knowing a little of what lay ahead, I resisted the urge to take a pull of water from the skin.

I had one last task to perform and that was to retrieve my stiletto from the bandit's dead body. I wandered over to where he lay and stared at the mess of blood and vomit, the hilt of my blade standing up in the middle of it. I gingerly grasped the sticky handle and pulled. I was surprised by the resistance to my effort as the soft flesh of his torso clung lovingly to the blade. I tried harder a second time and the blade came free with a wet sucking sound. I cleaned the blade as best I could with some leaves from one of the hardy desert shrubs that grew there before putting the blade back in its scabbard.

I offered the first ride on the pony I had ridden to one of the women who was particularly distressed, as I learned, by the death of her pilgrim husband and the abduction of her sister-in-law. Her name was Enid. I felt sad for her in her grief and gently assisted her to mount. I then took the lead by the reins and led pony and rider over to the caravan line. It was only a moment before Sir Giles waved his fist forward in the air and our tiny caravan moved off to the east.

About an hour later, Sir Giles called a brief halt to change riders. Raymond came up beside me, leading one of the destriers with the more seriously wounded knight in the saddle. At some stage, he had become unconscious and was strapped to the saddle's cantle to prevent him from falling. He was deathly pale.

'Ippolito, your face is redder than a cardinal's cap.'

'And my feet hotter than the Devil's kitchen,' I replied between teeth, lips and tongue that were becoming stuck together in a thickly cloying paste of what little saliva I could produce in my mouth.

Raymond reached down and picked up a small smooth pebble, wiping the dust off it onto his tunic.

'Here,' he said, handing the pebble to me, 'put it in your mouth and gently roll it around. It will help keep your mouth moist.'

I thanked him and put the pebble in my mouth. Within a few moments, it was working.

The day's heat and hardship drew itself out. Only after everybody had had a rotation on horseback did I allow myself to take my turn. The sun was mercifully setting behind us and the heat of the day slowly dissipating. I allowed myself a small mouthful of water to rinse and swallow. The temptation to guzzle more of the precious fluid straight down was enormous, but I resisted, stoppered the skin and put it back by my side. As I did so, I saw Raymond smiling and nodding approvingly at my self-control.

Sir Giles was unrelenting in keeping us moving on, even as darkness took hold of the land around us. Fortunately, the desert skies were clear and the stars and a gibbous moon were bright in the sky, effectively reducing the risk of injury whilst journeying at night. Even so, Edward, the remaining sergeant, went ahead with an improvised torch its light reflecting off his bald head.

As he went, he called out any potential obstacles such as holes and other trip hazards.

We plodded our weary way on through the night. Fatigue and the shock of the day's events kept us mostly silent with very little conversation passing between us. The desert night was cold and I was glad that despite my fatigue, I had to keep on moving. It did help keep me warmer than I would have been had we been resting and trying to sleep on the desert floor.

It was on one of our hourly change of riders that I saw Raymond lead his horse and its rider over to Sir Giles and quietly say something to him. Sir Giles moved his great horse next to Raymond's smaller pony and felt the neck of the rider in several places, searching for a pulse. He slowly looked down and then nodded his head to Raymond. Sir Giles got down from his destrier and quickly tied it to a nearby gorse bush. Together, he and Raymond unbound the knight from the cantle and gently lowered the body to the ground. Again, there was no time for a burial or last words.

Sir Giles was all business again as he mounted his horse and called out to the troupe, 'Spare mount over here for whomever needs it.'

It was the two surviving merchants who immediately moved to grab the chance of an hour off their feet by claiming the mount. What was ridiculous in this midnight moment was that both merchants came to blows with each other trying to mount the beast from opposite sides and headbutting each other as they tried to step into the stirrups and swing into the saddle. Amidst a lot of cursing and swearing at each other, Giles swung his gauntleted fist across both their heads, sending the two tumbling to the ground.

'Enid,' called Giles, 'the saddle is yours. These two fools can keep walking.'

Enid came up to the horse and Raymond assisted her to mount

bringing her almost eye to eye with Giles.

'Thank you, Sir Knight,' she said.

We continued through the night. I maintained the rationing of my water by only taking a small mouthful, rinsing and then swallowing at every change of riders. Despite this, I still felt tormented by thirst and my tongue was constantly dry. I was a growing thirteen-year-old boy and by this time was also ravenously hungry. I imagined Raymond felt the same. He was not complaining and I followed his example.

We continued making our slow way through the night in tiredness and silence. Eventually, the sky in the east began to lighten and before too long a burning, bright yellow sun began to bore into our tired eyes. In the distance, I could just see the silhouette of what looked like a monastery sitting atop one of the mountains in the range ahead of us.

'Behold,' called Sir Giles, 'Montjoie and Saint Samuel's. Be of good cheer. We shall be there before the end of day.'

A very brief and ragged cheer greeted this news. We were all just too tired, sore, thirsty and hungry.

3

Montjoie was at the top of a hill and the site of the monastery and church of Saint Samuel. The hill was named Mount of Joy as it was from there that the earliest crusaders first beheld the city of Jerusalem. It was beginning to grow dark on our arrival and the lights of Jerusalem could be seen on the eastern horizon. Many of the pilgrims knelt in worshipful and thankful prayer at the sight.

Used to catering to the needs of pilgrims and travellers, the monks offered us a hearty and nourishing repast of local goat's cheeses, olives, dates, cold chicken and wine from their vineyards.

Sated and weary, I collapsed into a comfortable cot and slept like a log for the rest of the night. No amount of snoring, farting and grunting around me in the dormitory could wake me.

I had expected to wake tired, stiff and sore after our tribulations the next morning. Instead, I woke refreshed and eager for the final stage of our journey into Jerusalem. The road twisted its way up through the central ranges of the kingdom. As we got higher and higher, the spectacular views that opened up to us were undiminished by dust and heat haze.

It was mid-afternoon when we passed under the arches of the Damascus gate and into the Holy City.

As the others were dismounting outside a monastery, Raymond rode up beside me and said, 'Follow me, Ippolito. I will guide you to Master Hadar's house and apothecary.'

I suddenly felt awkward, anxious and a bit ashamed. My clothes, hair and body were filthy after the travails of the last two days. I regretted I had no clean and respectable clothing in which to greet my new master in, particularly one who was a physician and, in whose footsteps, I hoped to follow.

'The Jewish Quarter is in the southern district, so we must cross most of the city to reach Master Hadar's premises,' explained Raymond.

We came to an intersection and I could not help but note a party of pilgrims, all in brown habits, slowly and painfully shuffling on their knees along the crossroad, their hands pressed together in attitudes of supplication and prayer.

'We are just crossing The Via Dolorosa,' Raymond informed me. 'Those pilgrims are hoping to emulate our Lord's suffering by progressing their journey on their knees to the place of skulls where our Lord was crucified.' Then added with some disdain, 'They could better spend their time learning to defend the city.'

His horse seemed to agree with this sentiment as it lifted its tail and deposited several lumps of steaming horse turd into the path of the pilgrims.

We passed by the old palace of the Hasmodean kings, what was left of the Wailing Wall, and entered into the Jewish Quarter of the city.

'Well, Ippolito, this is your destination,' announced Raymond as he pulled his horse up outside one of the shop fronts on the street. The shop was fronted by an awning that shaded a small selection of various potted plants. I assumed them to be herbs of medicinal value. Above the awning swung a sign with a mortar in the middle filled with leaves of different shapes spilling up and over the mortar's rim.

'I trust we will meet again, Raymond. Despite its difficulties, I have enjoyed my journey with you and will consider you my first friend in Jerusalem.'

'I too.' Raymond smiled as we shook hands farewell. I dismounted and handed him the reins of my horse. He turned his horse, leading the one I had ridden, and headed back through the city.

I stood alone outside the apothecary, once again considering my dishevelled state.

'Are you window shopping or would you care to come in?' came a voice, interrupting my self-deprecation.

I snapped out of my thinking and turned to the shop front door where stood an older-looking man, but one who nevertheless radiated a vitality about him that suggested the vigour of a much younger man. His moderately long hair and beard were both a silvering white and framed a wizened face, the most striking aspect of which were brown eyes so pale they could be described as yellow. He smiled and showed a full set of teeth.

'M-M-Master Hadar?' I stammered in surprise.

'Master Ippolito de Medici. I have been expecting you sometime soon and the departure of the young Hospitaller squire confirmed who you might be. Please come in.'

Hadar's residence was two-storied. Downstairs were the business premises which consisted of a shopfront with a heavily shelved interior packed with vials, sachets, jars, pots and other containers all holding various herbal, mineral and a few dried animal ingredients. This was where Hadar's principal business lay. Behind the shop was a small clinic and examination room with a high cot, a chair and cupboards for whatever medical or surgical equipment was needed for the procedures he carried out there. Behind the clinic lay the storerooms. I breathed a whiff of nostalgia as the herbs and other ingredients of the storeroom reminded me of the scents, aromas and fragrances of my father's spice and herb emporium warehouse in Acre.

In a corner at the rear of the storeroom was a cot, a chair, a small table and medium-sized chest for storage. A small oil lamp sat upon the table next to a handbell.

'This is your space, Ippolito. It is your bedroom, your study and your guard post. Should you see or hear any intruders on the premises, ring the bell as loudly as you can and try to sound like a guardsman giving the alarm. When your belongings arrive, you can store them in the chest.'

'I'm afraid everything I have is upon my person. Bedouin bandits made off with our caravan three days ago.'

Hadar's eyebrows rose in surprise.

'Perhaps, a little later, you might tell me about this.'

Along one wall of the storeroom, a narrow staircase led upstairs to the living and domestic arrangements of the building. The stairwell opened into a living area that was lined with shelves filled with books, scrolls and papyri as well as numerous jars of different sizes containing what I hoped were only animal parts. Two comfortable-looking lounges, a table, some simple wooden chairs, a Persian carpet and a lamp stand completed the room.

'Through there is my bed-chamber,' he said, pointing to a door. 'You may pass through it to the balcony roof when summer's heat will see us eating and sleeping out there.'

'Each day,' he continued, 'Hannah, a good woman in the Quarter, brings in meals and attends to cleaning and repairing clothes as needed. You will meet her tomorrow. But I forget myself. It grows late and you must be hungry and thirsty after your journey. Come let us see what Hannah has left us for our evening meal and perhaps you might tell me about these desert bandits.'

Thinking about my stiletto, I wondered just how much to tell this gentle and caring healer about the raid and my small part in its defence.

Later, after a meal of cold chicken, olives, salad greens with dates and cheese for dessert, Hadar and I both sat back in comfortable repletion.

'That is quite a tale for one so young and I believe every word of it,' he said before pausing to give me a wry smile and then continuing. 'I shall have to try not to get your anger up!'

It was good to share a laugh with him.

4

Early the next morning Hadar and I were downstairs in the apothecary.

'Your first duties will be here in the shop,' he said. 'What do you know of plants and herbal remedies?'

I was glad of everything I had picked up from Maria, our family nurse at home in Acre, and began a short recitation of the dozen or so common herbal remedies she had put to use.

'Well, that is a start, I guess.' Hadar sighed without any praise or enthusiasm.

'In my library, you will find a large book, the *Liber Herbalis*. Your father told me you speak and read Latin and Greek.'

I nodded but did not mention that I also spoke Arabic, Hebrew, as well as the *lingua franca* of the Mediterranean trading ports.

'I want you to bring this book downstairs and keep it as a guide. It will be the bible of your learning, so to speak. Naturally, I also expect that you will read it and learn from it in every spare bit of time you have in the shop and your cot space. Over dinner each night, I will test you on what you have learned, fill in any gaps and answer any questions you may have. Later I will introduce you to other healing treatments and cures that I keep and prepare for the public. You will need to know not just the herbs, but their individual qualities. You must learn which parts of the plant are efficacious and the individual preparations for their use.

'All the herbs and other curatives are stocked in alphabetical order on the shelves. Their names are in the Latin form. You will need to learn these, as well as their common names. Most of your customers will know what they wish to procure, but others will ask you for a cure or treatment for a particular disease or ailment. The *Liber Herbalis* will help you in this.'

'Yes, sir,' I replied. 'I am very much looking forward to this.'

'Good. Now go and fetch the *Herbalis* and start reading. When your eyes grow tired, you can dust the shelves and clean the vials.'

So began my introduction to herbalism and becoming an apothecary.

Most of the customers of the shop were the wives or servants of the local households seeking cures for common ailments and afflictions. These I quickly learned and my job became less worrisome to me as I grew in my learning and confidence.

It was a few months later a girl about my age came into the shop. She had a head of long, unruly black hair which was poorly contained under a scarf. Black curling wisps of it were escaping at the sides and along the fringe. Her eyes were hazel in colour, which was a welcome change from the almost universal dark brown colouring of most Mediterranean eyes. She was not as dark-skinned as others were in the east. Her skin was more a light honey in colour and her face unblemished by smallpox scars, pimples or moles. It looked silky smooth. I thought she was perhaps a little too skinny compared to the few other girls I had seen in Outremer. I did not mind. Her face was most pleasant: small and heart-shaped with a finely pointed and tilted nose.

'Is Master Hadar not about?' she asked.

She was obviously familiar with the business.

'He is upstairs at the moment. Perhaps I can help you. I am Ippolito de Medici, Master Hadar's new apprentice,' I responded.

'I am pleased to meet you, Master Ippolito. My name is Ruth.'

She had a beautiful smile. All her teeth were intact and flashed a pearly white.

'Ah, my mistress requests the following: one measure each of dried angelica, wormwood and pennyroyal.'

I knew these were the ingredients of an abortive and felt a little concerned for her. I hoped they were for her mistress and not her.

Ruth seemed a little awkward and embarrassed as she took the small packages and passed over a few local coins for their purchase. She thanked me for my service and before leaving, said, 'I look forward to doing business with you again,' and then she flashed that smile at me again.

I liked her.

That night, after dinner I asked Hadar about the hazards and risks of the abortives I had provided to Ruth.

He explained the common problems of abdominal cramping, overdosing and haemorrhaging.

'You seem concerned about something, Ippolito. What is it?'

Without mentioning Ruth by name, I told him about our encounter that morning.

'And was this young girl named Ruth?' he asked knowingly.

'Why, yes,' I replied. 'You know her?'

'She has been coming here for a couple of years now. It is a sad story but not an uncommon one. Her mother is the daughter of one of the fortune-seeking adventurers that came here just after the first crusade. He took a local wife, a Jewess, so I am told. He stayed on in Jerusalem but never made the fortune he was hoping for. Of course, the two are long dead now. Their daughter, Ruth's mother, married a sergeant of the Temple. Sadly, he was killed in a skirmish with Bedouin tribesmen about ten years ago. Unfortunately, through falling into poverty and being taken advantage of by an unscrupulous money-lender, her mother was faced with the choice of being sent to the dungeon or entering into a brothel wine-house to make a living. Either way, the life of her daughter would have been precarious.

'Ruth shares a room with her mother at "The Rocking Horse". She earns her keep by working in the kitchen, house-cleaning, doing the never-ending laundry of the premises and running errands for "the madame", as she did today.'

He paused for a long moment and then finished, 'The girl is wise beyond her years.'

I felt saddened by this story. Ruth had so much light about her. I remembered her flashing smile and I did not like to think of her as dwelling in the darker corners of this world.

She returned a week later to request a measure of wild amaranth for 'her mistress'.

'It is her moon flow and she suffers greatly,' she explained.

'The amaranth will lessen her flow,' I offered, 'but if she has pain and cramping, some raspberry leaves will provide relief. Mix them in the same tisane in equal quantities and take it with every meal while the flow is in progress or the symptoms persist.'

Ruth looked at me appreciatively.

'Thank you. My moth– er, my mistress will be grateful. Thank you.' Again, that flashing smile graced and gave light to her face.

'You seem very knowledgeable for your age,' she said.

'My father has sent me here to learn the basics of the business in the trade of medicinal herbs and goods, not so much its practice. I want to learn more about actual medicine and the science of healing. My father also wants me to learn about the trade in religious relics and antiquities. The priests tell us they have miraculous healing properties as well.'

'You seem to have a natural ease and ability in relating healing matters to people. I, too, would like to learn of the healing arts and be a wise woman one day. Many of the other girls and women in my mistress's household tell me I have a gift for it.'

Her smile brightened again with the telling of this.

'I have been learning greatly from this book,' I said, reaching under the counter for the *Liber Herbalis*. 'Do you read Latin?'

I opened the book on the counter before her. Her eyebrows rose in amazement and appreciation.

'No. I don't. But the illustrations are of passionflower and peppermint. Could you tell me what the writing below them says?'

I did so, and so our afternoon became a communion of shared knowledge.

Ruth knew and recognised many of the herbs from their illustrations and had a practical knowledge she said she had garnered from her 'mistress's' instruction. I did not tell Ruth that I already knew her 'mistress' to be the madame of 'The Rocking Horse'.

'Oh, my goodness. It is mid-afternoon. My mistress will be cross that I am late home,' Ruth said in a sudden panic. 'I must go.'

'Tell her I had to hunt for the amaranth in the warehouse,' I said, 'and there were other customers waiting in the shop.'

'I hope that will work.' And there again, that flashing smile. 'I will come again soon, Ippolito.'

I fervently hoped so.

5

Ruth visited the apothecary whenever she could over the next few months. Sometimes on the business of 'her mistress', when we would spend some brief time together poring over the *Liber Herbalis*, and at other times for just a fleeting hello before she went about other business.

These moments were to be interrupted when Hadar assigned me to the other key aspect of my 'apprenticeship', that of learning about the trade in religious relics.

One morning Hadar called me into his lounge and introduced me to a gentleman he simply introduced as Rudolphus.

'That is the only name you shall know him by,' said Hadar emphatically.

Rudolphus, by his accent, was of central Italian origin. I later learned he was originally from Tusculum in the Alban Hills not far from Rome. He had a weathered and tanned complexion that complimented what was an athletic build. His dark eyes seemed to be always moving around as if assessing his surroundings in search of any immediate risk or hazard to himself. His long black hair fell to his shoulders, where it had been recently and neatly trimmed. His beard had been trimmed as well and was rakishly pointed beneath his chin. He reminded me very much of an adventurer, albeit a somewhat roguish one. He bowed his head to me with a smile.

'You will be accompanying Rudolphus on a...' Hadar paused. 'What shall we call it? An... expedition.'

They both smiled at this turn of phrase.

'Have no concern, Ippolito, that you will be placed under any duress during this time. You will be visiting other cities and towns within Outremer and various monasteries and churches along the way. I expect you will be well accommodated during this time and your basic needs will be amply met. The expedition should be about three months in duration. In this time, Rudolphus will teach you about holy relics and where their markets will return the most profit. Your father has amply provided for you and Rudolphus in this venture.' This last piece of information was said with a knowing smile and a nod to Rudolphus.

There was something secretive going on between the two of them, and, I suspect my father knew about it as well. He was, after all, putting up the funding for the 'expedition', but I decided not to worry about it. Traders and merchants had all sorts of information and secrets they kept to themselves or sold on for a price. It was just business.

I was given three days to prepare, during which time I was able to tell Ruth about my impending departure and the nature of my journey, of which I really knew very little.

'How I envy you. It will be such an adventure for you. I sometimes wish I were born a man. I will miss you, Ippolito. Stay safe and come back.'

She placed her hand over mine and gave it a gentle squeeze.

I knew in my heart I would miss Ruth. My leave-taking was filled with a sweet sorrow. Still, I knew I would return and we would have much to talk about. She, like Raymond, had become another true friend in Jerusalem.

Three days later, Rudolphus and I departed Jerusalem, heading north on the Damascus road, bound, he informed me, 'for an out-of-the-way monastery'.

The road between Jerusalem and Damascus was well-travelled and we required no armed escort for this part of the journey.

Rudolphus began informing me about the business he was in once we were clear of Jerusalem's city gate.

'You must realise, young Ippolito, the trade in holy relics is at best a deceptive one, yet it brings much comfort and healing to the faithful. I have noticed that often, if you believe strongly enough in something, faith may bring healing or other miracles. It is to these believers, their churches and communities that we offer the fruits of our trade. You have no doubt heard of the holy cross upon which our Lord was crucified?' he inquired.

'Of course. It resides in Jerusalem under the protection of King Baldwin and the church.'

I knew something of the history.

'Correct. And it is largely intact, with the exception of a few small shavings and splinters that have been taken from it as gifts of holy relic to the Holy Roman Church, some of the other Eastern Churches, and a few kings and princes across the Christian realms. Yet all over the Christian countries there are supposed splinters of the holy cross that, amazingly, have seen actual miracles of healing delivered in their name. I suspect there are more than enough of these not-so-holy splinters to make a second cross. It is like the bones of the saints. If we took all the bones of Saint Peter lying in churches, cathedrals and monasteries across Europe and Outremer, we would find that the blessed saint existed in not just one body, but four or five.'

I had not considered all this, and in truth, was somewhat disturbed by this revelation.

'What makes a relic holy and valuable is its ability to perform miracles. I do not know,' Rudolphus continued, 'if it is the relic, the hand of God that is rewarding faith or something inside the individual faith of a believer that brings about the miracle. It does not matter to one such as myself, or for your father, for that matter. What matters is the pilgrims who travel to worship and pray at the sites of these relics. They bring enormous trade and benefit to the economies of the cities, towns and trading centres where these relics are kept. And don't forget this; when and where there is wealth, so is the church, the state, and of course, trade and business.'

I now understood my father's interest in holy relics. It was simply business as usual and not some religious obligation he felt. For hundreds of years, the very business of every church, cathedral or monastery was based partly upon the faith of believers in a supposed holy relic that was buried beneath its stones or encased in some fabulously jewelled reliquary.

'Tomorrow we shall be visiting a monastery of sorts. Not exactly the most holy and spiritual place, but one that does provide for the needs of the Holy Church and the faithful.'

We spent the night in a large inn that was stationed to accommodate travellers a day's travel from Jerusalem. Many travellers and pilgrims were spending the night there. The food was excellent, and Rudolphus and I had separate and comfortable beds in a quiet room at the end of a corridor in the dormitory.

Luxury.

6

The next day, around mid-morning, we turned off the road and into the wilderness. The ground had a predominantly grey, broken shale surface that held the heat more than the road upon which we had been travelling and I soon grew thirsty. There were the usual grasses and thorny scrub of the region interspersed by a few stunted trees and rocky outcrops. We progressed in a westerly direction with no road or signage to guide us. Rudolphus led me along what was little more than a goat track at best.

Around midday, we arrived at a small monastery with a graveyard and some small, ramshackle dwellings alongside it. The main building was in a poor state of repair and I noticed that much of the masonry was cracked or broken in places, and in other places, the mud and daub that had been used for repairs gave the outside of the building a very rundown, patchwork appearance. Alongside the building, some goats were foraging in the sparse grasses and scrub that surrounded the monastery. A lone milk cow was tied to a post beside one of the other dwellings while a newborn calf suckled at its teats.

We dismounted, tied our horses to the gate post, and entered the grounds of the monastery.

Rudolphus pulled on a rope beside the old, oaken door. In the distance, I heard a bell ring and shortly after, a rather dishevelled-looking old monk opened the door. He smiled warmly in greeting.

'Ah, Rudolphus. Welcome back to our humble monastery.' He paused and then turned a cautious eye on me. 'And who is your good-looking young companion?'

'Brother Dismas, this fine young fellow is Master Ippolito de Medici. He is accompanying me to learn something of our trade.'

He said the last word with a peculiar emphasis.

'Ah! A de Medici. I see. I see. All of the business it is then?' he asked, raising his eyebrows.

'Yes, Brother Dismas. All of it. Upon his father's instructions.'

'Master de Medici,' he said and turned to me, 'welcome to Saint Photius's.' He then dipped his head in deference to my name. 'And how is your father, Bartolomeo?' he asked me.

'The last I saw, he was doing well,' I replied, not giving away too much about his age and health.

'Well, come in. You are in time for a humble meal.'

We ate a filling but not very flavoursome meal of beans, lentils and peas washed down with a glass of wine. As we finished our meal, Brother Dismas dabbed his lips with the cuff of his cassock.

'So, shall we begin our tour?' asked Dismas.

'In its entirety,' replied Rudolphus again with some emphasis.

Dismas led us first to a storeroom lined with shelves upon which lay numerous desiccated and stained bones: whole arms with hands attached, individual fingers, leg bones with feet attached and unattached, a multitude of ribs, hip bones, and of course, skulls. On one shelf some of the fingers had rings placed upon them. Other bones had what appeared to be some remnant and faded archaic script scratched upon their surface.

'This is our warehouse where we keep the bulk of the relics we prepare,' said Dismas proudly.

Realisation dawned upon me that the monastery was, in fact, a factory where fake relics were being crafted. I looked at

Rudolphus in astonishment. He simply nodded as if to say yes, it is.

'But let us start at the beginning,' said Dismas.

Dismas led on and we progressed through the monastery past some dormitories, a kitchen that had seen better days, a small chapel that had a number of broken pews, and a library which I was keen to have a look at. Finally, Dismas led us outside to the graveyard.

'Many centuries ago, this site was not just a graveyard, but also the scene of an ancient battle. I know not which one, but there was a great slaughter and many bones lie beneath our feet. These bones are already beautifully aged and suit our purposes here quite well.'

I looked around the graveyard and noticed two of the brothers working at a large pit beside which were piles of brown dirt and assorted bones. Some of the bones were shattered and broken, whilst others, which were intact, had been placed on a bench not far from the pit.

After a brief examination of these 'treasures', as Dismas called them, we moved back inside to another room that contained several small vats lined up along the walls.

'Here the bones are cleansed of their dirt, sorted and selected for their various attributes. Take for example these bones.' He held one up for me to inspect. 'See how the mark of an arrowhead has cut into the bone? Such a bone we might present as having belonged to Saint Sebastion. He was executed by the Romans and died pierced by so many arrows, he resembled a pin-cushion.'

I was somewhat in dismay over all of this, but in truth, a part of me had to admire the industry of the monks.

In another small room, two brothers were busy with diluted inks and quills, inscribing some of the bones variously in either ancient Latin, Greek, Syrian or Aramaic. This, Dismas said, was to give some of the bones an impression of having ancient heritage and having been passed along through the ages.

The final stage of the monks' industry was the packaging of each of the relics. This took place in a woodworking shed where one of the monks and a skilled lay brother from a nearby village fashioned caskets in which the relic would rest. Each casket was skilfully fashioned, artfully carved and lined with a silken cloth.

I have to admit that the packaged result was quite impressive. I could not help but wonder if the shin bone of Saint Priscilla, resting in its silk-lined casket in the apse of Saint Peter's church in Acre, had not come from here. I had prayed for Giacomo, my dead brother's eternal rest whilst kneeling before it, and the thought that it might have been a fake disturbed me.

'Does the Holy Church not know about all of this?' I asked with some incredulity.

'My dear boy.' Dismas laughed. 'The Holy Father, the Patriarch of Jerusalem himself, was here just last month to inspect the premises and, of course, to place his own personal orders.'

7

Rudolphus and I spent that night at Saint Photius's and left early the next morning, Rudolphus's saddlebags containing several 'special orders' destined, he said, not to the churches or cathedrals of Christendom, but to the private family chapels of the rich and the royal of the Christian realms.

'Bartolomeo will make a tidy profit on this expedition,' he informed me.

I was still in a quandary over what I had learned the previous day and said nothing in response. In a way, I felt ashamed about my family's role in such a massive deception of so many hearts and souls.

We continued on for much of the day while I maintained my ruminating silence.

That night we sat around a campfire hidden between two gentle rises in the landscape so as not to attract the unwanted attention of any bandits that may have been about.

Later that evening, Rudolphus noticed that I was still brooding and asked, 'Have yesterday's revelations disturbed you, Ippolito?'

'Yes. They have,' I replied. 'I don't understand how the Holy Roman Church and the other churches, after preaching all they do to help make us worthy of redemption and resurrection, can engage in such bold, two-faced lies to the faithful.'

'If you only knew, Ippolito.' He laughed cynically to himself and then continued, 'The whole church is based on lies and control of the public mind. Believe me. I know.'

'What do you mean, "I know"?' I asked, suddenly defensive of my faith and my church, despite the inner misgivings I was having.

'It is a long story, Ippolito. Do you want to hear it?'

I was not sure I did, but I said, 'Let us hear it. Then I will decide what I believe.'

'Well, for a start, Rudolphus is not my real name,' he began. 'I was given the name Guiseppe at birth and was born into the Colonna family of Tusculum in the Alban Hills of central Italy. You may have heard of them.'

I had. The Colonnas had been trading and business partners with Papa. Their wealth and influence extended not just to the peasantry who farmed and worked their extensive properties all over the Mediterranean, but they were also powerfully represented within the Holy Church, counting several bishops, archbishops and cardinals from amongst their family. I told Rudolphus this.

'Very good, Ippolito,' he replied. 'And it was my destiny to join the Holy Church as well. Being the third son of the count of Tusculum meant that I should take holy orders, as per custom amongst Italy's foremost families. It also meant that I could use the auspices of the church to advance my own and my family's fortunes.

'I was nine years old when my father left me in the care of the priests and monks that surround the papacy. I was given over as a novice and acolyte into the care of one Father Sylvester. He was one of the principal linguists in ancient languages to be found in the Church of Rome. He was easily fluent in ancient Greek, Roman, Syrian, Aramaic, Hebrew and Arabic languages, as well as many of our modern tongues. He was also the head librarian and archivist. Only he and the Pope had a key to the archives.

He was very good to me and I have to admit that despite his use of me I still think of him fondly.'

'What do you mean "use of me"?' I asked.

'To use the language of those within the Church of Rome, I was his "manness". A bed-warmer. His night-comforter. Do you know what I mean?'

I was not sure I did and said so.

'Do the words sodomite or catamite mean anything to you?'

They did, thanks to my brother, Giacomo, having told me about them, along with the rumour that some of the Templars engaged in these acts.

'But God destroyed Sodom and Gomorrah for the sinfulness of their unions. You don't mean to tell me that a priest of the Holy Church would– do– do that.'

'Sylvester never practised penetration upon my person. He maintained that a man's fundament was designed solely as a portal of exodus for the body and that any intrusion into that part is to go against the will of God. Be it between men or between men and women.

'As I said, I was principally his bed-warmer and night-comforter. It was only on rare occasions that he would move his part between my thighs, kiss the back of my neck and shoulders until he had done his business.'

Again, I was shocked by yet another revelation about activities within the church.

'Couldn't you say something to someone or report him to a bishop or a cardinal?'

Rudolphus guffawed at this and slapped his thigh.

'What! When most of them were practising some form of sex either with each other or upon victims that they either procured, lured or forced to their beds, or some other squalid and convenient corner of a church building. They even use the Bible to justify themselves to themselves.'

'How so?'

'Johnathon and David, the beloved disciple, the naked youth at Gethsemane. I can even give you some quotes.'

I was aghast and said so.

'Ippolito. Do not believe for one moment that every monk, priest, bishop, cardinal, or even the Pope, is holy, chaste and celibate like the Lord Jesus Christ. Some of our Popes have been notorious.'

'Who? When? I don't believe you.'

These revelations were all becoming too much for my already shaken faith.

'Just over two centuries ago, Pope John XII was said to preside over what became called the papal pornocracy. It was said that he turned the Lateran Palace into a school for prostitution. Virgins, widows and female pilgrims were fair game to his lusts and their rape by the Pope was commonplace. But it was not just women he lusted for. He used the wealth of Rome and the Papal States to sate his appetites for gambling and just about every other type of sexual license, including incest with his nieces.

'He came to an early, bad end when he died, apparently of an apoplexy, in the arms of his mistress at the age of just twenty-seven. He had been Pope since he was eighteen years old.

'Less than a century later, another shameless debauchee, Pope Benedict IX, mounted the throne of Saint Peter. Over the twelve years of his enthronement, he so disgusted and upset the Roman people that they eventually rose against him and forced him to flee the city.

'Not every Pope of a sodomite inclination has been licentious though. Only twenty or so years ago, the English Pope, Nicholas Breakspear, who became Pope Hadrian IV, maintained a very private and personal relationship with his paramour, the great intellectual, John of Salisbury.'

'But surely this cannot be. Has not someone reported or complained about this breach of God's Law to the Curia or another court of law?' I interjected.

'Be sure some have tried. About a century ago, a young, fiery and ascetic priest named Father Pio Damiani wrote a book called the *Liber Gomorrhianus* in which he revealed the widespread prevalence of Lateran Palace depravities. He detailed sins of simony, clerical concubinage, masturbation, pederasty, as well as sodomy. At the time, Pope Leo IX praised the book as a revolution, but was quickly convinced by the members of his Curia that it was all an exaggeration, and so the Pope did nothing about it. Later, another Pope, Alexander, tried to gain possession of the book and have it destroyed.'

I was quite overwhelmed by all of this and did not wish to hear any more about it, and adamantly said so.

'Very well, Ippolito. Perhaps we can discuss the contradictions within the Bible at another time. But I say this truthfully to you: trust God, but do not trust the Church of Rome.'

8

Sleep was a stranger to me that night and I felt very irritable the next morning. Questions regarding what Rudolphus had told me had kept running through my mind but had led to no answers. I wanted to ask Rudolphus more about what he had learned of the Roman Church and the goings-on within the Lateran Palace but I was still angry with him for upsetting me with exactly those same kinds of revelations.

The next day, any conversation between us was somewhat sparse, but a day later I had let go of my brooding and we resumed being amiable travelling companions.

Our tour took us to towns and cities throughout Outremer and into their churches, cathedrals and monasteries. Rudolphus added to his collection of relics which he gained either by appeal, purchase, trading, deception or outright theft, which shocked me yet again. However, I had to admire his cunning and creativity throughout all of this. He really was a very likeable rogue and scoundrel.

There was one memorable incident that illustrated Rudolphus's daring and ingenuity that I shall briefly relate. We were visiting the tomb of an obscure saint, by name of Digitas, located in a monastery outside of Sephoria in the Galilee.

Rudolphus had a special order to acquire something of the saint's person. Father Demis, the abbot in charge, a huge man with an equally huge beard, told us there was absolutely nothing of the saint's remains that could be given away or sold. He was adamant about this and I could sense Rudolphus's mind scheming away to achieve the object of his mission.

Rudolphus appeared to accept the abbot's decision in good grace and then asked the bishop if he and I might pray beside the remains of the godly saint. The abbot acquiesced to this humble and faithful request and escorted us downstairs to a crypt where the remains were laid out on a stone coffin.

Rudolphus knelt in apparently humble prayer beside the saint. Upon finishing the prayer, he looked up at the abbot and said, 'Please, Father, may I kiss the blessed hand?'

The abbot again allowed the request.

Rudolphus gently raised the hand to his lips, his face hidden by his cowl. It seemed he lingered on the kiss for a moment too long, but the abbot said nothing and I wondered what he was up to. Rudolphus then returned the hand to its resting place and turned to the abbot with a most beatific look upon his face.

'Oh, my heartfelt thanks,' he mumbled to the abbot, his eyes scanning the ceiling as if there were angels circulating above us.

Thus, we left the monastery without saying another word. Rudolphus was beaming in an apparent ecstasy of joy all the way back to our horses.

Once outside and clear of the abbot's eyes, he turned to me and spat something into his hand.

On his palm lay one of Digitas's skeletal fingers.

'Time to move on,' he said giving me a conspiratorial wink, 'and quickly, I think.'

We rode off into the western desert wastes, leaving behind a shouting and gesticulating abbot, who obviously had now discovered the deception and theft, surrounded by a group of nonplussed-looking monks.

We hastened to the coastal plains of Outremer for the rest of the day and in the evening, had found the comfort of an inn by the docks of the coastal port of Haifa.

The next day we were up early and on the coastal road heading south to Caesarea Maritima.

'We should reach Caesarea Maritima this evening and the comfort of "The Pilgrim's Sandal" next to the old Roman Mithraeum. Tomorrow we will purchase some attire appropriate for our purposes.'

'Which is?' I enquired.

'To appear as scholars and not the dusty traders and adventurers we look now.'

'Scholars! Why?'

'Ceasarea Maritimae was where the supposed saint and apostle, Paul, was held for two years before being sent to Rome. It was one of the earliest Christian centres for theological study. The school boasted over thirty thousand theological treatises mostly written on scrolls and codices, with some in books. It was, at different times, home to visiting Christian scholars such as Origen, Eusebius and Pamphilius.'

'I have heard of Origen. Wasn't he the one who fully castrated himself so that he could be in imitation of our Lord's pure and celibate state?'

'Yes. And what a bloody fool he was for that,' came the terse reply. 'My hope is to pass ourselves off as a scholar, and his assistant from Rome, wishing to visit the archives of the bishopric. Our intention will be seeking early church correspondence relating to the Council of Nicea.'

'And what will be our real objective?' I asked, knowing what a devious nature he had.

'This is where I will need your help. Your scholarship in ancient Greek and Latin will be most helpful to me and it will be texts composed in them that you will be reading and examining. I will work on the ancient Syrian, Hebrew and Aramaic texts. We can save time like this.'

'And what will we be looking for?' I asked, wondering what he was up to this time.

'Anything that might damage the Church of Rome.'

9

Two days later, we were seated in the old scriptorium of the monastery, surrounded by shelves upon shelves that held scrolls upon scrolls and codices upon codices. Another room accommodated books in a similar manner.

'And how many years did you say we would be here?' I said a little caustically to Rudolphus upon seeing the scope of the task he was proposing. There was no order or attempt at cataloguing the mass of texts.

'First, try to ascertain when a text was written. If it is first century, as in dated from the reigns of either Tiberius, Caligula, Claudius, Nero, Vespasian or Titus, then put it aside for closer examination later.'

We were not bothered by any monks or priests during our times in the library, and it was on the fourth wearisome day of our search that I noticed something unusual about a papyrus. It seemed somewhat stiffer than usual. I turned it over and examined the back of the sheet and there, carefully cut to size, was another papyrus loosely stuck to the back of it. I held it up to the light and could see that there was a script on the inner aspect of the second sheet. Very gently, I began to peel the two papyri apart. Fortunately, they separated easily. I placed the page in front of me and saw that it was written in an ancient Latin text but the words made no sense when I tried to translate it.

I called Rudolphus over and showed the papyrus scroll to him, telling him the details of how it had been secreted behind another scroll.

'But the text does not make any sense,' I said.

'I believe it is written in a cipher,' replied Rudolphus. 'You have done well to find this, Ippolito. It is bound to be very secretive, high-level information. I just hope I can crack the code of it.'

He did break the code, and in a matter of minutes.

'We are in luck, Ippolito. It is in the Caesar Cipher. It is a simple cipher that substitutes the original letters of the text with letters three positions further on in the normal alphabetic sequence. I think this may be exactly what we were looking for.'

He sat down with a quill and a blank papyrus. An hour later, he had finished deciphering and translating the ancient text. He had a most gleeful look of satisfaction on his face.

'Well. What does it say?' I asked impatiently.

'Here. Read the translation,' he said and passed me the papyrus.

It read:

To our faithful servant Saulus in the twelfth year of the reign of our beloved Emperor Nero.

'This must be dated about sixty-five *anno domini*. Just before the outbreak of the Jewish war against Rome,' I said, making some quick calculations in my head, and then continued reading.

The news of your success in establishing temples of universal love and peace throughout the Eastern Empire has greatly pleased our beloved emperor and god Nero. He extends his divine gratitude. He is most desirous that you continue your exhortations in favour of co-operation with the authorities and the payment of taxes to Imperial tax collectors. He has read copies of some of the letters you have sent to these temples, or churches, as you call them, and is very desirous that you commence work on this concept of gospels to ratify and sanctify what you have already achieved. As you would know, the situation in the land of Judah is extremely unstable at the moment and, despite your successes in other territories of the Eastern empire, the pacification of the Jewish masses must be a priority in the region. Our agents are circulating news that you are languishing in prison. We trust this will keep you safe from the Sicarri and Zealot assassins you mentioned in your last correspondence.

Yours in service of his divine Emperor

Epaphroditus, secretary to the Imperium

My hands were beginning to shake as the ramifications of what I had just read began to dawn on me.

'Who– who is Saulus?' I asked Rudolphus, not really wanting to know the answer.

'He is the thirteenth apostle. Saint Paul. The Liar!'

10

We left the monastery with Epaphroditus's letter secreted beneath Rudolphus's cap and returned to The Pilgrim's Sandal.

'You knew that we would find something like that letter, didn't you?' I said to Rudolphus later in our room.

'Yes.'

'How? I mean, what made you think that we might?'

'I need to go back to my story about my experiences in the Lateran Palace as a youth. Is that alright?'

'It could not shock me any more than today has. Go on.'

'Father Sylvester noticed, very early on, my gift for languages and began to show me texts and documents that are – how shall we say – not generally available to most scholars... or many priests for that matter.

'He would retrieve the key to the archives from its supposedly secure location in his room, a location he never tried to hide from me, incidentally. Whilst in the archives, he would select certain codices and papyri. Most of the texts were letters of polemical defence from, or attack on, other Christian sects. Did you know there was a group – the Carpocratians, I think – who followed the example of the disciples in Acts and lived together with everything in common?'

'So? What was wrong with that?'

'Spouses were also in common.' He laughed. 'But I digress. Knowing where the key to the archives lay allowed me ample opportunity to slake my curiosity about the very early church. There was ample opportunity whenever Sylvester was on a spiritual retreat or staying the night at Castel de Sant'Angelo, which he did often after some of the regular welcoming feasts the Pope held for visiting dignitaries.

'During those months, I discovered and read much that changed my mind about the holy history and nature of the Latin Church. Most significant were the very early versions of the gospels that are considerably different from the ones that you hear in church as Holy Canon today. Aside from errors of fatigue and poor lighting, there have been deliberate insertions, deletions and very clear editing by a long line of theologians, copyists and scribes who felt they could improve the message, or more sinisterly, wished to insert their own agenda. There is enough of it to make you wonder about what real truth could lie therein. Added to this, there were damning documents that revealed the nature of the unwholesome relationship between the empires of Rome and Constantinople and the infant churches: a relationship of power, control, corruption, hypocrisy and depravity.

'On one occasion, I became overly bold and stayed late into the night and the light of the early dawn. Unfortunately, I had closed my eyes and fallen asleep. I was discovered by a Lateran Palace guard whilst in the restricted area of the library archives. In brief, I knew I was in big trouble and could easily wind up one of those unfortunate bodies that disappear into the Tiber on the basis of what I had discovered and read. I was a threat to the security of the organisation. I managed to flee but not before being recognised. Going home was not an option as I knew church agents would be watching out for me there.'

'What did you do?'

'I drifted north through Terni, Perugia, Florence and then Pisa, scratching a living by stealing food either in the marketplaces or the groves of the countryside. It was in Pisa that I met a kindly benefactor. To cut a long story short, that was the beginning of the long and lucrative relationship I have had with your father.

'I digress,' he continued, 'That letter from Epaphroditus to Saulus, or Paul as he renamed himself, will be worth more than any other antiquity I have brought to your father before.'

'Why would Papa want it? What could he do with it? The Latin Church would just dismiss it as another forgery from church history saying it was generated by enemies of the church,' I pointed out.

'Correct, Ippolito. You begin to see the wheels within the wheels. But it is not to the church that your father would offer it. It is to the Holy Roman Emperor, Frederick I, *Barbarossa* as they call him. To him, it would have huge value as a deterrent to Papal ambitions in the current dispute they are having over who holds real temporal power in this world.'

'The Guelphs and the Ghibellines,' I said, naming the two parties within the empire on either side of the dispute.

'Correct, Ippolito. Again, more wheels within wheels.'

After a short pause, I said, 'I think my head has had enough revelations for today.'

It was spinning.

My sleep was poor that night as my mind turned over question after question to which I could, again, find no answer.

As we broke our fast over boiled eggs, cheese and olives the next morning, there was a foremost question I had to ask.

'Why would Paul have made all this up?' I asked.

'I believe it was a combination of his flawed personality and political and religious opportunism on his part. A quest for wealth and influence. First, let me put it to you that Paul was a compulsive liar and what is the downfall of all compulsive liars?'

'They do not remember all their lies and to whom they said them and sooner or later are found out.'

'Let us take one of Paul's, or "Saulus", most obvious lies. Luke claims in the Book of Acts that while ship-wrecked on Malta, Paul was bitten by a viper. The locals fully expected him to swell up and drop dead on the spot. When Paul did not die, the locals supposedly began to say he was a god.'

'So, what is the lie?'

'Any Maltese local will tell you there are no deadly venomous snakes on Malta.'

I could not help it but a small irreligious chortle escaped my throat at this obvious stretching of the truth.

'The letters of Saint Paul, the Book of Acts, the gospels and letters of the disciples are full of distortions and contradictions about the life, teachings and miracles of Jesus. I think Paul even tries to justify his lying somewhere in Romans when he says something about his untruthfulness making God demonstrate His truthfulness. A somewhat spurious and convoluted argument, I think.'

'Okay. So, Paul cannot be relied upon to tell the truth. That does not explain why he went to all this trouble writing all these texts,' I queried.

'That brings us to another motive for Paul's activities. Fame and money. I think Paul liked being admired and popular. He was after all travelling all over the Eastern Empire and winning converts to his creed. He was fed and housed just about everywhere he went. At times, he is quite boastful about himself and what he believes he is achieving,' responded Rudolphus.

'I think that one of the big attractions for Paul,' he continued, 'was the money. I do not believe that anywhere are we told that Paul ever delivered any of the monies he supposedly collected for the Temple in Jerusalem or, for that matter, any of the other churches he claimed needed funds.'

'I admit that the prospect of fame and money would be an attractive proposition to just about anyone,' I concluded on this point. 'However, I believe that the real reason Paul or Saul or Saulus, as Epaphroditus and the historian Josephus refer to him, was that his work was politically motivated. At that time, and for decades beforehand, Israel and Judea had been hotbeds of insurrection, revolution and dissension against Roman occupation, taxation, and oppression. Not only that, their king, Agrippa II, was a puppet king for Rome and was too busy kissing Roman backsides to keep his position of wealth and power. All the dissension, disruption and protest of the Jews put Agrippa's kingship in jeopardy not only from the Jews but his dissatisfied puppet masters in Rome as well.'

'Now imagine if someone comes along with a supposedly divine and miraculous creed that preaches humility, obedience, charity to the poor, turning the other cheek, peacemaking, receiving your rewards in heaven, loving your enemies and the love that God has for everyone.'

As he was speaking, Rudolphus began to wave his arms around for emphasis, an egg in one hand and an olive in the other.

'What a wonderful solution to all of the problems Rome and Agrippa have with Jewish resistance. But, who to orchestrate all this? Who but the powerfully persuasive Saul or Paul? Gifted in Greek rhetoric and philosophy he was the perfect agent to bring about this huge change in Jewish thinking and also across the entire Roman Empire. I think Paul gave himself away when he preached obedience to the Roman authorities as placed there by God and the willing payment of taxes to them. I cannot see any faithful Jew swallowing this piece of Paul's promulgations.'

As if to emphasise this last point, he put the last olive in his mouth and made a deliberate gulping sound as he swallowed it.

I sat down and let out a long breath. I had not realised I had been holding it while Rudolphus was making this final, and to me, even more logical explanation of what appeared to be Paul's letters and gospel of lies and hypocrisy.

'You make my head spin, Rudolphus. Come, let us return to the road home so that I can think about all of this.'

11

It was good to return to Jerusalem after the three months spent on the road. I had grown and changed into another person whom I was not too sure I knew just yet. There was the boy who had spent three months on the road visiting some unusual and unorthodox locations, been an accomplice in the theft and forgery of holy relics and had the very foundations of his religious and spiritual beliefs shaken to the core. Quite a rite of transition.

I only knew two things as I stepped over the threshold of Hadar's household. First, I wanted a hot bath in the old water barrel that was kept by the back door for such purposes and to wash all the dirt, filth and sweat of three months journeying from my person. I could do nothing about the soiled nature of my religious faith as my doubts and disbelief could not be washed away so simply.

Second, I wanted to see Ruth.

The next morning, we farewelled Rudolphus. His saddlebags had been largely emptied, their contents now secreted safely in Hadar's storeroom. They would travel to my father in Acre under escort with the next merchant caravan leaving for the coast. I knew Rudolphus would have Epaphroditus's letter secure somewhere upon his person and he would take it personally to Papa.

I resumed my place at the apothecary counter and waited each day for Ruth to come in. I knew where she lived and worked but as she had never volunteered this information to me, I felt unable to visit her there.

When Ruth did eventually return to visit the apothecary, I saw that she too had changed in ways that I could not quite identify. She seemed older and wiser in many ways. I noticed she was wearing a new tunic and had her belt cinched in such a way as to reveal other, more physical changes about her. I was pleased that that flashing smile of hers was still the same, though.

Ruth noticed changes in myself.

'You have grown taller and leaner,' she commented. 'Your face is so tanned and your brown hair has golden tips through it from the sun.'

She asked about my travels and I told her many of my adventures and of what I had seen and learned along the way. I told her of Saint Photius's and its business of 'relic creation'. Ruth thought this story was rather funny. I did not tell her about the revelations at Ceasarea Maritima.

'I should like to meet this Rudolphus one day. He sounds an interesting fellow.'

She sighed and turned the conversation to the reason for her presence.

'Can you help me with a treatment for the watery flux? There is much of it about and many of the women in... our household are unable to work.'

'There are many treatments for the flux depending on its cause,' I said, pulling out the *Liber Herbalis*. 'Let us review the signs and symptoms.'

We were deep in discussion about the availability and best use of the different herbs when I noticed Hadar quietly leaning against the door jamb to the shop. I had no idea how long he had been observing us from there.

'Greetings, Miss Ruth.'

'Greetings, Master Hadar.'

'I see the pupil is now becoming the teacher,' he observed as a slow smile crept across his face. 'Are you interested in herbal lore, Ruth?'

'Yes, Master Hadar. I very much would like to be a wisewoman that is able to offer healing and comfort to the sick.'

'She already knows a great deal,' I offered in support.

Hadar raised his eyebrows at this.

'Ippolito has shown and taught me much from this wonderful book,' she said, moving a hand over the *Liber Herbalis*. 'I want to know everything that is written in it and Ippolito is helping me.'

'I see,' responded Hadar thoughtfully. 'Noble and worthwhile objectives for a girl your age. If he is not busy with customers or other duties, please feel free to call upon Master Ippolito's extensive knowledge anytime.'

He was smiling broadly as he said this and then added, 'I'm sure Master Ippolito would not object to you joining our table in the evenings and we can further discuss matters of herbs and healing as part of your education.'

Ruth and I were momentarily stunned by this offer and then we spontaneously turned and hugged each other, laughing and clapping for joy as we did so.

'Yes! Yes! Thank you, Master Hadar. Thank you so very much.'

I had never seen Ruth looking happier.

12

Ruth and I were able to meet most evenings at Hadar's dwelling where, when he was not visiting patients, he maintained his practice and household. Somehow, through natural charm and an obvious yearning to be a healer, Hadar readily accepted Ruth into our circle of learning. He said there was definitely a future for her as a wise woman – 'a much more learned one than others of that calling,' he said. It was only a matter of a few short weeks before we had both absorbed the entire contents of the *Liber Herbalis*. Hadar had quizzed us both closely and separately on our knowledge of the book before he allowed us to move on.

'This is only the beginning. As you both know, the herbs and plants of the *Herbalis* are predominantly western ones. There are many more herbs and plants in the east which have beneficial and healing properties. Then there is learning the most effective form or preparation within which to deliver the medicine be it in a tisane, a paste or a tincture, and how to mix combinations of the herbs and plants. And that is just the botanical kingdom. There are the animal and mineral therapeutics to learn of as well.'

Ruth and I looked at each other. Our road together seemed to stretch on forever if we were to realise our dreams of being healers.

Of most interest to Ruth and myself was the portfolio of sketches that Hadar had copied from texts he had studied while travelling and studying in the east. These were anatomical drawings of the musculature, organs and skeletons of both men and women. Hadar informed us that he had made the copies from texts by Galen, a court physician of ancient Rome, and ibn-Sina, a philosopher physician greatly respected in the Islamic world. Both had been heard of in the west, but their texts had been lost or unavailable. Unseen in the west, the only copies available were in one or two of the great universities and libraries of the east. Fortunately, Hadar had made his own notations beside the sketches describing the weight, shape, colour and supposed function of the various organs. Ruth and I both laughed at each other's interest in the anatomy of our opposite sexes.

Ruth was unable to personally attend to the patients that Hadar and I visited or came to his practice. Women were not recognised as being suited to being physicians. She had to be satisfied with my accounts of what I had heard, seen and felt of the patients in Hadar's care and their relevant diagnoses and treatment. I allowed her to press and feel various appropriate parts of my own body to assist in her learning. I liked it the day she pressed her ear to my chest to listen to my heart and breathing. It was nice to have her so close to me and I think she enjoyed it in the same way as she lingered a long while listening. The different sounds our intestines made while gurgling and bubbling away was another source of humour between us.

In time and over some months, we both satisfied Hadar that we had a functional knowledge of herbs and anatomy as described in the texts, sketches and notations he provided us with.

Not everything in the acquisition of knowledge, however, was a pleasant experience.

I learned there was much one could diagnose from the expulsions of the bowel. There were various features to consider, most obviously consistency from watery to pebbly and whether undigested foods were present. Then there were the characteristic odours of various ailments. Colour was a determining factor in whether there was internal bleeding or perhaps a malaise of the liver. Inspection using a spatula might reveal the presence of worms and other parasites. The breath, vomitus, mucous and pus from wounds and infections could be investigated and interpreted in a similar manner. I would later share all this with Ruth in the evening.

'I am rather glad I can learn this second hand,' Ruth commented upon my description of a particularly unpleasant stool.

One evening, Hadar announced to the both of us, 'It was the great ibn-Sina who stated that the "urine is a faithful guide for the knowledge of the illness". This evening you will learn just how.'

Before us, he had placed some glass vials evidently containing various samples of urine.

'How would you describe the colours you see before you?'

Our responses were varied; 'Straw, brown, clear, reddish, golden.'

'And their clarity?'

'Some are clear others are cloudy. This one has sediment at its bottom and,' said Ruth, pointing to another vial, 'there are tiny bits of something floating in this one.'

'Now remove the corks and describe the odour of each sample,' directed Hadar.

We did so. Some smelled strongly of urine, others had a slight metallic odour, one smelled strongly of ammonia and one reeked of the fish market at the end of a long hot day. Hadar then explained the diagnosis and treatment accompanying each sample we had examined and smelled.

'It was Apollonius of Memphis who first recognised a disease in which there was an excess of urination. He named it "diabetes". Which means, Ippolito?'

'In ancient Greek, it means "to go through",' I responded.

'Other symptoms of this disease may include increased thirst and hunger, weight loss, fatigue, loss of concentration and a tingling or numbness in the hands and feet. In India, the urine samples of sufferers are sometimes called "honey urine" as ants are attracted to it.'

Hadar then placed a sample of urine in its glass vial in front of us along with a small jug of water, a cup and a bowl.

'Do either of you notice anything unusual in this sample's visual characteristics and odour?'

Neither of us noticed anything unusual about the sample and said so.

I had an uncomfortable feeling about what was to come next.

'The most precise diagnostic test for the physician in the case of diabetes is the taste test.'

'Oh no, Hadar,' spluttered Ruth. 'Surely not.'

'I will take the first sip to lead the way. Simply hold the sample behind your teeth and taste it with the tip of your tongue. Then, when you have tasted it, spit and rinse your mouth with the water.'

Hadar did as he said he would and then looked at us with expectation and a small smile upon his face.

'You first,' said Ruth.

'Thanks.'

I did so. The urine tasted sweet. I spat and then rinsed thoroughly. After a moment's hesitation, Ruth did likewise.

'It is indeed sweet,' commented Ruth.

'Hadar,' I tentatively queried, 'we won't have to do a similar test in the examination and assessment of stools, will we?'

13

It was a few weeks later that a party of three Templar Knights leading a spare pony arrived in the street and stopped at Hadar's shop front. They were attired in standard Templar uniform: mail coat and leggings over which was a white sleeveless tunic with a red cross emblazoned in the centre. By their sides hung long swords inside plain and unadorned scabbards.

The captain introduced himself as Sir Jean de Lyon.

'You are Hadar, the physician?' he inquired respectfully.

'That is correct, Sir Jean, and this is my assistant, Ippolito de Medici.'

I bowed my head respectfully to the knight before exchanging an uncertain glance with Hadar, both of us wondering what this was all about.

'Master Hadar. I have been directed by Sir Guy de Lusignon, regent to his majesty King Baldwin the Fourth of the Holy Kingdom of Jerusalem, to request your presence at the royal court at your soonest convenience. To be blunt, sir, I am to return with you.'

'Certainly, Sir Jean, but I would like my assistant to accompany me.'

The knight quickly acquiesced to the request.

'Then Sir Jean,' continued Hadar, 'if you would allow us to

have a few moments to dress in attire more fitting attendance at court, we will do so.'

'Of course.'

I only had one other shirt and tunic to wear, and I was glad they were clean. I donned a pair of hose and quickly buffed up my boots. I only looked cleaner, not resplendent.

Hadar, on the other hand, was wearing a fine yellow cotton shirt beneath a green tunic with a red hose. Over this, he had donned a black velvet cloak embroidered around the collar, cuffs and hem. About his neck, he wore a gold chain with a heraldic device of some sort hanging from it. Upon his head, he wore a flouncing cap with brocade around the edges. Short fine leather boots completed his outfit. He had taken the time to comb his hair and beard out as well. I had forgotten about this latter aspect of grooming. Hadar looked much younger for his efforts.

Hadar was offered the spare horse as his mount and, once seated in the saddle, looked like a nobleman. I climbed up behind one of the other knights.

We rode at a sedate pace through the streets of Jerusalem, eventually arriving at David's Gate on the western wall of the city. Beside the gate stood the Citadel of Jerusalem and the Court of King Baldwin.

We clattered gently through the gates and into the forecourt of the Citadel surrounded by towering brick walls. Milling in the forecourt were numerous knights, sergeants and squires, four of the latter running to hold our horses and assist us to dismount.

Sir Jean led us along hallways and corridors past richly embroidered wall hangings where guards were posted every ten feet or so along the way. Eventually, we arrived at a spacious and richly decorated anteroom where Sir Jean invited us to sit while he went ahead.

Hadar and I were surrounded by an opulence that neither of

us had ever seen before. I had thought our family home in Acre was well-appointed but it paled beside these surroundings. The wall hangings were beautiful works of tapestry detailing hunting scenes, colourful gardens and orchards, battle scenes or scenes from the life of Christ. Three or four other hangings were simple damask designs and patterns that caught the eye with their silken threads and the reflected glow of the beeswax candles illuminating the room.

'My palms are sweating,' I whispered to Hadar.

'This is a new experience for myself, too. I have been to the houses of many of the lords of this realm and other realms as well but this is the first time I have been requested to be in the presence of a king.'

It seemed only a minute or two before Sir Jean returned to us.

'When I lead you into the hall, follow my lead a step or two behind. Bow when I do and only speak when spoken to by any of nobles, knights and lords present. The king will be at the head of the hall but will not be speaking with you for reasons that will become obvious.'

Hadar and I followed Sir Jean through the great arch of the doorway into the grand hall of the citadel. The walls of the hall were adorned with picturesque hangings, pennants and shields of differing heraldic designs. High windows gave the hall a feeling of light and space.

Before us, numerous court dignitaries were gathered below a dais upon which sat Baldwin, King of Jerusalem. The king was motionless, his arms resting in his lap, his hands hanging limply between his thighs. He was clothed in loose silks of red and gold the sleeves of which fell to cover his hands and fingers. Most strikingly, his face was covered in a light gauze veil that revealed only his eyes. I was shocked to see they were without eyelids and seemed to be staring sightlessly ahead.

We stopped about ten feet from the dais where we followed Sir

Jean's lead and bowed deeply before the throne and the lords.

'Your majesty, my lord regent and lords of the realm and church,' began Sir Jean, speaking in Latin. 'May I present Hadar, physician of Jerusalem, and his assistant, Ippolito de Medici.'

We briefly bowed again before the gathering.

A tall noble stepped forward. He was wearing a richly embroidered red cloak over an off-white surcoat with a faded red templar cross upon it. Beneath this, he wore a mail hauberk, leggings and upon his head a mail hood. He had a long face and nose surrounded by reddish-brown hair and beard. Piercing blue eyes flashed beneath thick eyebrows.

'I am Sir Guy de Lusignan, regent to his majesty King Baldwin IV of Jerusalem.'

His Latin was heavy with a Frankish accent.

'May I present my fellow lords and dignitaries? Foremost may I present his Holiness Heraclius the Patriarch of Jerusalem.'

A richly attired priest wearing a long golden-coloured cope over heavily decorated vestments dipped his crosier in our direction as if administering a blessing. He was the only member of the court who was clean-shaven.

'To his Holiness's right is Sir Arnold de Torroja, Grand Commander of the Knights Templar.'

Sir Arnold was a tall dark-haired man with a swarthy complexion dressed in soldiers mail with a red-on-white Templar's Cross displayed on his surcoat.

'Next to him,' continued Sir Guy, 'is Sir Roger de Moulins, Grand Commander of the Knights of Saint John.'

Sir Roger had known my father and smiled at me in recognition of the times he had visited our house in Acre. His hair was thinner and his beard whiter than I remembered. He still wore the same long black cassock with a white cross emblazoned on his chest.

'Greetings, young de Medici. You have grown. I trust that you are well?'

'Yes. I am, Sir Roger,' I stammered, suddenly aware of my lowly status in this company.

'On the Patriarch's left is Sir Reynaud de Chatillon,' continued Sir Guy.

I had heard of Sir Reynaud. He had been a captive of Saladin for many years. There had been a rumour that he was so troublesome no one would pay his ransom. He was very lean and had a rapacious aspect that suggested to me the story may have been true.

'Next is Sir Godfrey de Caen and beside him Sir Caspar del Calabria.'

Sir Godfrey looked many years the older of the two knights with the grizzled and hardened features of one who has survived many battles and fights. This was amply attested to by the many scars on his hands and wrists. His hair and beard were long and a silvering salt and pepper in colour. It was his eyes that stood out. They were an intense blue that made him stand out amongst all his brown-eyed Mediterranean companions.

Sir Caspar was much younger, blonde-haired and only sported a sparse beard and moustache. He had a warm smile which I immediately liked and I suspect women would have found him attractive. A scar across his right cheek somehow added to his facial appeal rather than detracted from it.

'Lastly, is Father Benedict,' said Sir Guy with what I thought was a little disdain.

Father Benedict had been standing just behind the Patriarch and momentarily stepped forward and briefly nodded his head to Hadar and I before stepping back behind the Patriarch. He looked uncomfortable and his eyes kept furtively sweeping the great hall as if expecting some kind of calamity.

'No doubt you are both wondering why you have been asked here,' began Sir Guy, getting down to the purpose of the meeting.

'Hadar, your reputation as a physician is well-known in Jerusalem and beyond Outremer. You are widely travelled and have many skills as a linguist and diplomat. These are the principal reasons you have been asked here.'

'You are generous in your praise, Sir Guy,' responded Hadar.

'You are no doubt aware that the king has been afflicted since youth with the leper's disease. Previously, this has not stopped him from leading our armies against the infidel and winning victories against Saladin for the glory of God and Christendom.'

At this I observed the king bowing his head slightly in Sir Guy's direction, his sightless eyes seeming to take in all gathered before him.

I remembered that a few years ago, King Baldwin had led his army in what looked like a hopeless one-armed charge against Saladin's army, guiding his horse with his knees and laying about himself mightily with a sword in his one remaining good hand. The Saracen army had broken and fled. It was the stuff of legend and a feat of great courage well-known throughout the entire kingdom.

'Word has recently reached the court that a cure for the disease is to be found in the east beyond Persia in the lands of Hind. We propose to send a small expedition to the east with the purpose of finding this cure and bringing it back to Jerusalem. It is our intention to send someone skilled in healing with a small party of knights to accomplish this goal.'

A thrill of excitement ran through me as I realised where this was leading to. 'Go on, Hadar. Say yes,' I thought to myself.

'Hadar of Jerusalem. It is our opinion that you are best suited to lead this expedition. We, the king and court of Jerusalem, humbly request, without order or duress, that you accept this commission. What do you say?'

Hadar put his hand to his chin and rubbed it in contemplation. 'I have travelled much in my youth towards these lands but never reached them. I believe I have yet another journey in me still and for this reason, I accept the commission.'

A collective look of relief spread across the faces of the assembled court. I saw Baldwin's veil ripple slightly as if the muscles of his face too were moving in a smile.

'How do you propose that this mission be carried out?' continued Hadar.

'We believe that a very small party will travel most quickly and be less likely to attract the attention of Moslem or bandit forces whilst enroute. You are to travel overland as the sea lanes are closed to us. You will be accompanied by Sir Godfrey de Caen, a proven and powerful knight in battle, and Sir Caspar del Calabria. His talents are many. Do not be fooled by his youthful features.'

Sir Godfrey and Sir Caspar nodded their heads towards Hadar and I in acknowledgement. Sir Godfrey's face was grim while Sir Caspar's smiled warmly.

'Sir Godfrey will lead you east of Jerusalem to Baghdad. From there your group will have to determine the best route to Hind and beyond depending on factors such as weather, terrain and hostile forces.'

'You will meet their sergeant, Edward, and their squire later. Both have skills to recommend them to this task. Finally, so that the mission has the grace of God's blessing and guidance, you will also be accompanied by Father Benedict here.'

The priest stepped forward again but did not smile or nod his head in any form of acknowledgement to Hadar and I. He simply looked decidedly grim-faced about his relegation to the mission.

'My knights and their entourage are ready at a moment's notice to leave on this mission. Hadar, how long before you can be made ready?'

'My assistant and I will need but a few days to prepare. We will need a little time to sort the medicinals and curatives that such a trip will require.'

'So be it. Friday is not too soon?'

'Friday it is,' answered Hadar.

14

Hadar and I were escorted back to his house in the same manner and with the same group of knights we had left it.

We dismounted, said our thanks to the knights and went inside.

'I can be packed and ready to go in five minutes,' I told Hadar.

'My personal belongings will not take much longer either,' answered Hadar. 'However, the preparation and packaging of the necessary remedies and cures for the diseases that we will encounter on our journey will take some time. The forces of Islam and banditry are not the only adversaries we will have to face.'

I was surprised that Ruth did not visit that evening as I was bursting to tell her of my news. I supposed her 'mistress' had duties for her, which was occasionally the case, and that I would see her tomorrow.

The next morning Hadar and I were busy in the apothecary.

'Our main dilemma in preparing curatives for the journey will be in ensuring we have enough supplies but in small enough quantities so as not to encumber our limited baggage space. It is for this reason that we will have to reduce many of our curatives and herbal treatments to tinctures based in oils or alcohol. I have not yet taught you this so pay close attention.'

Hadar opened a cupboard and withdrew some unusually

shaped glassware I had not previously seen and a small device I recognised as a spirit burner.

'The Arabs call this an *al-kas*. You may prefer to simply call it a beaker. Now, I want you to prepare these herbs in the mortar and pestle and grind them down to the finest powder you can.'

I did so as Hadar continued his instruction.

'The curative agents of the different herbs, animal products and minerals are not all soluble in the same solutions. Some may be distilled in water whilst others require distillation in oil or spirits of wine. The correct solvent is important in preserving the curative elements of the substance in its most concentrated form.'

I absorbed all that Hadar imparted to me that day. I realised that, although the process was time-consuming and more expensive, it seemed that tinctures and oils of whatever substance would be far more palatable when taken with wine, food or some other drink rather than taking them in their raw unrefined form or in a tisane where the taste is often disagreeable.

We poured the various concoctions into a collection of dark brown vials. Once each was filled, they were firmly stoppered and labelled. Hadar informed me that the purpose of the dark brown vials was to prevent light and air from denaturing the contents within.

I had been so busy that I had not noticed Ruth's absence yet again in the afternoon and evening of the day. It was not until late that I wondered if she was not ill or indisposed.

I fell into bed that night with my head full of the formulas for the preparation and distillation of all the numerous tinctures, oils and treatments we had prepared that day. Hadar had informed me that disorders of the digestive tract would be the principal malaise we would have to deal with thanks to contaminated water and spoiled food. He detailed how the ointments we had prepared would be useful against parasites infesting the skin and hair that could be picked up anywhere. Hadar informed me that prevention was better than cure and stressed that the best preventative of illness was meticulous personal hygiene and cleanliness, particularly in the preparation of food.

'I don't know how I am going to get those filthy Frankish knights and the priest to observe this, but I will insist upon it as leader of the group if we are not to be halted due to illness and disease.'

Our work continued apace the next day, which was the Wednesday prior to our departure. Hadar supervised the careful packing of vials and containers into special leather satchels that were lined with numerous pockets inside. We packed straw around them to prevent any breakage enroute. Each satchel was then numbered with a list of the ingredients inside to facilitate quick and easy access in an emergency.

It was mid-afternoon when we heard Ruth's voice calling in clear distress from downstairs. We both moved quickly to see what the matter was.

I was not prepared for what I saw and was shocked on entering the room where Hadar held his clinic. Ruth was hiding behind the door and only emerged when she saw there were just the two of us. Her face was bruised, her eyes blackened, lips swollen and there were cuts and abrasions on her hands and arms, and, I suspected, on other parts of her person. She immediately burst into tears and ran into my arms.

I had never felt so protective of anyone in my life up until that moment, nor had I felt so much anger in my being. I truly wanted to kill whoever had caused this harm to Ruth. I barely understood the intensity of the feelings coursing through me.

'Who– what– why– how has this happened?' I stammered in my shock.

Ruth just continued to sob uncontrollably in my arms. All I could do was hold her against me and stroke her hair and shoulders.

I had not noticed Hadar's disappearance nor his return with a bowl of water and some cloths.

'Come, Ruth. Let me clean you up.'

Ruth seemed to accept the wisdom of Hadar's instruction and submitted to his ministrations while she held her head low and quietly sobbed.

My heart was aching for her.

Eventually, Hadar had completed his work and Ruth seemed more comforted and secure in our presence.

'What has happened, my child?' queried Hadar, taking her hand and looking into her face. I sat beside her and put a protective arm around her shoulders. She leaned softly against me.

It took her a moment to respond.

'I'm so sorry,' she began, 'but I have not been honest with you about myself.'

She broke off, trying to hold back more tears.

'If this is about you and your mother living in "The Rocking Horse", we already know and it does not matter to us,' I told her as openly and honestly as I could.

'You mean you have known and still have welcomed me here?' she stuttered in surprise.

'Ever since the day you came into the apothecary to ask for the angelica, wormwood and pennyroyal – supposedly for your mistress. I was concerned and asked Hadar about you. He told me your mother's sad story and your situation. It has not mattered to me.'

'Oh, Ippolito. You are too good. Thank you so much. I have been so ashamed about it.'

'That is in the past. How is it you are so battered and beaten?'

Ruth hung her head in some embarrassment and then began, 'My woman's flow has started.'

'Congratulations,' said Hadar. 'You are no longer a child.'

'No! It is a curse. Abigail, the mistress of the brothel, expects that since I am now a woman, I must begin working the beds if I am to have a roof over my head. She has already made it known throughout Outremer that a young virgin is on offer and she has received many bids for my maidenhead.

'My mother just hangs her head and will not help me. When I tried to run away, Abigail set Ishmael, our eunuch guard, upon me to teach me a lesson. It was he who did this to my face while the mistress took the whip to my back and thighs. I managed to escape this afternoon while Ishmael was called to a disturbance upstairs. Please help me. I have no one else.'

She began sobbing into my chest again and I held her close.

I looked up at Hadar, the obvious question in my eyes. He simply looked at me with a great smile of compassion on his face.

'We will help you, Ruth,' he said. 'We will take you far away from all this and you will be safe, I promise you.'

My anger suddenly melted away into an intense joy as I realised that Hadar was inviting Ruth to accompany us to the east.

15

Hadar and I attended to the rest of Ruth's wounds. As Ruth had commented, they had been designed to hurt and punish but not to scar and disfigure in any way. Ruth eventually settled after a warm cup of valerian and chamomile tea. Before she fell asleep, Hadar and I escorted her to my bed space where we let her rest and heal.

I endured the discomforts of lying on the floor at the foot of the bed, where I stayed in case Ruth awoke in distress. She did not and slept soundly till the next morning when she arose refreshed and more herself. I was somewhat less so after my night on the floor. I did not mind.

We agreed that Ruth should remain hidden in the house and should not venture outside, lest Abigail have Ishmael or other agents out looking for her. Ruth spent the day assisting Hadar and I with the final preparations for the journey. She was very interested in the medicinal preparations contained within their brown vials. She taxed me greatly on what I had learned about their preparations and properties. In one morning, it seemed she had gleaned as much as I had in three days.

Around mid-afternoon, there was a knock at the door. It was Sir Caspar with two others standing behind him whom I did not immediately recognise. None were wearing mail suits or surcoats but were dressed as everyday citizens of Jerusalem.

'Greetings, Ippolito,' said Sir Caspar.

'Greetings, Sir Caspar. Please, come in.'

It was just then a voice I recognised said, 'Ippolito. Why, hello. How are you? This is a surprise.'

I looked past Sir Caspar to the young man behind him. It took me a second or two to recognise the face. He was leaner, the puppy fat gone but the freckles and shock of unruly hair remained. It was over a year since I had seen him.

'Raymond!' I exclaimed, recalling my companion on the journey from Acre to Jerusalem.

'This is a welcome surprise. Please, come in. All of you.'

Raymond and I clasped hands.

'You remember Sergeant Edward, who was also with us.'

Edward smiled warmly at me, bowing his bald head in acknowledgement. I remembered him as a grim fighter. I noticed that his nose had been broken since I had last seen him and it was slightly skewed to the left.

'I do. It is unusual seeing you both unattired in Hospitaller uniforms.'

'It is how we will be travelling. Not so hot to wear, more comfortable and very much incognito so as not to attract unwanted attention.'

Later, as we were all gathered into the small space of the salon, Hadar announced to the knights and their entourage that Ruth would be travelling with us.

'I do not see a problem with this,' commented Sir Caspar. 'In fact, it may even be an advantage to us. We shall maintain the deception that we are escorting a young bride to her new home and that we are assorted family members. It will work very well with the overall plan to avoid attention. We will work out the finer points in a moment.'

Hadar, Ruth and I breathed a sigh of relief as we were concerned that the knights might prohibit Ruth from joining the party. We said nothing about the circumstances that had led her to this situation and, thankfully no questions were asked by the Hospitallers.

'I will bring an extra pony befitting a young bride on the morrow then,' commented Sir Caspar in summary.

'One more thing. As of tomorrow, I am Caspar and Godfrey is Godfrey. No more titles. We are a family travelling together. Hadar, you are the family patriarch, Godfrey is your brother, I, his son and your nephew. Edward is your son and father to Ippolito and Ruth, your grandchildren. I suggest we get used to the idea of calling each other Father, Brother, Sister, Uncle, Son, Daughter as the case may be. Father Benedict will serve as the family priest. He refuses to travel incognito any way. He claims it would diminish his role as "God's emissary" for the journey.'

Later that evening the three of us sat in the salon reviewing the day and exploring our thoughts and feelings about the long quest ahead of us.

'I want the two of you to travel as much as possible by my side on the journey. There will be ample opportunity for instruction and I very much wish for your education to continue.'

'An excellent idea,' agreed Ruth. 'There is only one thing that is a worry to me. I am not sad about leaving my mother. She has only been a very small part of my life these past years. She has worked evenings and nights and has slept for most of the day. There have been times when I did not see her for days and she did not seem to care that I was absent in the evenings or ask of my whereabouts when I have been visiting you both here. I do, however, wish to let her know that I am safe. Would it be possible to send her a message at a later date informing her that I am safe, far away but in good hands?'

'This can be easily arranged from one of the towns along the way. Do not fret on this matter,' advised Hadar.

He got to his feet and said, 'Well, it is time we all retired so we can be alert and ready for the early start we can expect tomorrow.'

The delights of the floorboards at the foot of Ruth's bed beckoned once more.

16

Friday morning saw the three of us up before dawn and breaking our fast with a filling meal of flatbread, cheese and olives. We had just finished when we heard the clatter of hooves and knew it was time to depart.

Outside, Godfrey, Caspar, Edward, Raymond and Benedict sat astride palfreys leading three saddled spares, a team of four laden donkeys and a fifth as yet unburdened. I threw our baggage over the fifth and with Raymond's help, secured it to the donkey.

'A good day for travelling, I think,' observed Raymond, looking to the east where a reddening sky was greeting the dawn.

I assisted Ruth up into the saddle of what I hoped was a gentle and tractable young mare.

We made our way along streets that were largely empty of people and passed by the church of Saint Anne where the priest was just opening the doors of the church. He nodded to the knights in greeting and then looked in surprise at Father Benedict but said nothing. Benedict looked the other way as if pretending not to have noticed the priest and thus avoiding any potential conversation with him.

I could not help but wonder why Father Benedict should choose to do this. What was he avoiding?

We passed through the Gate of Jehoshaphat and looked out

onto the Vale of Jehoshaphat through which ran the Kedron brook. To the north was the Mount of Olives, ahead lay the Tomb of the Virgin and, to the southeast, Gethsemane. The countryside ahead of us was lit in oranges, yellows and reds that were reflected off the sky and the few small clouds that were drifting by.

We soon fell into an order which we would maintain for some time. Leading our group by about half a mile was Caspar, acting as scout. Even though we were close to Jerusalem and its peaceful surrounds, Caspar sat straight and alert in his saddle vigilant for any unseen hazards or foes. Behind him and at the head of the rest of our band rode Godfrey. He too had a very businesslike look about him as he scanned the way ahead of us. Then came our little trio. We had grouped ourselves as Hadar had suggested the night before, Ruth and I riding either side of Hadar. Behind us followed Father Benedict who seemed content to ride on his own and avoid conversation. Most of the time he spent fingering his rosary whilst his lips moved in silent prayers. He was followed by Raymond leading the pack donkeys. Edward rode somewhat further back bringing up the rear. He too seemed to be constantly scanning the surrounding landscape.

Hadar did not waste any time recommencing our education.

'What would you like to learn about today?' he asked.

This was the first time he had ever asked this question. He usually dictated the learning agenda to us.

'The road ahead could be hazardous and injuries may occur,' said Ruth. 'I would like to know more of how to treat such ailments and injuries, should they occur.'

'So be it.' Hadar smiled. 'Thirst may be one of the main hazards we face,' he began.

And so, the first few hours of the day, as they would for many days to come, were devoted to instruction in medicine.

We broke our journey for a small repast around noon and to stretch our legs. I was decidedly uncomfortable after so many hours in the saddle and I could see that Ruth was moving with difficulty in what I could only describe as something of a bow-legged waddle.

'What is wrong?' I asked.

'It is my buttocks and thighs. It feels like the skin has been rubbed raw from them.'

'Ah. I know what ails you. You have saddle sores. Your skin is unaccustomed to the rubbing and frictions of prolonged riding. Hadar and I have something packed that will help relieve the discomfort.'

I went to our pack donkey and felt around for the jar of comfrey unguent we had prepared. I brought it and a small piece of cotton gauze to her.

'Use this sparingly,' I said. 'It is all we have until we can purchase or prepare some more. Go behind those gorse bushes over there and apply it.'

Ruth headed towards the bushes, jar and gauze in hand.

Ruth sat more comfortably that afternoon. Raymond had noticed her difficulty after dismounting and had thoughtfully provided a sheepskin for her saddle. He had done this without being asked and had said nothing about placing it there. Ruth picked him as the only one in the troop who would have done this and thanked him for his kindness, as did I.

'I should have thought of it earlier.' He smiled. 'It would be a shame to see Ruth not looking her best at her wedding because of a pain in the backside.'

We laughed at this and fell into an easy camaraderie. Raymond and I shared the task of leading the pack donkeys. It was an afternoon of pleasant conversation for the three of us and helped to while away the rigours of the journey.

Raymond recounted what a miserable creature I had looked like the morning after our night in a filthy rundown travellers' inn at Bethinople.

'You should have seen him, Ruth. His face was a red spotty mess of insect bites, he was scratching from head to foot with fleas and he had more bags under his eyes than an old man.'

'I had no sleep because someone else in the bed snored and farted all night long,' I said to Ruth, pointing my thumb at Raymond.

Raymond had an acute sense of humour and a warm and caring nature, as was demonstrated in his gifting of the sheepskin to Ruth. He spoke highly of his Hospitaller companions, telling Ruth and I of some of their acts of bravery and courage. Sir Godfrey had been in the leading charge at the Battle of Montgisard riding beside King Baldwin. Sir Caspar, he told us, had orchestrated the skilful capture of several leading Islamic nobles right from under the noses of their knights and armies.

Late in the afternoon, we arrived at a settlement of monks known as Bethfage Monastery. Godfrey had decided it was enough riding in one day for Hadar, Ruth and myself, stating that we would have to become used to much longer and more difficult days of journeying.

He called a meeting that later that afternoon before the evening prayers of the monks and the last meal for the day.

'I am concerned that we are under armed for the defence of this mission. At the moment, Caspar, Edward and myself are the only skilled warriors. Raymond is able to mount a reasonable defence with a sword but there are four more who could carry arms and it is this I wish to discuss.'

This was unexpected. I suppose I had been a little bit naïve to think that we could journey to the Far East without the kind of mishap Godfrey was concerned about.

'Hadar,' continued Godfrey, 'have you any skill at arms?'

'Well, believe it or not, in my younger days I was a fair shot with a hunting bow and believe I could still draw a string with a degree of accuracy. I would not be much good with a war bow as I no longer have the strength.'

'This is good news,' responded Godfrey. 'We shall be able to purchase a bow, quiver and arrows for you in the next large town we visit.'

I looked at Hadar with yet another new appreciation of him.

'Ippolito,' Godfrey continued, 'we have brought a spare light sword with us. You will begin training in its use with Edward tomorrow. Raymond, you will join Ippolito in this.'

I looked at Edward in excitement. He merely nodded and said, 'Do not look so keen, young Ippolito. You will not be smiling after your first sessions with me, I can assure you,' and then he laughed a big belly laugh to let me know it was all part of the learning and nothing personal.

'Father Benedict,' began Godfrey but was cut short by the priest.

'You don't expect a man of God to use a weapon, do you?' responded Benedict with some indignation.

'Only one that does not draw blood and which is in keeping with church dogma on the use of weapons by men of the cloth. For that, Father, I have the hammer in mind for you. You can break bones and skulls without drawing the blood that is forbidden for you and you will learn from me just how to use it.'

Benedict started to say something but was cut short by Godfrey's abrupt order: 'No arguments, priest, or else.'

'What about me?' piped in Ruth.

'Caspar and I have thought long and hard about how to deploy you in a fray. You are to be Caspar's special pupil in the use of the throwing knife. It is… a… speciality of his from the south of Italy.' Godfrey smiled knowingly at Caspar as he made this last comment.

Ruth looked excited at this news while Caspar grinned enigmatically.

Something inside me told me that Ruth would emerge as quite deadly in this skill given her determination and ability to apply herself to anything she wanted to.

<h1 align="center">17</h1>

The next day saw our party descending into the Valley of the River Jordan. Ruth and I rode beside Hadar for the morning as he reviewed yesterday's discussion on thirst.

'How would you recognise dehydration in an unconscious human being?'

'I would open his mouth and inspect his tongue. If it were not moist in appearance, I would suspect dehydration,' I responded.

'Yes, but one has to be cautious that the condition of the tongue is not because of breathing through the mouth as may occur in an unconscious person,' added Ruth.

'Go on, Ruth.'

'One can assess for dehydration of the body by assessing the elasticity of the skin. It loses elasticity when the body is not hydrated and a sample pinch of the skin on the back of the hand will reveal if the skin has lost elasticity by not reforming quickly to its normal flatness.'

The morning continued in a similar vein.

Ahead of us, the Jordan River came plainly into view just a bare mile distant across a slowly descending plain. To our right, and to the south, the opal vastness of the Dead Sea opened up before us, the salt-encrusted shoreline brightly reflecting the sun.

'One can easily die of dehydration in such an environment as the one you see before you,' cautioned Hadar. 'The salt on the land and in the sea leaches water from the body and will quickly dehydrate the unwary traveller.'

Caspar led us further north along the banks of the Jordan River to a place where the river widened into a shallow crossing.

'Give the horses a good watering before we cross over,' said Godfrey, making sure they too would not dehydrate in this hostile environment.

Ruth and I led our horses to the riverside and let them drink their fill.

'I have decided to name her Esther in honour of the Jewish heroine in our Bible,' Ruth informed me.

'A good strong name, I think. Rather like yourself, Ruth.'

'I hope I will be strong enough for what lies ahead of us. At times, I wonder what I have gotten myself into. One moment I can barely contain my excitement, the next I am considering all the terrible things that could happen to us. I have to admit, I am looking forward to learning the skills of the throwing knife from Caspar.'

'And I the sword with Edward.'

We replenished our canteens from the river and as the horses had finished taking their fill, we led them across the narrows of the ford that Caspar had found for us. Once across, we remounted and made our way back south to follow the Dead Sea staying away from her salt-encrusted shoreline.

Later in the day, I rode beside Raymond while Ruth rode ahead with Caspar. I noticed he was showing her how to hold a throwing knife between her thumbpad and forefinger. Ruth looked very intent.

'Tell me something about your home,' I said to Raymond.

'I am fortunate in that both my parents are very much alive

and living in the Occitan region of southern France. It is very picturesque with its own unique culture and its own religion.'

'Own religion?' I queried. 'I thought the Holy Church was practised everywhere in Western Europe.'

'So it is. But it exists alongside our religion of Catharism which is similar to Christianity in many ways. For instance, we believe in the true teachings of Jesus Christ. My father follows the Holy Church, as does my mother in many ways but she is also interested in the Cathars and the fact that so many of them are such very good people who actually do live and practice the real teachings of Jesus. They dislike what they see as the corruption of the Church in Rome by its popes, bishops and priests who are often seen as merely feathering their nests with gold and corruption.'

We had been unaware that Benedict was riding close behind us until his voice suddenly boomed in loud damnation at Raymond. 'You have been worshipping at the Synagogue of Satan, you vile and worthless wretch.'

Benedict was red-faced in his fury and self-righteousness. 'You will be damned for all time. Don't you know this? Repent now of your wickedness or die a thousand deaths in the eternal fires of hell.'

Godfrey and Hadar had been riding in front of Raymond and I. Godfrey had heard the priest's outburst and came riding back to where we were.

'You speak of the Synagogue of Satan, priest. Do not quote that unholy book around me. It should never have been placed in the Bible,' interjected Godfrey.

'The Book of Revelation is God's Holy Word as revealed to the apostle John,' retorted Benedict in surprise at Godfrey's spirited defence of Raymond.

'I doubt it very much, priest. If you have read the Testaments in their original Greek, you would note the beauty of the language and verse of John the Apostle's gospel. It is a beautiful example of the high Greek spoken by the learned and influential in the ancient world of Jesus's time. That book you quote from is written in the *koine*, the *lingua franca* of the market and trade. It is some of the worst and clumsiest Greek I have ever read. You cannot tell me that the authors of those two texts are the same person.'

'The elders of the early Holy Church have deemed it God's will and the revealed word for mankind,' spluttered Benedict no doubt surprised that Godfrey had turned on him with such cynicism and with such biblical knowledge.

'The elders had it wrong. There is nothing of Christ's gentleness and love in that book. It is a book of fear and frightful visions designed to bring terror into the lives of good Christians. I do not see or hear our Lord Jesus in its pages at all. I suspect that this John of Patmos had eaten some very unwholesome mushrooms and they were the real source of these so-called visions of his – not the Lord, as you bloody fools would maintain.'

Godfrey was angry with Benedict for attacking Raymond.

'I am surrounded by heresy and untruth,' bewailed Benedict. 'I will pray for your souls.'

'Do so, priest. Just do it quietly. I will not have anyone attacking another for their religious beliefs in this party. Do I make myself clear to you?'

'You do, Sir Godfrey. On my return, I will make a full report to the Patriarch on this matter,' retorted Benedict, now regaining some composure.

A silence descended on our party after these words and no one spoke for a while.

Hadar and Godfrey rode on ahead together. Hadar made some remark to Godfrey which brought an amused guffaw from him.

This lightened everyone's tension with the exception of Benedict, who had ridden away and off to the side of the party.

About mid-afternoon, Godfrey called a halt to the day's riding in the foothills overlooking the Dead Sea. A freshwater creek ran nearby and the area was surrounded by green pasture. We hobbled the horses and donkeys in the pasture where they could eat and drink at their leisure.

Raymond and I set about putting up the small tents and awnings for our camp quickly and efficiently. I laughed quietly to myself when I realised that Benedict's small shelter was placed over some stony ground while the rest were pitched on the grass. Raymond smiled mischievously at me and placed his forefinger to his lips. I nodded and smiled back.

The next thing I knew was Edward had given me a friendly whack across my buttocks with what looked like a long wooden baton. He had one in each hand.

'Time for some lessons in defending yourself, young Ippolito.' Edward laughed in his cheerful manner.

'In time I hope to do more than just defend myself.'

He handed me the wooden baton, the mate of which was in his other hand.

I realised the baton was merely some freshly cut green wood that had been shaved down to give it some pretence of being a sword.

'We will begin with these fine sticks to teach the rudimentary lessons. Duelling with real swords will come later.'

So, we began. I learned the postures and stances that a swordsman would use that afternoon and the beginnings of some lunges and blows. Always, Edward was ahead of me countering and occasionally delivering a blow to my arms, shoulders and ribs to illustrate how slow and predictable I was.

'Always watch your opponent, Ippolito. In time you will be

able to read his next move from his eyes and preliminary hand and arm gestures.'

I was weary and my body was hurting and bruised.

'I think we might call this a day, Edward. I had not realised just how much is involved in learning the craft of swordplay – let alone the cost of actually learning it!' I said, rubbing my bruised elbow with emphasis.

Edward laughed with a cheery and friendly smile.

'Most of your bandits and ordinary foot soldiers know little more than you do right now. Do not be disheartened. They have never really been taught how to use a sword to its maximum efficiency. In a few short weeks, I will make a swordsman of you. Not the greatest by any length, but not the worst. Hopefully it will keep you alive.'

'I hope so too.' I laughed.

'Soon you and Raymond will commence your competition with each other.'

I looked over to the trees where Ruth and Caspar were throwing knives at a tree. Caspar turned to Ruth and clapped his hands, a clear expression of praise on his face. Ruth looked delighted by this.

It seemed I had the harder road in our party's need for better defences.

18

The next day, we travelled south, keeping the Dead Sea and its salty shoreline to our right. Godfrey informed us that we were travelling an old trade route that had grown into disuse ever since the First Crusaders took possession of Jerusalem. Our routine remained much the same. Godfrey, Caspar or Edward would wake the camp before dawn to break our fast and perform whatever ablutions we wished before breaking our camp and setting out for the day. Ruth and I spent the morning riding with Hadar who continued our education in medicine and Edward and Caspar training us in our respective weapons in the afternoons and evenings.

It was about mid-morning on the fourth day out from Jerusalem when Godfrey called a halt after Caspar alerted him to a dust cloud on the horizon. Godfrey reassured us that from the size of the dust, it was a small party and reminded us of the 'no, sir' directive. The horsemen were still coming towards us and I think we all felt a sense of apprehension. We had, after all, left the Kingdom of Jerusalem that morning and were now in Oultrejordain. It was outside of the jurisdiction of Jerusalem; still a Christian domain but not a very secure one.

Our anxiety was relieved a short while later when a troop of about twenty Templar Knights and sergeants came into view and joined us on the road.

'Sir Godfrey. Sir Caspar. Your disguises don't fool anybody who knows either of you by face.' Their leader laughed.

'Thank you, Sir Pierre,' replied Godfrey, appearing a little embarrassed. 'What news can you tell us of what lies ahead to the east?'

'The truce of Jerusalem and Damascus still holds. We passed by some mounted Moslem scouts patrolling to the south yesterday. They did not seem intent on bothering us. Nor were we them. Saladin has been amassing troops to the north. We believe he is intending to travel south to Egypt to settle some scores there. He and his army may well be on his way south as we speak.'

'You see no danger in our proceeding east to Baghdad?' Godfrey asked more than stated.

'Only with bandits, mostly small and cowardly, and the odd local warlord who has not gone over to Saladin yet.'

'What lies ahead of us to the east?'

'Easy travelling, I should think. Gentle hills, fresh waterways and game aplenty. You should not starve or die of thirst.'

'I thank you. Your counsel has been welcome, Sir Pierre. I gather you are keen to finish your patrol and return to more comfortable surroundings sometime soon. We shall not delay you any further,' concluded Godfrey.

Sir Pierre raised his hand and motioned it in a forward direction at which he and his troops set off in the direction of their base to the southwest. Our party did likewise in the opposite direction.

Later that day we pitched our camp in a green meadow beside a welcoming creek. I was once again bruised and battered by Edward's punishing lessons in swordplay and decided to take a wash a little further downstream in the creek. Cleanliness was, after all, one of Hadar's injunctions for staying healthy during the journey.

I stripped off my clothes and left them neatly piled by the

creek's edge. I had brought along an old horse cloth to towel myself dry afterwards. The water was brisk and refreshing. I grabbed a clump of reeds and, rolling them up in my fist, used them to scrub the dirt and dust from my body. Once clean, I then rolled on my back and gently floated by the bank before emerging to dry myself.

It was as I was towelling myself dry overlooking the creek that Benedict crept quietly up behind me.

'You bare your nakedness and your shame openly before the Lord. Ippolito, your brazenness is a vile sin.'

In some shock and surprise, I quickly turned around to face him. He was standing very close to me.

Suddenly, he painfully grabbed my stones in a tight grip. His face moved closer to mine.

'Repent, Ippolito. Repent. Say the Paternoster now aloud so the Lord may hear your anguish and repentance.'

He squeezed further, kneading my stones against each other, causing me even greater pain.

'Our Father who art in heaven. Hallowed be thy name…' I began uncertainly wondering why this was happening but frightened of the power the priest was suddenly showing. I screwed my eyes shut in pain and continued the Paternoster.

'That is good, Ippolito. Keep saying it aloud over and over and feel the Lord's forgiveness washing over you.'

He eased his grip on my stones, his hands taking on a gentler more fondling quality rather than the brutish squeezing he had inflicted on me moments before.

'That is good, Ippolito. Keep praying. Keep praying.'

I did even if I was very confused at this point. I was in his power.

'Can you feel the Lord's kindness and forgiveness, Ippolito?'

His hand took on another quality and started to move from my stones to the base of my manhood. His face had moved closer to mine and he was staring intently into my eyes. I could feel his breath on my face as he whispered at me.

'Keep praying. Feel the Lord's mercy. Feel his kindness, Ippolito. Can you feel Him on...' He did not finish.

Suddenly he let go his hand on me and I looked up to see Godfrey's forearm around Benedict's neck, roughly pulling him away from me.

Godfrey's voice was full of whispered menace as I heard him say, 'I know you, priest. I know what you have done. I know you do penance for your sins and that is why you are here. You and your filthy kind deserve to die. One more time, Benedict, and I will kill you. Priest or no priest. Do you understand me?'

'Stop it. You are strangling me,' cried Benedict in terror and pain.

'Do you understand me, priest?'

'The boy had sinned in his nakedness and was being punished by the hand of the Lord.'

Godfrey pulled his arm tighter around Benedict's neck.

'Do you understand what I say to you, priest?'

'Yes. Yes. I do. Let me go.' He gasped against the pressure of Godfrey's forearm against his throat.

Godfrey's hand gripped Benedict's shoulder and he flung him to the ground, releasing him. Benedict lay sprawled at our feet one hand, massaging his neck.

Godfrey gave him a kick and told him to be on his way lest he receive worse treatment. Benedict got up and scrambled away further downstream away from the camp.

'Get dressed, boy.'

I quickly finished towelling off and put my clothes back on as quickly as I could. I was not sure just what I had been rescued from but I knew that Godfrey had saved me from something unpleasant and unwholesome. Shades of what Rudolphus had revealed to me about his mentor, the priest Sylvester, came back to me.

'Thank you for coming along and getting him away from me,' I said. 'I'm not sure I know what he was about.'

I suddenly felt a sense of shame and embarrassment, but for what reason, I was not wholly sure.

'He was doing wrong to me, wasn't he?' I questioned Godfrey.

'He was, boy, and at your age, you were not to know quite what his intentions were. Just accept that you have done nothing wrong in the eyes of your Lord. Do not be ashamed or feel you have sinned in any way. To save you from any further discomfort of the soul, I think that we shall say nothing to the others of this incident. It will remain a secret.'

I was relieved to hear Godfrey say this and felt a wave of gratitude wash over me.

'Thank you. Sir Godfrey.'

'Godfrey. Remember, no "Sirs",' he said giving me a friendly cuff around the shoulder.

'Godfrey,' I said feeling a new warmth and trust toward this gnarled and grizzled old warrior I had not felt before.

19

Godfrey and I returned to the camp where nothing was said and no one seemed to notice that anything had been amiss. I was secretly grateful for this. Benedict did not return to the camp that night for which I was also thankful. I did not know how I would react to his presence again and was still trying to determine what it was that he had been about. I was glad that Godfrey was around.

I spent the first part of the evening talking with Ruth. I was very glad to have her company as she was a distraction from the events of the day. The evening became even more pleasantly distracting when Raymond joined us and told us some more amusing anecdotes about some of the Knights Hospitaller.

'They say that when his suit of iron was finished, it held more iron than three others and was so heavy that not even, he, Gotfried the Fat, could rise up in it!' concluded Raymond to one of his stories. We all laughed at the preposterous story of the fattest knight in Christendom.

The next morning there was still no sign of Benedict. Hadar, Caspar and Ruth expressed some concern about his whereabouts but I think the rest of us were secretly glad he was lost or keeping his distance from us.

He was keeping his distance as later that day, Edward informed us he was bringing up the rear by about half a mile. When we stopped for a midday meal, he eventually made his sorry way into the camp. It was obvious he had been engaged in scourging himself through the night. There was dried blood on what we could see of his neck and his wrist and hands showed the same signs. He moved as if one in pain and would not meet anyone's eyes.

For some reason, I found his misery deserved and wished him more although I still had not worked out exactly what it was that he had tried to do to me.

We continued on our way and Benedict resumed his position at the rear of the party, falling back behind Edward, who did not seem to care about the priest's self-imposed exile and let him be.

We journeyed on in this manner until Caspar pointed out another, albeit larger, dust cloud rising from the horizon. It signified a troop of many more horsemen than the twenty who had composed the Templar party. We continued on our way towards the dust cloud as any attempt at avoidance or flight would have quickly aroused their suspicion and attention.

Just as we could begin to make out the figures beneath the cloud, Edward alerted us to another still larger cloud arising much further away to the north of us. We had become caught between two large groups.

'Just stay calm and let me do the talking,' cautioned Godfrey. 'Edward, ride back and bring that damned priest in. Make sure you tell him he is not to utter a single word or I will skin him alive!'

Benedict and Edward had re-joined us by the time the company of Saracen cavalry rode up to us. Their commander and three officers, all dressed in cavalry armour, greeted Godfrey and Hadar peacefully and with respect enquiring in Arabic of where our party was bound and on what business.

'To deliver my granddaughter to her new family in Baghdad,' was Hadar's reply.

'What is in the satchels and under your saddle blankets?' asked the commander suspiciously.

'Our belongings, gifts, medicines and other goods for the journey,' replied Hadar.

'And what about weapons?'

'Yes. We have weapons,' answered Godfrey. 'We would be foolish to travel without some kind of arms even in times of peace such as these.'

Suddenly there was a slight commotion in the ranks of the Saracens.

'Hadar. Hadar. Is that you? I don't believe my old eyes.' An elderly man with a long white beard and dressed in a plain woollen caftan was guiding his horse through the troop. He was smiling and laughing loudly.

Hadar too laughed out loud and then called out, 'Usamah, is that you? You old camel thief. Ha-ha. Well met, dear friend, well met.'

Usamah dismounted with a sprightliness that surprised me. The two friends came together in a laughing and slapping embrace, periodically breaking off to take each other's face in their hands and then begin laughing and embracing yet again. Their performance held the attention of everyone present. It seemed for the moment that the pair's laughing and smiling was catching as almost every face watching held a smile as well. Their final act was in losing their balance together and falling to the ground in yet another round of laughing and slapping.

'Ah, my dear, dear friend.' Hadar gasped, catching his breath.

'How many years has it been? Too many I am sure,' said Usamah, trying to catch his breath as well. 'Come, you must spend the night with us in camp, at least.'

'I would not dream of refusing the esteemed Usamah ibn-Munqidh. How many titles do you have now?'

They laughed again.

Godfrey had come up and dismounted beside the duo. Hadar made the introductions between the two and both gave the greeting of peace with their hands to each other. Godfrey and Hadar briefly conferred before Godfrey nodded his head and turned to the rest of us, announcing we would be spending the night under the truce as guests of Usamah in the camp of Saladin.

Raymond turned to me with a grin and said, 'I think this should be a very, very interesting evening.'

Over his shoulder, I could see Benedict crossing himself and mumbling some prayers at the prospect of being surrounded by infidels. He looked even more uncomfortable and unhappy than he had earlier in the day.

The commander of the troop spread his horsemen ahead, behind and around us as we formed up in a single file and moved out toward the growing dust cloud to the north.

As we rode, Hadar made a point of taking Usamah down our column and introducing us all individually and telling something of us each to him.

'So, you would learn from this great master of medicine and universal quackery?' he inquired of me, smiling as he did so.

'Yes, Usamah, sir. Ruth, my colleague here and I have learned much from Hadar and hope to learn much more of his... "quackery",' I jested in reply.

Usamah laughed again and turned to Hadar. 'A bright student. You will have to guard against the apprentice outshining the master.'

'And this must be Ruth,' continued Usamah, turning to face her.

Ruth performed a small bow to Usamah before informing him, 'I would be what is called a wise woman in my culture, and I will be the only one that has had the opportunity to learn from a real physician such as Hadar.'

Usamah looked pensive for a moment then turned and conferred briefly with Hadar.

'Mistress Ruth. You are no doubt aware of the traditions in our religion that require a certain amount of segregation of men and women.'

Ruth nodded her head.

'It would be considered a great impropriety, and against the will of Allah, if I were to allow you to stay and sleep under the same tent as your companions. I would request that you make yourself available to the hospitality of the Emir's harem this evening. In the harem is a wise woman named Noor who looks after the wellbeing of the women. I believe you and she could find much to discuss of mutual benefit to both of you.'

I hoped Ruth would accept this temporary separation with good grace. I need not have worried.

'I look forward to meeting Noor and the other women of the harem,' responded Ruth. 'I'm sure there is much we can share.'

We rode towards the dust cloud, which had stopped moving and was slowly dissipating over the horizon. Within two hours, we were guiding our horses through the huge Saracen campsite. The vast majority of soldiers did not give us a second glance and continued with setting their tents, guiding horses to the lines or preparing cooking fires. There was a general bustle of sound: horses neighing, armour tinkling, hammers banging, pots clanging and the sounds of a multitude of conversations going on around us.

At Hadar's request, Ruth had donned a veil to cover her face and hair and rode beside Raymond and myself. Hadar and Usamah rode ahead of us, still engaged in a lively conversation broken only by guffaws of laughter. Neither Ruth nor I had ever seen such a light-hearted and merry side of Hadar before. Their laughter was contagious and was attracting some attention from the soldiers.

Eventually, we arrived at a complex of larger more colourful tents than those we had earlier ridden by. In the middle of this complex was erected one tent taller and grander than any of the others nearby. The tent was red and a large green pennant with golden Arabic script upon it flew from the central pole of the tent. Around the tent was a squad of fully armoured guardsmen. They eyed us suspiciously and watched our party move on past the tent.

'Our headquarters and the tent of our commander and general Salah-ad-Din Yusuf ibn-Aiyub, may Allah bless his fortunes and family,' Usamah informed us. Shortly after this, Usamah bade farewell to the escort we had been travelling with and our little group followed him to the front of a large green and gold tent.

Soldiers standing outside the tent moved to hold our horses while we dismounted.

'Your horses will be watered, fed and groomed while you rest. Do not worry about them,' Usamah reassured us.

Usamah then called to someone inside the tent. A moment later, a servant appeared. He was dressed in very loose flowing robes with painted facial features and a perfumed air about him. I suddenly realised he was a eunuch but unlike any of the others I had occasionally seen before.

'Mistress Ruth. Would you be so kind as to follow Malik to the women's compound where I'm sure your every comfort will be attended to?'

Ruth turned and smiled to us all and then cheerfully stepped behind the eunuch and together they strolled away to the compound.

'Now the rest of you, please, if you would remove your shoes and then come into my comfortable home away from home where you can refresh yourselves.'

Usamah led us into his tent.

20

I was amazed at the opulence with which Usamah surrounded himself – and this was in a tent in the middle of a desert. Most amazing, I realised, was the fact that this portable palace was struck, packed up, transported and reconstructed each day by what must have required a small army of servants.

Beneath our feet were carpets so lush and luxurious it truly was a new experience to feel. I wriggled my toes just to feel the pleasure of it. The carpets were woven with hunting scenes where men, clad in an Eastern style, riding horses brought down gazelles, lions, bears and other animals with spears, swords and arrows. Laid over the carpets were placed dozens of similar embroidered pillows and cushions upon which Usamah bade us sit.

We did so and immediately servants appeared, offering us ice-cold fruit-flavoured sherbets to wash the dust from our throats and cool us down. I chose a sherbet from the tray. It was reddish-pink in colour and had a refreshing sweetness and flavour I had never tasted before. I wondered what the other coloured sherbets tasted like. The sherbets were accompanied by offerings of sugared dates, grapes, apricots, almonds, pistachios, olives and some small sweet pastries.

'Delicious,' mumbled Raymond between mouthfuls. 'I could eat the whole plate!'

I looked around and noticed the other members of our group

smiling and gesturing appreciatively over the delicacies. All were engaged in conversation. Hadar and Usamah most of all.

We had only been seated a short while when an officer entered the tent and stood to attention until beckoned by Usamah to his side. The officer whispered in Usamah's ear to which he nodded and waved his hand in dismissal.

'It would appear you are to be honoured,' announced Usamah to Hadar. 'My lord Saladin has requested that you attend him as soon as you are refreshed.'

'Myself, or all of us?' asked Hadar.

'Just the two of us, I believe, but you may take your young friend as your attendant.'

'Ippolito, finish what is in your mouth. We must not keep the Emir waiting.'

'Gulp, hah, yesh,' I responded, wondering if there would be more food in Saladin's tent.

Hadar and I tidied ourselves as best we could: washing our hands and faces in rose-scented water, brushing the dust off our coats and trying to look at our best. Usamah clapped his hands and made some urgent looking hand signals to a servant who disappeared quickly from the chamber and returned a moment later with two richly coloured and patterned silken overcoats, which Hadar and I placed over our tunics.

'Ah, now you both look more the part,' said Usamah, eyeing us over.

Usamah then led us outside toward the command compound with its grand tents and pavilions. We strode past numerous guards on duty and towards the largest pavilion in the compound. Outside the pavilion were six tall and powerfully built guardsmen. Usamah immediately raised his arms out to the side, telling Hadar and I to do the same. We did so as Usamah indicated to the guards they go ahead with their search. We were all searched thoroughly, not once, but twice by different guards each time.

Once completed, two of the guards ushered us through various hanging silks to the main chamber of the pavilion. Within the chamber, three men were seated upon cushions and awaited us. I noticed one of the silk hangings behind them move with an unexpected ripple. I suspected there were other guardsmen hidden behind the many hangings and curtains around us.

Usamah stepped forward and bowed. Hadar and I followed his lead.

'*Salaam* and greetings, Great Lord. May the peace of the Prophet be upon you,' said Usamah.

The Great Lord bowed his head to Usamah in acknowledgement.

'Saladin, Righteousness of the Faith, Yusuf ibn Ayyub, *malik* of Egypt and Emir, commander to the Sultan Nur al-Din, may the Prophet smile upon him. May I present to you Hadar, Jewish physician of Jerusalem and his assistant, Ippolito de Medici.'

Hadar and I bowed again.

'Please. Be seated.' The Emir gestured.

The Emir's complexion was paler than many of his companions although he was still tanned by the sun. His eyes were brown and surmounted by dark curving eyebrows, giving his face a gentle, almost searching look. His dark brown beard and moustaches were long and flowing. He was dressed in a buttoned cotton shirt with a darkly woven woollen surcoat, while loose black silk pantaloons completed his attire. On his head was the most unusually wound turban I had ever seen. Instead of being a neatly rounded head-covering, it was crafted so that five cloth horns appeared to be rising from his head. I noticed that one horn hung a little more limply than the others, giving the whole accessory a slightly comic look. I kept this to myself, of course.

'*As-salam-u-alaykum*. Peace be upon you,' said the Emir.

'*Alaykumu s-salam*. And peace be upon you too,' Hadar and I responded together.

We sat down on the cushions provided and immediately more sherbets and trays of delicacies were brought before us. I chose a light green sherbet this time, which tasted like melon. I noticed Hadar's eyes upon me looking as if to say, 'Do not stuff your face in here!' and held myself back, taking only one of the proffered delicacies.

'May I introduce Al-Adil, my brother in blood and in arms,' said Saladin, indicating the man sitting to his right. Family blood was evident in the facial features of the two brothers but there the similarity ended, al-Adil carrying considerably more weight than his brother seated beside him.

'And on my other side,' continued Saladin, 'is Imad-ad-Din-al-Isfahani, my loyal secretary, biographer and confidante.'

We bowed our heads again to the two companions.

'I am curious,' began the Emir, 'about a number of things concerning your party of travellers. How is it that you, Hadar, a respected physician and a Jew, have taken on young de Medici here, a Frankish Christian, as your apprentice?'

'A good question, my Lord,' responded Hadar. 'The making of a fine physician is not solely determined by whichever master he studied under or whatever university he attended. Nor is it governed by religious teaching be it yours, mine or his. The truly real physician is born with the desire to heal within them. I perceived this innate desire in Ippolito, and in his companion, the maiden Ruth, when I first met them. It is strong in both of them and they will drive themselves to learn all they can for their whole lives. It is my belief that only God determines into whom this desire will be born.'

I was surprised Hadar had chosen not to lie to Saladin about us not being a marriage party. I suspect he was worried Saladin may already have known the real truth.

'Ippolito. Why is it that you have chosen to study under a Jewish physician here in the east rather than one of your own or at one of your Frankish universities in the west?'

'It was rather a matter of circumstances, my Lord. I believe those circumstances were dictated by a power greater than I and have led me to the best possible teacher I could have.'

'Interesting, Ippolito. You do not talk of Allah, God or Yahweh, simply a greater power than you. What do you believe in or worship?' said the Emir, leaning forward to glean my response.

'I was born into the faith of the Latin Church, my Lord. Within that, I was taught to have faith in the Love of The One God, that of His Son and of all the saints. However, I'm not sure that all who claim to serve and walk with Him are worth listening to or following in their dictates. Nor do I believe that everything that is written in our Holy Book, the Bible, is truly the revealed word of God. It seems to me the thoughts and agendas of other men have been at work on our scriptures and texts.'

I thought of Rudolphus and his painful revelations as I said this.

'An interesting and wise answer from one so young. Islam too has some imams and clerics who speak more of what is in their mind rather than that of within Allah. Personally, I can do without them but some of them hold incredible power in the minds of the misguided among the faithful.'

'Do you speak of Shia Fatimids in Egypt, my Lord?' I asked. 'I have been told you are of the Sunni Faith and that there is much dispute between the two.'

'It is as you said – there are some who walk as though they are men of The One God but are mightily misguided. This is the case in Islam between Shia followers and those of the Sunni. We each believe the other is misguided.'

'May I ask in what ways?'

'Take, for example, how Islam's spiritual leader is chosen by the two parties. The *Sunni* believe their Caliph or leader should be elected from amongst those most capable and virtuous. The *Shia* believe that their imam or spiritual leader should be chosen from amongst the Prophet's family and descendants. But this is only one of many points of division between the two beliefs.'

I thought about this for a moment and then offered the following to the Emir: 'Could it be possible for *Sunni* electors to choose a leader for Islam from *Shia* nominees from within the Prophet's family?'

Saladin laughed in some surprise. 'It is a commendable thought from one as young as you, Ippolito. Unfortunately, the division between *Sunni* and *Shia* is so great that there will not be peace until one or the other is no more. Besides this, there are many other sects complicating these matters. There are the *Khawarijites, Ahamdiyya, Twelvers, Seveners,* amongst many others such as the widely accepted mystical *Sufis* and the murderous *Ishmaeli Assassins* that complicate our faith even further. All have different versions and interpretations of what the Prophet said and did. Others totally reject as unreliable some of the Prophet's sayings recorded in our second Holy Book, The Hadith.'

I had heard of The Quran but I had not heard of this last text.

'I wish I had more time to converse with you, Ippolito. I sense you could offer me perspectives on a number of issues I had not considered before. Alas, I must turn to more mundane matters such as the security of Nur ad-Din's realm.'

'Hadar. As you are aware, I am not deceived by the outward appearances of your party. Within your company are two knights, Sir Godfrey and Sir Caspar I believe, and a sergeant and a squire. Is this not so?'

'It is so, my Lord,' stated Hadar, making no attempt to deny the deception.

'To what purpose do you travel through these lands?'

'Lord Saladin, you are no doubt aware that the King of Jerusalem, Baldwin IV, suffers mightily with the skin disease leprosy.'

'I am,' acknowledged Saladin.

'News has reached the king's court that certain physicians and healers from the land of Hind are rumoured to have a cure for the disease and it is in search of this cure that we are bound.'

'A noble quest,' commented Saladin. 'I had worried that there was more to your subterfuge in disguising the Hospitallers. I do not believe that your party is intent on spying or espionage in this realm as has been suggested to me.' He eyed his brother Al-Adil briefly as he said this. 'I have great respect for the King of Jerusalem. Even when severely afflicted with the disease, he was able to lead his forces against mine at the Battle of Montgisard. It was a bitter defeat for me. My respect for Baldwin is immense and I see that this is a matter of honour.'

He paused briefly and stroked his beard.

'The Prophet instructs us to assist the poor, the widowed and the sick. I believe that my assisting you in this quest would be in keeping with the Prophet's instructions to his followers. With this consideration in mind, I will issue you and your party a safe passage, a *firman,* through those lands currently under my control. It would be dishonourable of me to deny you or your king this assistance.'

'Thank you, my Lord,' said Hadar.

'Thank you, my Lord,' I said, following Hadar's lead.

We both bowed our heads to the Emir.

For some reason, I was grateful I had not lost mine.

With a nod to Usamah the Emir indicated the interview was at an end.

21

Usamah, Hadar and I made the short journey back to Usamah's pavilion where the others were keen to know what had transpired.

'This is a good outcome,' commented Godfrey, concluding the discussion. 'I believe we will be able to travel with more certainty of achieving our quest with the Emir's *firman* to pass with safety through his lands.'

It was now late afternoon and the sun was low on a red horizon, casting the camp in a warm glow. All around us, the soldiers of the camp were preparing for the sunset *al-Maghrib* prayer. Wherever they could, soldiers performed their ablutions, unfurled their prayer mats and took their position for the prayer. Usamah joined them. Out of courtesy, Hadar suggested we should remain in the pavilion rather than appearing as 'gawking' at the spiritual privacy of their prayer.

After the evening prayers, Usamah returned to his pavilion and invited us to join him for an evening meal. We sat on cushions in a horseshoe arrangement set up by attendants. Sherbets were brought in and I tried another differently coloured and flavoured one to the one I had earlier. By its sharp tang, I knew it to be a citrus fruit but the flavour was one that was unknown to me. This was followed by dishes of spiced lamb with sauces of honey, yoghurt, mint or rosemary. After the lamb, various spiced dishes of lentils, beans and peas were presented along with a delicately flavoured flatbread. Marinated olives, dates, plums, apricots and more of those delicious sweet pastries made up the final course.

The meal was a leisurely one as Usamah encouraged us to take our time and enjoy each dish to its fullest. We needed very little encouragement.

'Some wine would have made this meal perfect,' said Raymond very quietly to me.

'Was it not Saint Ambrose who said "If you are in Rome, then live in the Roman manner"?' I whispered back.

'Touche, Ippolito.'

At that moment, Usamah clapped his hands for attention and as a signal to a servant to bring out what looked like a large one-handled vase with a long spout. Accompanying this was another servant carrying a tray of small cups.

'Dear friends,' began Usamah. 'I should like to offer you something new in the way of beverages which comes from the far-off mountains of Abyssinia. There is a legend related to its discovery, which I should like to briefly relate.'

We all stopped eating and ended our conversations and gave our attention to Usamah.

'Some time ago in Abyssinia, a goatherd named Kaldi was tending his goats in the mountains of that country. One hot day, after taking a rest, Kaldi looked up to see his goats dancing and prancing about and bleating joyfully. Curious to understand why his goats were so energised he got up and found they had been eating the red fruit of some trees growing there in the mountains. Sensing no harm, Kaldi decided to consume some of the "fruit" himself. Sometime later, a local imam was walking by and noticed Kaldi dancing and prancing and ululating with joy alongside his equally joyful goats. The imam naturally asked Kaldi what he was doing. Kaldi told him the story of the red berries, and it is from those red fruits that we obtain this unique beverage called *qahwa*. I like to call it "the drink of the dancing goats". I trust you will all enjoy it, and…' Usamah paused for some emphasis. '… its effects.'

The two servants poured Usamah a cup of the steaming beverage and then proceeded to pour small cups for the entire party.

Raymond and I glanced into our cups at the thick tarry black fluid then at each other.

'If you are in Rome,' said Raymond, winking at me and proceeded to take a sip from his cup. He immediately recoiled.

'Be careful, Ippolito, it is very hot. I have scalded my tongue.'

Others amongst our party had noticed the same thing and were letting their *qahwa* cool down. Usamah, obviously an experienced imbiber, had finished his before the last drink had been poured for his guests and sat awaiting a refill.

Eventually, our *qahwa* cooled enough to taste. The aroma was most pleasant and reminded me of the exotic spices my father had stored in his warehouse. The taste was unusual in that it had a bitterness that, at first, was a little off-putting but behind the bitterness was another flavour that made the drink quite enjoyable to taste. Raymond and I agreed, after finishing our cups, that it was a good drink. After watching Usamah finish his second cup, we decided another one was acceptable and signalled to the servant to pour us some more.

When we had both finished our second beverage, Raymond said to me, 'I say this "karwa" or whatever it is called is rather good. I feel refreshed and somewhat stimulated. Joyful like wine but in another less befuddling way.'

I felt the same way and said so. Around us, the conversations had become increasingly animated with more facial and hand gestures going on. The only exception was Benedict who had declined the beverage, no doubt thinking it was some kind of pagan poison. He had a decidedly grim aspect and no one was engaging him in conversation.

The evening progressed in lively talk and amusing anecdotes shared mostly by Usamah with the rest of us.

Raymond and I had just finished our third cup when Usamah again clapped his hands and bade us sit back against our cushions and to enjoy the entertainment he was about to provide.

I could see Raymond was, like me, wondering what this entertainment might be in the middle of an army camped in the middle of nowhere.

Usamah clapped his hands again and sat down. Three musicians entered the room, sitting near the entrance to the horseshoe arrangement of our cushions. The instruments were familiar to me, having seen them played in both the markets and squares of Acre and Jerusalem. One was an *oud*, a multi-stringed instrument somewhat like my father's *citole,* another was a simple drum called a *kudum,* while the last was a single-stringed instrument played with a bow called a *rababah.* The musicians took their places and commenced playing.

The beat was lively and the melody transporting. The musicians of the markets and squares of Acre and Jerusalem were nothing compared to the three who played to us.

Quickly the music reached a crescendo and as the drumming grew louder, six dancers emerged from behind a curtain.

They were all dressed very much the same: loose gauzy veils hiding their faces and hair so that only kohl-lined eyes showed through, tight-fitting bodices that accentuated the curves of their upper bodies and loose-fitting pantaloons that swirled about their ankles. Jewellery hung across their foreheads, around their necks and from their wrists and ankles.

Their movements were matched perfectly to the rhythms of the music and the whole performance seemed to take on a hypnotic quality such as one finds watching waves roll in and out.

Slowly the music changed pace, guiding the dancers into more sinuous movements. Singling out the guests before them the six dancers moved directly in front of myself, Raymond, Edward, Godfrey, Caspar and Hadar.

Each dancer performed differently, using their arms in beckoning gestures before their chosen guest but at the same time keeping their hips swaying in time to the regular beat of the *kudum* and the *rababah*.

The kohl-lined eyes of the dancer in front of me stared deeply into mine as she swayed and beckoned. Her gaze drew me in with its secret and seductive quality. I very much wanted to see the rest of her face, wondering if it would match the beauty of her eyes. I was entranced.

I suddenly became aware of Raymond nudging me in the side. 'Careful, Ippolito, I don't think it is polite to stare so intently back at the dancers.'

I shook myself out of my reverie and assumed a more polite and respectful pose just as the music came to another crescendo. The dancers did a final small leap in the air then bowed before their audience. They turned and exited in a flurry of silken colours.

22

We woke early to the noises of a large military camp stirring and preparing itself for another day's march. I had not slept well. Intermingled images of Ruth and the dancer, both with kohl-lined eyes and floating veils had drifted through my dreams and stayed clearly in my mind's eye as I arose and readied myself for the day. I felt confused by the images I had seen during the night.

I was even more perplexed by the fact that the loin-cloth I had slept in was sticky and adhering to the pubic hairs I was then beginning to sprout.

'You made a lot of noise in your sleep last night, Ippolito,' commented Raymond as we dressed. 'I thought at one stage you were dying. But then I realised you were experiencing the little death of a night spill.'

'A what?' I stammered, having no idea what he was talking about.

Raymond explained, in a young warrior's way, what had happened to me.

'It is nothing to worry about, Ippolito. In the squires' barracks of the Hospitallers, such things are freely talked about. We often share the details of our dreams to entertain each other. Tell me, what happened in yours?'

'I can't. I won't,' I said, suddenly feeling confused by a rush of thoughts.

'As you wish,' said Raymond, sounding a little disappointed.

I felt defensive about Ruth and did not wish to share the details of what I had dreamed of. I also felt ashamed about having thought of Ruth in ways I had not felt before.

'What did it all mean?' I asked myself.

My confusion and discomfiture were only increased when Ruth was escorted back to Usamah's pavilion later that morning. She was wearing two veils, one to cover her face and the other over her hair. Her eyes seemed to glitter joyfully at seeing me and I knew that underneath the face veil, she was flashing her beautiful smile.

Suddenly any awkwardness I had experienced vanished and I once again knew the same comfort and closeness with Ruth that I had always felt toward her.

Our horses were saddled and packed outside the pavilion when we emerged. Usamah was there to wish us a safe journey and we all thanked him individually for his hospitality. Once again, he and Hadar engaged in much laughing, hugging, back-slapping and shaking of each other. I wondered just what those two men had got up to together in their younger days that could engender such jocular friendship.

Ruth and I fell into place beside Hadar as we wound our way eastwards through the camp in the early light.

'Tell me, Ruth. Did Noor or any of the other women teach you anything of substance concerning their healing practices?' asked Hadar.

'Some variations on the treatment of common women's health problems that will be handy to know if our current stocks of curatives run out or become damaged. I notice we do not have a lot.'

'Well,' responded Hadar, 'at the time Ippolito and I were preparing them, we were not aware that we would be accompanied by a woman on our travels. It is good that you will be able to find or replenish those supplies if needed. I appreciate this.' He paused 'So what should we review this morning?'

And so, the next few days unfolded. Lessons in the healing sciences during the morning, a short break for a mid-day meal, conversations with Raymond or Edward, preparing our campsite and then painful lessons in swordplay with Edward, which would leave me bruised and looking forward to bed.

According to Caspar, Ruth was developing as a knife thrower very rapidly. She had an eye and a feel for the balanced weight of the knife and could hit a target eight out of ten times from a range of twenty or so yards. Caspar commented that her next challenge would be to develop the strength to make her knives truly penetrating when hitting a target whilst still maintaining accuracy.

It was on our sixth day out from Saladin's camp that we came across the hermit mystic.

We saw him first from a distance and could not make him out or exactly what he was doing.

As we drew closer, Godfrey came up beside us on his horse. 'Ippolito. Your eyes are younger than mine. What is he doing? Is he dancing?' he asked in some perplexity.

I had only just been able to get the figure in the distance into a clear focus. 'I believe he is dancing or maybe just whirling around. I do not think he wears any clothes either. He is naked.'

'A demon of the desert, surely,' interjected Benedict. 'Hold fast to your faith and the Lord will protect us. Follow me in prayer. Our father–'

'Shut your sanctimonious mouth, priest,' ordered Godfrey. 'It is probably some poor lost individual who has become quite demented in the desert. Let us be ready to help him.'

The man did not need any help and, in fact, he seemed as happy and full of wellbeing as any man I had ever met.

'My name is Abubakar – "father of the camel".' He laughed in introduction of himself. 'I dance and laugh and sing because I know that the One True God is my lover and I am his.'

'Heresy! Beware!' blurted Benedict at the mystic. He had a venomous look on his face.

Abubakar stopped his dancing and simply stared in silence at Benedict.

'Can you not answer me? You prophet of falsehood,' continued Benedict, almost spitting his vitriol.

Abubakar continued staring at Benedict, a blank look on his face. Suddenly his eyes widened and his eyebrows arched with inspiration. 'It was the great Imam Ali who once said, "Silence is the best reply to a fool".'

Each member of the party quietly snickered at this pithy response.

'I think the mystic speaks true, Benedict. Keep your comments to yourself. That is your last warning priest,' snapped Godfrey impatiently at the priest.

Benedict was patently wary of Godfrey and had been since the incident by the river. He did shut up.

Abubakar held up his hand. 'It is alright, Sir Knight, I have already forgiven him. For is not forgiveness the fragrance that flowers release when they are crushed?'

I found myself liking this smiling, laughing, singing, dancing and forgiving person. I looked over to Ruth who had a smile upon her face that suggested she too found this unexpected stranger likeable and interesting – despite the fact that he had no clothes upon him.

'Why are you naked and alone in this wilderness?' she asked him.

'I am clothed in love – the love of myself, the love I have for humanity and most importantly, the love of The One God who made all things. With myself, humanity and The One God, I have the best of company and the most elegant clothing I could have. I see that the beauty you see in me is but a reflection of that beauty in you.'

'But what do you live upon? You carry no supplies – how do you survive?' I asked.

Abubakar had recommenced his whirling dance, arms out to his side, eyes gazing up to the sky with his manhood flying out comically in front of him.

'I listen to silence and it has much to say, for you must see darkness dancing before you can hear silence singing. The morning dew quenches my thirst as every drop is happy to die in the river of my life. The locust gives thanks that he sees the teeth that deliver him to The One.'

'Oh, my Father,' moaned Benedict.

Abubakar started laughing again. This time it was more of a cackling sound and his eyes took on a more excited look.

'Judge me not for I do not follow the words that some call truths but the truths that already lie inside me. You must only look within and you will find your own truths for happiness and the blessed communion of being at One with The One.'

I was about to ask if he needed anything when he said, 'Before you speak, let your words pass through three gates. At the first gate ask yourself, "Is it true?". At the second ask, "Is it necessary?" and at the third ask, "Is it kind?"'

He began skipping instead of whirling and commenced to move away from us. He turned tind bowed low to us before uttering, 'I could speak of love and drive you mad, that is until you worship love with your own madness but always make sure you have tied your camel before plunging into the sea of riches.'

With that, he bounded off in his ecstasy of joy and madness and left us all wondering just what this encounter had been about.

'I hope he will be alright,' said Ruth quietly by my side.

'He seems to have lasted this long in the middle of nowhere and does not seem physically ill or worn out. Somehow, I think it is a kind of faith that sustains him in all this... madness.'

'Are you sure it is not a madness that sustains his faith?' came Ruth's quietly perceptive response.

23

Three nights after our encounter with Abubakar, I was awoken in darkness with a hand over my mouth and something stinging sharply beneath my jaw.

'Silence or die, infidel,' said a whispered voice full of menace in Arabic.

I made no sound. Next to me, I heard the same command issued to Raymond by another voice. I heard no sound from Raymond except his breathing. Or was it mine? I could certainly hear my heart pounding away in my chest. I could hear muffled sounds and rustlings coming from the other tents and awnings around us.

My assailant grabbed me by the hair with his other hand while the knife remained at my throat. I stood up as best I could and was roughly manhandled outside, closely followed by Raymond and his attacker. We were both shoved to the ground to lie on our bellies with our heads turned away from each other.

I was feeling panicky and could see the other members of the party being pulled or pushed from their shelters and forced to the ground on their stomachs. I heard Ruth squeal softly as she was forced to the ground and onto her stomach as well. Near the fire, I could see the slumped form of Edward by the fire's low light. There was blood across his forehead. I wondered if he was dead or alive.

Around us, shadowy figures dressed in black were moving around while others stood guard. I thought there might have been ten of them in total.

'On your knees,' came the command from one of the assailants. 'No talking.'

He was wearing a larger turban than the others and from the way he spoke, I took him to be the leader of the group. He turned and barked an order in Arabic which I did not catch and immediately two of the black-clad warriors mounted their horses and spurred away to the east.

We were kicked and pulled to our knees and turned to face the speaker who simply nodded to his fellows. The next thing I knew a blindfold was placed over my eyes and pulled tightly around my head.

'Stand up,' came the rough voice of the commander.

I started to stand when I was suddenly jerked up by my hair, the knife still beneath my jaw. We all stood there in silence, each of us no doubt wondering what would come next. My panic settled with the thought that if they were going to kill us it would have happened by now. Something else was going on.

I could hear the sounds of activity coming from the direction of where we had hobbled the horses for the night. I heard our assailants rummaging through our packs and belongings. From the direction of the packhorses, I discerned the sound of glassware softly tinkling and realised the vials Hadar and I had prepared were being loaded onto the packhorses. Other sounds suggested that other items too were being salvaged and loaded onto the packhorses. What was going on, I wondered?

My thoughts were interrupted by a shove in the back and the rough command, 'Walk. Slowly,' whispered in my ear while the knife still pricked and scratched away beneath my jaw.

I moved in the direction indicated and came up beside one of the horses. My hand was placed upon the pommel of the saddle and I was commanded to mount. In the darkness of my blindfolded night, my foot found the stirrup and I hoisted myself up into the saddle. At the same time, I felt the knife had been repositioned and was now poised to puncture me in the groin. A fatal wound should my assailant press his knife home.

'Give me your hands,' came the voice again.

I did so and felt rough cordage being wound around my wrists and pulled tight. My captor did not seem to care that with each tightening tug of the cordage he was chaffing away layers of the skin on my wrists. I winced. He laughed.

I could hear the others being directed into their saddles and similarly bound. The sound of water being splashed about followed by the mumbled grunts of Edward coming around reassured me that he was still alive. His startled protestations were quickly silenced by the thud of a meaty fist.

Our assailants continued to work largely in silence and it was not long before I heard the voice of the man with the large turban speaking in Arabic to us again.

'You will not speak whilst we journey. Your guide will lead you and your horse. Your wrists are bound but you can still use your hands and fingers to grasp the pommel of your saddles. Do as you are told and do not try to escape.' He paused and then said in a loud and clear voice to the others. 'Move out.'

We took off at a slow and leisurely pace, which was probably a safety precaution as night was still around us and the ground very uneven. I had no idea who was in front or behind me nor whose horse I was upon. I suspected it was Shadow, Caspar's horse, as he was skittish and difficult to control even when being slowly led. This did not make my journey any more enjoyable as I was worried the temperamental horse might throw me. I did not have Caspar's strong arms or the commanding relationship with the horse that he had developed with it.

An hour or so later, a change in the intensity of the darkness and the appearance of a small area of light in my blindfolded darkness below my left nostril told me that dawn had arrived. I could feel some weak warmth on my right cheek and knew we were heading north towards the mountain ranges that had been to our left as we rode across the plain the day before.

For the rest of that morning, we continued at our sedate pace with only the occasional sounds of our captors communicating with each other, and that was at a minimum. At some stage, a water bottle was placed in my hands and the order, 'Drink,' was given. I took a mouthful or two before it was grabbed off me.

'Enough!'

These were men of few words.

I had been aware of a growing pressure in my bladder and asked, 'Piss? Please.'

'Yes. Piss. Please,' came Benedict's voice from behind me. He sounded pleading and uncomfortable.

'Piss in saddle. No stopping,' came my captor's reply followed by a throaty chuckle.

Somehow with my wrists bound, I managed to lower the front of my hose and grasp my manhood and point to the side before letting a healthy pent-up stream issue down Shadow's shoulder. I sensed him turning his head back to bite me in retaliation. I jerked my legs back and he missed, his teeth coming together with a loud clack.

Behind me, I heard Benedict making protesting sounds of difficulty as I imagined him trying to raise his cassock from underneath himself and take a piss. I secretly hoped that he would wet himself thoroughly.

A minute later a disgusted 'ohhh' told me I had my wish.

This did cause me to wonder how Ruth was faring with her

needs and how she would handle this in front of our captors. I hoped she was alright.

The heat on the top of my head told me that it was around midday when we started ascending a track that led upwards and I guessed we were in the foothills of the mountain range that had been off to our left the day before. The changing positions of warmth on my face told me that our path was a winding one whilst the constant position of my back against the cantle of the saddle told me we continued uphill.

The air became cooler as we ascended higher into the mountain range. I was beginning to feel sleepy and my head began to nod onto my chest when I heard the first of the calls issuing from someone at the front of our party and a reply coming from somewhere above and ahead of us. This happened two or three times before I felt the track level out. The calls became shouts of recognition and questions and answers flew back and forth. Finally, I heard the sound of Shadow's steel-clad hooves clattering on stone and I knew we had arrived at a built-up location. A moment later someone called, 'Halt' and then, 'Dismount.'

I grabbed the pommel of my saddle and dismounted just as my guard deftly removed my blindfold. I blinked in the late sunlight and became aware of the general laughter from my captors around me.

I looked around and saw the source of their laughter. There was Ruth, her blindfold still in place, squatting on the courtyard stones with a rapidly growing puddle issuing from under her skirt.

I knew Ruth well enough to know she was not just answering a need, she was making a statement.

She wanted to piss on the lot of them.

24

When Ruth arose from her squat, her captor removed her blindfold. She turned to look at all the men surrounding her and gave them such a withering glare that their laughter quickly ebbed to be replaced by quiet smiles of amusement and respect for this bold girl.

I was still restrained by my captor's hand upon my arm and could only give Ruth a look that I hoped would say, 'Are you alright?'

She understood and nodded.

I looked around at the others in our party. Raymond seemed unscathed but Edward was pale and dried blood covered much of his forehead. He looked sick and miserable. Caspar and Godfrey appeared more indignant than ill-treated. Benedict was trying to look disdainful but the large stain on the front of his cassock gave the lie to his hauteur. Only Hadar appeared unruffled by the experience. He was quietly surveying our surroundings and nodding his head in greeting to anyone his eyes met with.

We were in the middle of a fortress forecourt and bailey that was surrounded by high and very thick walls. Dozens of men were milling along the parapet, leaning against bastions or sitting between the crenels of the wall. All were armed and all, like our captors, were dressed in a variety of loose-fitting black garments. Around the bailey were stables, barracks and storehouses. A well stood not far from one of the walls. In the centre and taking up most of the fortress space was a towering, tiered and expansive citadel. The whole complex seemed impregnable and highly defensible.

'Where are we?' mumbled Raymond from the side of his mouth.

I shrugged my shoulders in ignorance.

'Prisoners. Follow me,' said the leader of our captors. Our blindfolds were gone but our wrists were still tied as we were led into the citadel.

The first thing I noticed inside was the variety of suits of armour and weapons that were displayed around the walls. They were eastern in design, either Arabic, Persian or Egyptian in style. One or two did not seem either western or eastern in design and I wondered from what culture they had originated. Every so often the display was punctuated by the occasional European suit of armour, heraldic shield or long sword. Above us, hanging from the ceiling were various banners and pennants, some by their insignia and heraldry were related to those upon the armour and armaments below. We passed by numerous corridors and hallways similarly lined with arms and armour or with rich tapestries and hangings.

Eventually, we arrived at two great doors of a dark stained wood. The doors opened into a good-sized hall also decorated with armoury and hangings. At the head of the hall on a raised dais sat an old man on a pile of cushions. He too was attired in black and wore a very large turban. The only thing of colour about his apparel was a large blood-red ruby sitting in the middle of his turban. Beside him lay a sword in a beautifully jewelled scabbard. Behind him stood two tall guards dressed in black with their swords bared and crossed over their chest.

Most striking about his appearance were the scars from three diagonal sword strokes that had crossed down his face from the upper left-hand side to the lower right-hand side. The tracks had made a carnage of his face; his left eye was a closed and empty socket, his nose, which was missing its tip and left nostril, and the left side of his mouth and upper lip had been forced into the scarred rictus of a perpetual sneer. His one 'good' right eye was a bloodshot red that seemed to peer into one's most private thoughts. He truly had an intimidating and fearsome appearance. I noticed Ruth shiver ever so slightly at the horror of it.

'Bring cushions and drinks for my guests and unbind them immediately,' ordered the old man in what was a quiet, almost whispering voice.

Our captors immediately drew wickedly curved knives from their belts and slashed the bindings at our wrists. I looked down at the raw welts around my wrist and made a mental note to apply a healing salve as soon as I could. I noticed the others had been similarly roughly bound and had bloody red welts as well.

Servants dressed in rough pale woollen garments appeared with numerous cushions for us and, upon the old man's gesture, we all sat down. A moment later other servants emerged carrying trays of glasses and jugs of cool water. Again, the old man made a gesture, this time of raising his hand to his mouth at which all of us raised our glasses and drank deeply with our first mouthful. Once our thirst was slaked, the old man addressed us.

'Welcome to *Ash al-Nasar*. I believe you would call it "the eagle's nest" in your tongue,' he began. 'I am Mohammed Alaeddin Sabah and I have the honour of being master to the Ismailite Assassins in this region.'

I noticed Hadar bowing his head and upper body in acknowledgement from his seated position and, along with the rest of the party, did likewise. Only Benedict, in his self-righteousness, abstained. One of the assassins stepped behind Benedict and, grabbing him by the back of the neck, roughly shoved his head down against the floor with a dull thud. When Benedict raised his head a bead of red spittle escaped the corner of his mouth. I was hoping he had bitten his tongue off but knew he hadn't.

Mohammed ignored all this and continued, 'I know that you travel to the east to Hind and perhaps beyond to find what is only a rumoured cure for your king Baldwin's leprosy. You'—he pointed at Hadar—'are Hadar the physician and your knightly companions are Sir Godfrey of Caen and Sir Caspar del Calabria of the Knights Hospitaller. You are accompanied by one Father Benedict of whom I have heard about from other… less salubrious sources.'

He scowled and looked at Benedict with a penetrating stare that visibly made the priest shrink back down into his cassock.

'I apologise for the injury to your sergeant Edward. No doubt you will be able to tend to his wounds once your belongings are brought to you, or if you like I will have our surgeon attend to him.'

Edward waved his hands in thanks and bowed his head to the master and then pointed to Hadar, indicating he would prefer that Hadar ministered to his needs.

'Your two young men here are Raymond de Toulouse and Ippolito de Medici.'

Raymond and I both bowed our heads to acknowledge him as correct.

'I have not been informed about the young woman who travels with you.'

'My name is Ruth and I am apprenticed to Hadar so that I may learn the skills required to become a wise woman to my people. If you would prefer, I shall wear a veil whilst in your company.'

The assassin master looked somewhat shocked and surprised that a female should speak unbidden in his presence but then appeared very pleased a moment later by Ruth's display of courtesy and respect.

'I thank you for your politeness and consideration in this matter, Mistress Ruth. I would prefer you to wear a veil to cover your face and hair whilst in the common areas of *Ash al-Nasar*. This is for both propriety and your safety. I am sure you understand.'

Ruth nodded her head.

'No doubt you are wondering to what purpose I have sought to detain you here? The answer is simple. You are my hostages for whom I hope King Baldwin will pay handsomely so as to see you released and once again pursuing your mission.'

'But that could take months,' stammered Sir Godfrey. 'The king is very unwell and our mission is urgent.'

'That is why fast-riding emissaries to the king were dispatched the moment you were taken hostage.'

I remembered the two horsemen who had left the party at speed the night before.

'They will be in Jerusalem within the week and will approach the appropriate personages to negotiate your ransom and release. Hopefully, you will be on your way again inside a month. Oh! And I might add that any thought of escape from "the eagle's nest" is pointless as a walk around the parapets will reveal to you. While you are here, you have the freedom of most of the barracks and grounds of the fortress. Those areas where you may not go will be guarded against intrusion so there is no chance of you wandering into forbidden areas.'

We all looked at each other with looks of frustration and amazement.

Sir Godfrey looked about to explode but kept his composure as did Sir Caspar. Hadar simply turned to Ruth and myself and said, 'More time for learning. Your time will not be wasted here.'

He turned to the old man.

'Master Mohammed, I suspect that you have a surgeon here in *Ash al-Nasar* who I am sure is very capable of attending to the wounds and cuts and contusions your followers may gain in training and at their work. I suspect that you do not have a physician who can attend to the illnesses and ailments that may attend your followers. Is this not so?'

'It is, Master Hadar,' came the cautious reply.

'I would then ask that myself and my two young apprentices be allowed to attend to those of your followers who are unwell or troubled by illness outside of the wounds and injuries sustained in the line of duty. To this could we add the men, women and children of the settlement we could hear as we passed by not far from here as well.'

The master assassin looked pleased with this offer.

'I can think of no better way for you three to pass your time and it would certainly benefit all parties including those of the village below us and maybe even further afield,' he said with a calculating smile and then clapped his hands.

'Hassam!'

One of the attendants immediately came to the alert.

'I have changed my mind. The northern officer's barracks are to be the residence for our guests. See that all their needs are well met,' he commanded and then, turning to us, added, 'We will talk more tomorrow. For now, please take your comfort in the humble quarters I offer you.'

25

'This is bad news,' said Godfrey. 'The king's condition was growing graver by the day prior to our leaving.'

We were seated on cushions around a softly glowing brazier that kept the chill of the cool mountain air out of the barrack's room. Around us were our bunks, a table that served for meals and some storage shelves where our belongings had been placed.

'I suggest that as we have our freedom to move around the fortress we do so as thoroughly and as discreetly as possible. Try to find out what the surrounding landscape and terrain might offer, any under-guarded gates or doorways, where the assassins' armoury is located. That sort of thing. We also need information. Hadar, Ippolito and Ruth, you have been given a position of trust and are best positioned to gain any details from your prospective patients about the fortress routines, who comes and goes or anything else that may be useful to us. We cannot just sit here twiddling our thumbs and doing nothing.'

We were all in agreement but I seriously wondered how we could make an escape when we barely knew where we were. In any case, as soon as our absence was discovered the hills would be crawling with assassins who knew the terrain like the back of their hands and there would be little chance of making a successful bid for freedom. I kept these doubts to myself.

The next morning, we had an opportunity to discover just how hopeless our situation was. The fortress was built into the side of a rocky mountain and on three sides the walls of the fortress rose from tall cliffs that descended in an almost sheer drop into a river valley far below. From atop the gatehouse, we could see that the path we had been led upon to the fortress was little more than a goat track along a narrow ridge with long and steep drops on either side of it.

'I am glad we were blindfolded when being led here,' I said. 'I would have been trembling in fear that my horse would have shied or lost its footing upon that knife-edge of a track.'

Raymond and I continued our reconnaissance.

'I do not think much of our chances for escape,' commented Raymond after we had walked around the fortress's parapet perimeter.

A little further behind, us I could see Godfrey, Caspar and Edward deep in conversation. Godfrey was shaking his head and Caspar looked forlorn.

Later in the morning, Hadar and I were informed that our first patients were ready to be seen.

'Try to find out who delivers food and essentials to the garrison and who can come and go without suspicion,' directed Godfrey as Hadar and I stepped out towards our barracks where a queue of half a dozen assassins were standing waiting.

Ruth had already set up our little clinic with instruments and vials neatly ordered on a nearby shelf. She was to sit behind a latticed screen where she could not be seen by the patients. From there, she could see and hear all that transpired during our consultations.

Three of our patients were carrying wounds gained in training that had been poorly treated by the fortress surgeon and had become corrupted. The first was angrily gangrenous and – from the extent of the corruption and swelling extending up his leg and into his groin – it must have been a torture of throbbing agony for the assassin. There was little we could do beyond treat his obvious pain with tincture of poppy and hope his time passed quickly. The wounds of the other two we swabbed and cleaned out with vinegar as there was no wine to be had in the fortress. Behind the screen, Ruth prepared poultices of honey, garlic and dried chamomile which we then applied to the wounds. They would need to be changed daily. Hadar and I had not taxed these men for information as each was in too much pain.

Our fourth patient could barely speak due to a large tumour growing under his tongue. Again, there was nothing we could do for the man except provide the poppy juice to relieve his pain.

The fifth man to come to us had eyes so red and encrusted, he had to be led in. He was unable to open them. Using a solution of peppermint and watered vinegar, I gently bathed the orbits of his eyes clear of all encrustation until he was able to open them. Ruth prepared a bath of elder leaves, eyebright, hyssop and althea with which I irrigated every aspect of his infected region. He, too, would have to return for treatment tomorrow.

Our last patient was a youth about the same age as Raymond and myself. He informed us his name was Ahmed and he was nervous and embarrassed but obviously in great pain. When he lowered his pantaloons and revealed his testicles to Hadar and myself, I could see the reason why. One side of his scrotum was extremely enlarged and dark purple in colour.

'Ah,' said Hadar. 'Look, Ippolito. The swelling and pain are due to a twist in the cord from which the testicles hang inside their sac. Left too long, the testicle will be strangled of blood and die. Leaving it in turn to corruption and ultimately a painful death for the victim.'

I felt my own scrotal muscles tighten and retract at this piece of information.

'Have you seen the fortress surgeon about this?' asked Hadar.

'No. That butcher would just cut everything off. I do not want that,' said the youth, looking worried and anxious.

'Ahmed, I will need to cut you but only a little bit so that we may untwist the cord that carries your testicle. We will give you some poppy juice so you do not feel any pain while I correct the twist in your testicle.'

Ahmed's face lost its look of horror but I could tell he was still very anxious.

From behind the screen, I could hear Ruth unstoppering the large vial of tincture of poppy that we kept.

'Gain his confidence,' whispered Hadar to me. 'He may talk when under the effects of the poppy.'

'Where are you from?' I asked Ahmed as I helped him onto the table where Hadar would operate.

'A village. Not far from here. It has no name. My family lives there. It was they who sent me here to serve the assassins and perhaps one day join their ranks. Many boys from our village have come here before and done just that. It can be a hard life but at least there is always enough to eat and drink, which is more than life offers in the village.'

'Ahmed. This does not taste wonderful but it will lessen the pain of the cutting.' I handed him a glass of tincture and water. 'Drink it all down.'

Ahmed did so while I casually chatted with him about life in the village and the fortress.

Whether it was the poppy or whether it was that Ahmed was a naturally open and honest youth, I don't know, but he told Hadar and I a lot about life in Ash al-Nasar and that of the assassins. We were able to establish that the nearby villages did provide the fortress with food and other necessities. There was no set day for the arrival of these much-anticipated stores. Often, deliveries would be accompanied by family members who would visit with former men of the village now living in the fortress. All the villagers in the area were devotees of the Ismaili sect and held everyone living in the fortress in great respect.

I watched Hadar with fascination as he deftly cut the affected side of Ahmed's scrotum.

'Oooh. That stings,' commented Ahmed with some surprise.

Hadar quickly removed the testicle from its home.

'See the twist in the cord and the blood vessels around it,' said Hadar.

The malformation was clear.

Hadar then unwound the single loop and I noticed a renewed blood flow immediately pulsing in the redder of the two blood vessels.

Ruth had prepared needles and sutures by soaking them in vinegar and was watching from behind the screen.

Hadar placed the glistening testicle back in its sac and proceeded to sew up the incision. He then placed a gauze swab soaked in vinegar over the wound.

'I am going to bandage your scrotum to hold the gauze in place. You will need to come here each day so we can change the dressing,' instructed Hadar as he neatly tied the loose bandage off.

'I will see you tomorrow then,' said Ahmed, rising a little bit uncertainly from the table. The poppy was still affecting him.

'Ippolito will accompany you back to your barracks and inform your officer of your need to see me tomorrow and in the days after. Ippolito, make sure you tell his officer he is to be on light duties only for the next few days.'

Ahmed was happy to take hold of my upper arm as we walked across the compound to his barracks. The effects of the poppy were making him unsteady on his feet.

'It is a bit like hashish in its effect. The poppy juice, I mean,' commented Ahmed. 'There are bricks of it in the master's stores, you know.'

'I have never had to take either the poppy or the hashish, although I know of their uses in medicine. What is it like?'

'The hashish? Why… it brings one to paradise.'

26

As the days passed, Godfrey, Caspar, Benedict and Edward became more morose and frustrated both by inactivity and their inability to seize upon a possible escape plan or route. The assassin fortress was truly impregnable and inescapable. Hadar was the only adult in the party who seemed unaffected by this state of affairs.

Ruth, Raymond and I shared the company of youth and found conversation, practising our skills at arms and other ways in which to pass our time. In his spare time, Ahmed would join us as we were the only other young people in the fortress compound and he enjoyed our company as we did his.

The master of the assassins, in keeping with the laws and customs of hospitality, regularly invited the males in our party to his table. Ruth did not miss out on any delicacies as Mohammed specifically directed dishes from the meals we were being served were also delivered to our barracks where Ruth would be eating with either Raymond or myself for company. Mohammed understood that we valued and respected Ruth and apologised that his own customs forbade unmarried women eating in the company of unmarried men unless they were her father, brothers or uncles.

Mohammed was an interesting and entertaining host. He was also quite charismatic and when he put his mind to some argument or debate, he could be powerfully persuasive simply by the use of logic and reasoning. He demanded and received absolute loyalty from his followers who all seemed somewhat in awe of him and were ready to carry out his least command immediately.

The extent of his power over his followers was demonstrated very clearly to us one afternoon. One of his men had been detained for stabbing another in the hand. It was fortunate it was his left hand. Had it been his right, he would never have held a sword again as the knife had slashed the tendons He would be able to carry a shield strapped to his forearm. Hadar and I had treated the wound and it would safely heal but with loss of function.

Mohammed listened to the senior officer's report and then summoned the accused to stand before him. He quietly spoke to the man who stood perfectly to attention, staring straight ahead at Mohammed. Mohammed quietly said something else to him and then withdrew his knife from the jewelled scabbard by his side. He handed it to the assassin who nodded his head in understanding. The man then held his left hand up and spread his fingers. With one swift and precise action, he cut down through the webbing between his fourth and fifth fingers till the slice met resistance at which he began a sawing motion and in just a few seconds had liberated his fifth finger from his left hand without making a sound. He held the thumb of his right hand down on the stump to prevent blood pumping and spraying onto Mohammed. The finger lay in the dirt. The assassin looked up at Mohammed who simply nodded in response and the warrior marched back to his ranks. Hadar and I treated the wound later that day in our barracks.

It was a week later when Ahmed approached Raymond and myself in a somewhat furtive manner.

'I have the keys to your paradise,' he whispered in a conspiratorial manner.

'How so, Ahmed?' asked Raymond.

'These.' He thrust his hand forward and opened it, revealing several brown and black pellets each the size of a sheep dropping. 'Pellets of hashish. There are enough for each of us and more.'

'But how did you get them? You said they are the master's property and kept securely locked away. Surely you will get into trouble for this.'

'The master and the senior officers had an entertainment last night. I saw the pellets lying on the floor when I attended to clear and clean up this morning. Some clumsiness on the part of an officer or a servant. They will not be remembered or missed.'

I was unsure if I really wanted to be a part of this. I had drunk wine in small amounts and was aware of its more extreme effects from watching family members become inebriated on occasion. Raymond changed my mind.

'Paradise, you say,' said Raymond. 'This sounds like it might be worth a try. What do you say, Ippolito?'

'Well. I'm not sure,' I replied.

'It is only the once and as Ahmed says, the pellets will not be remembered or missed. I'm game to give it a go. When?' he said to Ahmed.

'Tonight. The west tower. It is no longer used for observation and is far enough away from the barracks so that we will not be seen or heard.'

We assembled in the west tower as planned that evening.

'... and there in the gardens of Paradise, surrounded by fruit trees of every variety, the most beautiful and fragrant flowers on Earth and fountains of wine and milk the *houri* took me on such heavenly transports of delight that my senses left me entirely. When my senses did return to me, I was back in the fortress wondering if I had truly tasted Paradise or merely been the victim of a hashish phantasm. Tonight, I will find out and so shall you, my friends.'

We were sitting on the floor of the tower house atop the western tower of the fortress. To the east, a gibbous moon was casting enough light for the three of us to see each other. By the moon's path, I estimated it had been about an hour since we had ingested the hashish pellets.

'I feel rather heavy,' observed Raymond. 'My arms seem to have weights upon them,' he said, waving them about. He seemed to find this amusing and started giggling to himself. For some reason Ahmed and I, too, both started to laugh at Raymond waving his arms around in front of himself and above his head.

'It is beginning,' said Ahmed.

'Bring on the *houris*.' Raymond laughed.

I had been lying back supported by the wall of the tower house. A deliciously warm feeling of falling into myself was taking over my body. I tried to speak but found my mouth so dry my tongue was stuck to the top of my mouth. I reached for the water skin that lay at my feet and found that I too had limbs that felt weighted down. My efforts to reach the water skin amused Raymond and Ahmed and they began laughing at my efforts which made me laugh as well. I finally reached the skin and took a deep draught swilling it around my mouth before swallowing.

'Mmmh, this feels nice. I know I am still on the floor of the tower house but I feel like I am floating and could just drift away,' I said.

'Close your eyes for a while and let the dream begin,' advised Ahmed.

I did so and allowed myself to wriggle down into a more comfortable recumbent position. It was only moments before images started appearing behind my closed eyes. At first, they appeared as phosphorescent dots and short flecks that darted and flickered around my field of vision. I found these scintillations something of a novelty and very entertaining. I watched the light show with interest. Gradually, the dots and flecks changed into parallel lines and flickering zig zags that seemed to be leading me to something further ahead of me. These lines and zig zags gradually changed into spirals that seemed to turn faster and faster and became narrower in their circumference. I felt as if I was falling into a spiral.

Then the spiral became a vortex into which my spinning head felt it was being pulled along. Ahead of me seemed to be a white light that shimmered into haloes of the lightest pinks, blues and greens. As the haloes moved towards me, their interiors became filled with images that were confusing to me. Hadar was in one halo but his beard was a bright purple, which made me laugh. In another halo, Ruth danced and blinked kohl-lined eyes in time with the pulsations of the shimmering halo surrounding her. I tried to follow the image but it moved away and others replaced it. In another of the haloes, Godfrey and Benedict had their hands around each other's throat, which also made me laugh. Papa was in another halo, his head nodding and face smiling. It seemed that he was looking straight at me.

The faces that floated before me were all familiar and had something to say to me but I was not always sure just what the message was meant to be. They came quickly before my eyes and faded just as fast. One of them I am sure was Umm Sawda, my mother. She had died shortly after giving birth to me. I wanted to reach out to her and hold her just as she seemed to want to do to me. I became aware that tears were forming in my eyes.

Just as I felt Umm's hand stroke my cheek very softly, she and all the other haloes tumbled away from my vision in various directions. I could still feel Umm's hand gently stroking my cheek and I turned to speak to her but the hand was not Umm's. Instead, the kohl-lined eyes of Ruth were very close to me and examining me intently. Her eyes seemed to fill my whole vision as they came closer and closer to my face. Her eyes were still filling my vision when she seemed to close them in a swoon of ecstasy. I held her in my arms and stroked her hair, her neck, her face.

I suddenly became aware of hysterical laughing and my eyes opened to see an unconscious Ahmed sprawled beside me, his arm resting across my chest and shoulders.

'Oh, Ippolito,' laughed an amused Raymond. 'If only you could see yourself.'

<h1 style="text-align:center">27</h1>

Somehow the three of us made it on very unsteady legs and several fits of laughter down the staircase of the tower and out into the night. By the position of the moon, I could tell five or six hours had passed since we had ingested the hashish. My arms and legs still felt very heavy, my head was foggy and Raymond was making us laugh with his recollections of what Ahmed and myself had said and done in 'our state of transport'.

Ahmed was quite disappointed he had not met his *houri* again. Of the three of us, his memory of the experience was the most impaired. Raymond stated he thought this was because Ahmed had quickly stood up at one stage and then proceeded to pass out in what Raymond called 'the most graceful collapse' he had ever seen. I did not say too much about the latter part of my experience as I was somewhat shocked to learn that instead of stroking Ruth's hair, I had been running my fingers through an unconscious Ahmed's hair.

I slept well that night but woke up very sluggish. Hadar noticed the difference in my behaviour only commenting that whatever we boys had done the night before we were to avoid doing so again lest we bring down the wrath of the assassins upon us. After considering that I had run my fingers through Ahmed's hair thinking he was Ruth, I agreed with him about 'avoiding doing so again.'

Our group had fallen into a routine of meeting each morning while we broke our fast. It gave us an opportunity to discuss issues and to let each other know what we were planning to do with the day and where we would be if needed. I suppose this met Godfrey and Caspar's need for some military order to be maintained. Both were keen that Ruth and I continue our training in the knife and sword respectively. We were happy to oblige. Hadar had even been given an old hunting bow and a quiver of arrows to practice his archery.

We were all quite surprised by Hadar's accuracy with the hunting bow.

'Like riding a horse. You never forget how,' he said with a rueful smile, pulling his arrows from the target set up for him.

Godfrey was in an unusual mood this morning. 'I believe I have a plan that may assist us to leave this place. Caspar and I have had time to assess the mettle of these warriors that hold us prisoners. Whilst many are capable and strong warriors, neither Caspar nor myself have observed any of them during their training that could best either of us in a trial by combat. It is for this reason that we shall challenge Mohammed to allow us a trial by combat with one of his selected warriors to gain our freedom.'

'How do you know Mohammed will agree to this challenge?' asked Hadar.

'Have you not noticed how he often stands on his balcony overlooking the training contests going on in the fortress courtyard? His fist is often clenched and he urges on his warriors with words of praise and encouragement. He is obviously a very competitive man as well as the proud leader of these assassins. I think I can appeal to his sense of competition and pride to make this challenge and wager our freedom upon it,' replied Godfrey.

We waited until the next time that Mohammed chose to share a meal with us before Godfrey skilfully issued his challenge. Mohammed rose to the bait and it was agreed that Godfrey would fight Mohammed's champion.

'But!' said Mohammed. 'To make it interesting, the fight will be to the death, not to the first man to yield.'

'So be it,' agreed Godfrey. 'Arms and armour as chosen by each warrior according to his preference.'

'Agreed. Tomorrow then in the forecourt of the fortress at noon.' Mohammed smiled.

'Agreed,' answered Godfrey and then proceeded to indulge himself in his meal as if he had not a care in the world and would not be fighting for his life the next day.

The next morning saw us all assisting Godfrey in readiness for the trial by combat. Raymond spent the morning honing Godfrey's sword to an edge that could have split a hair. Edward reinforced Godfrey's shield by edging it with metal strips and sharpening the boss into a small but wicked point. Hadar had prepared a tonic for Godfrey that he said would give him extra stamina should the fight be protracted. Ruth and I cleaned Godfrey's hauberk of rust by rubbing sand into it and then polishing the rings till they shone. Caspar and Godfrey were immersed in a conversation about tactics. Benedict assured us that he was praying most fervently for Godfrey's success.

We could tell by the growing noises from the forecourt that a crowd of warriors was assembling to watch the upcoming battle of the champions.

'Well, let's not keep them waiting.' Godfrey laughed, trying to add good cheer to his voice. I thought it sounded a little strained.

'I cannot watch this,' said Ruth. 'Whoever wins or loses, there will be blood spilled and I do not wish to watch.'

I was torn between my feelings for Ruth and my loyalty to Godfrey who had not only saved me from Benedict's interfering with me but who also had my respect as a knight and the leader of our party.

'Go and support Godfrey,' said Ruth, noticing my indecision and uncertainty.

There was a ragged cheer of derision and also of expectation as we emerged from our barracks into the mid-day brightness of the forecourt. Warriors were positioned around the walls and Mohammed was seated on his balcony, overlooking what was to be the combat arena. This was all as we had expected. What was not expected was the champion who was to battle Godfrey. We had not seen him training with the other assassins in the courtyard before.

He was a giant of a man. A good head taller than Godfrey, broader across the shoulders and chest and with legs and arms as thick as the boughs of a tree. The top of his head and forehead seemed disproportionately large in comparison with his already oversized body. His nose and lips were also large but disfigured from either injury or an accident of birth – we could not tell. His irises and pupils were dark black pits sitting in yellow and blood-veined eyeballs.

He carried a curved and large scimitar with a vicious hooked blade emerging from the shaft a few inches below the point of the weapon. His shield was a small circular buckler-like guard that, similar to Godfrey's shield, had a sharpened point for a boss but also pointed barbs around the perimeter of the guard enabling it to be used as a weapon as well. Unlike Godfrey, he wore no body armour and was adorned solely in a loin cloth. He grinned evilly.

Mohammed called out to him in a language none of us recognised to which the giant replied with what sounded like, 'Gurk! Gurk orush havid.'

He then turned and held his arms and weapons up to the other assassins observing along the walls and from the few balconies surrounding the yard. His comrades gave him a fearsome and ululating response crying, 'Gurk. Gurk.'

Looking at the two warriors about to fight to the death made me feel sick to my stomach. How was Godfrey going to defeat this monster? I almost wished I had stayed behind with Ruth so that I did not have to watch what I felt was certainly going to be Godfrey's demise.

From the balcony, Mohammed raised his arm and then dropped it suddenly, signalling the start of the combat. There was no circling to size each other up. Instead, Gurk, as I assumed he was named, simply rushed at Godfrey with a blood-curdling yell, his scimitar raised to slash down at his foe. Godfrey neatly side-stepped the unexpected rush and twisted his body to avoid the swipe of the blade as it travelled within an inch of his left shoulder and arm. Gurk's momentum carried him on past Godfrey, allowing him to avoid being opened by Godfrey's blade in its counterstroke. Immediately Gurk turned and resumed his onslaught of Godfrey. This time their blades crossed and met in mid-air, momentarily locked between the two warriors. The giant had the advantage of height and was gradually forcing Godfrey down to his knees. Suddenly, Godfrey ceased his struggle and leapt backwards, landing on his back and rolling to his side. He jumped to his feet just as Gurk's scimitar crashed down to where his head had been only a second before. Again, Gurk allowed Godfrey no respite to catch his breath or plan tactics and rushed straight at the Hospitaller with scimitar raised, ready to slice into Godfrey. This time, Godfrey lifted his shield and stepped into Gurk's stroke using the newly sharpened boss in the centre of the shield to push it into the giant's breast bone. The giant gave a mighty yell of pain and stepped away from Godfrey but not before unleashing a devastating stroke that opened a six-inch gash down Godfrey's thigh.

Both combatants were now bloodied; Godfrey along his thigh and Gurk from his breast bone. Neither seemed to notice their wounds or show any sign of pain. Godfrey then took the initiative and stepped in low with a sweeping stroke designed to take the monster out from below. With surprising agility, Gurk launched himself from standing into the air and Godfrey's blade swept harmlessly beneath his feet. In the time it took Gurk to jump he had turned his blade and brought it down catching Godfrey in the same position as his previous thigh wound opening it further and hastening the loss of blood. Godfrey grunted in pain before stepping back and testing his weight on the leg before blocking yet another blow from the rapidly moving scimitar.

More and more, Godfrey was being forced into defensively blocking Gurk's scimitar and unable to launch an attack against the giant. Three more times Gurk missed a killing stroke as Godfrey ducked and weaved away from the whirling blade whilst trying desperately to launch his own offensive. Despite Godfrey avoiding the full force of Gurk's blade, he was now nicked and wounded in both thighs, his shield arm and shoulder. It was only a matter of time before he weakened and bled out.

Godfrey seemed aware of his diminishing chances of a victory and resumed his dance of ducking and weaving away from Gurk's scimitar. He was getting slower and slower when a vicious overhand sweep of the scimitar swept down Godfrey's back, opening a long wound and causing him to stagger. This gave Gurk another moment to turn and sweep around with a stroke that did the same to Godfrey's chest and abdomen. Blood was now running freely from his wounds yet still, Godfrey stood, albeit somewhat unsteadily.

Gurk seemed to sense the Hospitaller's battle was done and stepped in for a killing stroke when Godfrey suddenly leapt forward with a lunge that sent the point of his sword through the side of Gurk's cheek, dislodging teeth and taking most of his ear off. The giant bellowed and looked surprised, holding his hand to the side of his face and examining the blood all over his hands. Godfrey stood for a moment, catching his breath before launching into another lunge at Gurk's body. With surprising speed, the giant wheeled away from the thrust and turned to face Godfrey, bringing the edge of his blade down the side of

Godfrey's helm slicing it and the face below it deeply. Blood pumped and flowed all over Godfrey's face as he fell backward to the ground, his sword resting limply in his hands. He did not move.

Gurk stood over the supine and seemingly unconscious form of Godfrey, turning to the cheering crowd, accepting their applause and cheers of victory. Still, Godfrey did not move. I turned to look at Raymond whose eyes were welling with tears over the fall of his mentor and friend. Caspar stood with head bowed, not wanting to watch the delivery of the death blow. Edward and Hadar were similarly looking away. Anywhere but to the dreadful sight of seeing Godfrey slain like this. Only Benedict stood apart, his eyes never leaving the scene unravelling before us.

Gurk accepted the praise of his comrades while spitting teeth shards and blood from his mouth. He turned and looked down at Godfrey. He raised his sword, the pommel in both hands set to drive it down into Godfrey's chest and end his life.

Suddenly, just as Gurk was at full stretch in readiness for the final blow, Godfrey's arm came flashing up with sword gripped in hand. It was joined by his other hand as the sword point was driven through Gurk's bladder, bowels and backbone. Gurk stood for a moment as Godfrey twisted his weapon free in a gut-wrenching movement that saw the contents of bladder, bowels and blood vessels pour all over him. Gurk's legs folded beneath him and then he collapsed to lie motionless on top of Godfrey who could only spit to clear Gurk's blood and wastes from his mouth.

The courtyard exploded in a mass of yelling and curses as Gurk's supporters roared their protest. Suddenly, the noise ceased as Mohammed stood and raised his arms for silence before declaring, 'Godfrey de Caen is the winner. The hostages may go free. Now.'

The last word was spat out almost as a curse.

28

We could tell that Mohammed was not pleased by the result of the combat, but neither were we. Godfrey's wounds were hideous and he was barely alive by the time we got him back to the barracks. Caspar and Edward laid him out on the table while Hadar, Ruth and I prepared all that we would need to try and stitch his life back together again.

'Caspar! Edward! Raymond! Clean Godfrey up as best you can. Strip him naked. Get as much of that giant's muck off as you can. I don't want any filth in or near those wounds,' called Hadar to the Hospitallers.

Mercifully, Godfrey had passed out as we moved him from the courtyard to the barracks. We would do all we could to save his life whether he was oblivious, or not.

Within a few short minutes, all was ready.

'Ippolito! Ruth! Go to work on those thigh wounds. Cleanse them thoroughly. Drainage wicks at both ends of the wounds, tight stitches and peppermint oil swabs underneath the binding. When you are finished there, start on his arm and shoulder. I will do what I can with his chest and abdomen,' said Hadar, snapping out his directions. 'Caspar, to me. I hear you are good with a knife. Edward and Raymond, be ready to hold Godfrey down should he come around. And Benedict! Stop that infernal bleating. We cannot concentrate.'

Benedict stopped midsentence in his prayers. His eyebrows shot up and his jaw dropped, obviously shocked at what Hadar had just said to him.

'Better yet, send the pompous toad outside. He is only an annoying distraction,' added Ruth.

Ruth's manner surprised me. I had not heard her speak ill of anyone before.

'Don't you dare talk to me like that, you pair of murderous and blaspheming Jews,' snarled Benedict, not wishing to be admonished by one Jew, let alone two and one of them, a girl.

Edward did not waste a moment. He grabbed Benedict's cassock and pulled him through the door. 'Stay here and keep guard. Let us know if anyone approaches. You can be useful that way.'

With that, Edward turned around and took up position holding Godfrey's leg for Ruth and myself.

Ruth and I worked on Godfrey with only a word or two said between us. We could anticipate what the other required and we found ourselves moving, thinking and working as one. It was a spiritual melding of both our healing skills and, I realised later, of our hearts. Mercifully, Godfrey did not moan or move throughout the entire procedure and less than an hour had passed before we had Godfrey's thighs, arm and shoulder stitched, wicked, padded and bandaged.

We both had time to look up at Hadar and Caspar who were desperately trying to find a bleeding vessel on Godfrey's chest and close it off before Godfrey bled bone dry.

'Got it,' said Caspar, perspiration dripping from his forehead as Hadar closed in with stitches and tied off the errant blood vessel.

'Thank heaven.' Hadar sighed, looking weary and pale from exertion and worry. 'Ippolito. You and Ruth sew up his face. It is only a great fleshy flap and once stitched back in place it should hold and heal. Small wicks every two or three inches. He won't look very handsome from now on.'

'He never did.' Caspar laughed, helping us to make light of the situation for just the briefest moment.

Just then, the door flew open and banged loudly against the wall as an agitated and worried-looking Benedict rushed in. 'They are coming. Mohammed is with them. What are we going to do?'

Hadar looked up from where he hovered over Godfrey's inert form. 'Talk, I suppose.'

Hadar turned to the door as Mohammed, accompanied by three assassins, came into the room.

'I believe I told you to leave...' Mohammed trailed off as he took in the scene before him. On the table lay a savagely wounded and deathly pale warrior. His eyes saw two children sewing together the torn flesh of the man's face and two more blood-drenched men performing desperate surgery on the mangled torso.

'And so we shall, Mohammed, but until that time we claim the protection afforded to those of *dhimmi* status as outlined by your prophet, may his name be praised, in your holy book the *Koran*. All of us here are People of the Book. Let there be peace between us. Please allow us to finish here and we will be gone by sunset this evening,' said Hadar. He spoke in a commanding tone that gave his words a spiritual authority that surprised all of us, including Mohammed.

Mohammed appeared momentarily uncertain. In front of him were what looked like a band of blood-soaked *djinns,* one of whom was using the directives of the prophet to justify their continued presence in the fortress in open defiance of his explicit commands.

'I hear you, Hadar. The Prophet cannot be ignored. Let it be so.'

With that, he turned and exited, followed by his guards.

'I do not know if his patience will extend beyond sunset,' offered Caspar.

'Then back to work,' commanded Hadar.

An hour later, Godfrey was still unconscious, barely breathing and swathed in blood-stained bandaging.

We hastily packed all our belongings while Hadar kept a watchful eye over Godfrey.

The problem was how to safely transport Godfrey in his parlous state.

It was Ruth who suggested tying a straw palliasse to the saddle of one of our horses.

Soon enough our sorry expedition departed through the fortress gates, watched by Mohammed and his assassins.

Ruth and I walked beside and just ahead of the palliasse, picking up and removing stones and rocks that would have disturbed Godfrey or torn the already somewhat threadbare sacking.

We had arrived at the assassin fortress after a full day and half a night of travelling blindfolded.

Now that we were leaving, none of us really knew exactly where we were.

29

The path between the assassin's fortress and the plains below was mostly worn smooth by the passage of assassins and local villagers travelling up and down the mountains, making the transport of Godfrey's palliasse much easier than we expected. Yet the many treacherous twists and turns and a sheer drop of hundreds of feet into the valley below required us to remain cautious and vigilant. At various places, we could see defensive platforms in the mountainside above us where rocks and boulders had been stockpiled for launching onto any invaders coming up the mountain path.

Godfrey drifted in and out of consciousness. Ruth and I took turns using a dampened cloth to drip water into his mouth and keep it moist in the rare moments when he was alert and able to swallow safely. When awake, he was often confused and Ruth and I had to watch him closely, lest in his agitation he opened up any of his numerous wounds. I suggested to Hadar that some poppy milk would help settle him, keep him free from pain and less likely to cause harm to himself.

'Well done, Ippolito. I should have thought of that myself. The nature of our departure from the fortress distracted me,' responded Hadar.

Godfrey settled well after taking the soporific and was resting peacefully when we arrived at the small settlement. It was the one I remembered hearing as we passed through on our way up the mountain.

The settlement was no more than half a dozen crude huts and animal pens clustered around a small spring and rivulet that trickled off down the mountainside. Mehmet, the headman of the settlement, spoke Arabic and, despite some initial reservations about hosting our party, agreed that most of us could stay overnight in one of the shelters normally used for the animals of the settlement during the worst of the mountain winter. He suggested that Godfrey and one other of us could be his guests in his small dwelling as it had a brazier that would help keep Godfrey warm overnight.

We all agreed that Hadar as the eldest and only physician should stay with Godfrey while the rest of us sought whatever comfort we could in the animal shelter.

'Sweet Jesus, comfort me,' intoned Benedict when he saw where we were to spend the night. 'These idolaters insult us with this... this... pigsty!'

'Perhaps you would like to share the mountain track with the wolves and scorpions,' responded Ruth with unusual sarcasm. 'You could spend your night in peaceful prayer. I'm sure that will keep you unharmed until the morning.'

We were all exhausted, worn out and irritable after the events of the wearying day.

'Do not take that tone with me you little piece of whore spit. I will—'

'You will nothing, Benedict, except shut your mouth and take the first watch,' interjected Caspar who was now in charge. 'Edward, Raymond and I will share the watch with you overnight. Ruth and Ippolito. You have walked beside Godfrey all afternoon and evening while the rest of us rode. You have earned an uninterrupted sleep and you will probably have to walk beside him all of tomorrow. Get some rest, the pair of you.'

Ruth and I lay down in a corner at the rear of the shelter and with a horse blanket for warmth, settled down almost immediately into a night of dreamless and restorative sleep.

The next morning, it was a relief to see Godfrey awake and lucid although he was still wracked with pain and unable to move without making it worse. He had lost so much body fluid and moisture that he was parched dry and craving water. I sat beside him and gently assisted him to take small regular sips from a water skin. Too much too quickly might make him vomit causing his wounds to rupture all over again. Before setting out, Hadar had Ruth and I change the dressings around the wounds. As each still weeping and slightly bleeding wound was exposed, Hadar would lower his nose and sniff the wound for odours of corruption before Ruth or I swabbed the area with peppermint oil and applied fresh bandages.

After attending to Godfrey's dressings, Zana, Mehmet's wife, served us a small meal of gruel flavoured with some mountain herbs I did not recognise to break our fast. She had no food to send with us on our journey as might have been expected from a more prosperous settlement. We set out on our journey shortly after.

Below us, the mountain levelled out to gentle hills leading to the plains we had left nearly a month before our captivity and ransom had begun. I briefly wondered why there had been no response from Jerusalem to Mohammed's emissaries. The plains road was littered with more rocks and stones than the mountain path which meant more work for Ruth and I to clear Godfrey's passage than the day before. Even so, we had ample opportunity to walk and talk together without the others in our party overhearing us.

'It is funny,' said Ruth. 'Despite the horrors of yesterday, I have never felt so much as one with another when we were working together yesterday to save Godfrey's life. It was like I was part of you and you were part of me and as one we did what had to be done.' She looked up at me. 'Did you feel that way too?'

'I did, Ruth. I too felt as one with you. It was as if we saw the same things together in the same way and our hands did each other's bidding with no words needing to be said.' I turned to face her. 'I liked it, Ruth.'

With that, Ruth placed her hand in mine and my heart seemed to skip a million times over in happiness.

<h1 style="text-align:center">30</h1>

We made our camp that night beside a small stream that was surrounded by lush green grass for the horses and mules and provided a source of sweet freshwater for all of us. Hadar, Ruth and I attended to the dressings on Godfrey's wounds that were blood-soaked and needed changing.

'Hygiene and cleanliness are the keys to the successful healing of most wounds,' said Hadar, carefully sniffing each wound and then declaring they were still free from corruption.

Ruth and I applied a liberal coating of peppermint oil to keep them that way. Godfrey still slipped between a confused consciousness and the healing balm of sleep. He needed constant supervision as in his confused and poppy-driven delirium he would try to get up and move his limbs when awake. One positive sign we noted was that his lips were no longer blue and his face was not drained of colour. He was mending but still a long way from the vigour of his old self.

The next morning, Caspar called us all together for a meeting.

'Edward and I have taken a look at our supplies of food and they are in need of urgent replenishment. We do not know exactly where we are or when and where we may get the chance to purchase more. I have also spoken with Hadar about Godfrey and another day of rest will help his wounds to heal more effectively without the bump and grind of being dragged upon the palliasses. It is for this reason that I propose we stay here by the water for another day and use it for hunting and foraging. The plains around us seem to have an abundance of wildlife. This morning I have seen wild deer and goats, rabbits, birds' nests in the trees and there are fish in the stream. I am sure with further searching we can find nuts and berries albeit, probably unripe. There are different varieties of grasses and plants growing upon the plains which may yield up a grain or pulse that will be good for a ground meal.

'What I propose is this,' continued Caspar. 'Raymond and Ippolito are young and are best suited to climbing trees and invading birds' nests for eggs and any young birds that could go into the pot. Hadar, you have the best knowledge of herbs and plants and therefore are best suited to gathering what you can of leaves, nuts, berries, grains and pulses. Edward and I will try to track and run down some larger prey. Ruth, you will need to stay by Godfrey and see to his needs while Benedict can keep you company and try his best to catch some fish in the stream nearby.'

I could not help but notice Ruth rolling her eyes at the prospect of Benedict as her companion for the day.

'Are we in agreement about this?' asked Caspar.

All agreed that this was a sensible plan that saw us all putting our talents and skills together to the best advantage of the group.

We spent the next hour preparing for the day. Ruth deftly wove two narrow-necked grass baskets that could be used as fish traps while I trimmed a bough and attached it to a line of coarse woollen thread unravelled from one of the horse blankets. To the end of this, I tied a hook made from a medallion that Edward supplied. Raymond had been digging in the mud by the stream and had turned up a cup full of wriggling and writhing big fat blood worms for bait.

I approached Benedict and said, 'If you take all this over to that rock by the little pool there, I think you may have some luck fishing. Remember that no fish will be too small for the pot.'

Benedict snatched the fishing tackle, worm bait and traps from me without a word of thanks and walked away mumbling to himself.

'I will call you if I need your assistance,' cried Ruth to the departing priest and then adding, 'Otherwise you will have no need to disturb Godfrey or myself.'

Ruth then turned to me and quietly continued, 'Try not to be too long. That priest makes my skin crawl.'

Edward and Caspar had spied some rising dust away to the east, which they thought might be some herding animals and spurred their horses off in that direction. Hadar had taken a saddle-bag and had promised us all that he at least would have some salad greens for a meal if no nuts or berries could be found. He had gone north where the pastures were the greenest around our camp. Raymond and I did not saddle our horses as there was a coppice of small trees and undergrowth just over a half-mile distant from the camp that we thought might have nests in their branches and or other small animals for snaring in the undergrowth.

I did not like leaving Ruth behind as after the intimacy of our conversations the day before, I very much wanted to be in her company and feel the joy of her nearness.

Raymond, of course, had noticed everything the day before, as I supposed, had all the other members of the party, and said to me with a grin, 'You like Ruth a lot, don't you, Ippolito?'

'I do, Raymond. I have never had these feelings for anyone before. I know I loved my Papa but this is a different feeling. He never obsessed my thoughts the way that Ruth and everything about her stays in my mind. I never had daydreams about members of my family the way I daydream about Ruth. I admit it is all a bit confusing and sometimes I stumble over my words when we are together.'

'I envy you,' responded Raymond. 'I know I want very much to be a Knight of Saint John and the Hospitallers but the oaths of celibacy and poverty are very demanding. I don't know if you know this but many of the Hospitallers, and the Templars as well, have mistresses, some even wives. It is rumoured in the barracks that Caspar courts and woos the Lady Isabella.'

'Really!' I said in surprise.

'It is only a rumour but have you noticed the small ribbon of blue silk tied to the pommel of his sword?'

'I have, but thought nothing of it.'

'It is a love token from the lady.'

'Does he not risk punishment?'

'Only if he flaunts the affair. It seems there is an unspoken code of silence about these arrangements and that the vow of celibacy is broken even by those at the highest levels of the church and the knightly orders. They say even the Patriarch has an unofficial 'bed warmer' in his chamber. She is as old as he is and has served him... "faithfully"'—Raymond laughed at his use of this last word—'for over twenty years.'

I was not quite as surprised by this information as I could have been. Rudolphus had already opened this tub of worms for me.

As we journeyed to the coppice, Raymond kept up a discourse on all the scandalous rumours and stories circulating about the royal court, the knightly orders and the religious orders of Outremer. Some of it was entertaining and some of it was outright scandalous. I could not believe that such behaviours and hypocrisy were rife in all these organisations.

It took most of the morning climbing high into the trees to get at the nests. There was also more than one tumbling falling-down through the branches to have the wind knocked out of each of us as we hit the ground. Somewhat bruised and battered from our tumbles, Raymond and I did manage to collect a dozen small eggs. They were light grey in colour with small blue specks on them.

Not wanting to risk any broken limbs, Raymond and I decided to investigate the undergrowth for any edible wildlife. After a short while, we found a burrow sited amongst the uppermost roots of one of the trees in the coppice. We began cautiously digging it out with our knives.

'Get the bag ready and hold it over the opening while I poke around in there with my sword,' directed Raymond.

I did so and within a few moments, two adult ground squirrels had come charging and chittering in outrage out of the hole and into the bag.

'Gotcha!' I gleefully declared, holding the bag up by its neck.

Raymond put his hand underneath the bag and felt the weight in his hand as best he could while the two squirrels frantically scrambled about inside the bag.

'Not much but they will help fill the pot with some meat,' he declared. 'We will kill and skin them when we get back to keep the meat as fresh as possible.'

'Good idea,' I said. 'Let us head back now. At least we have something to offer the pot!'

In the distance, I could see Hadar was approaching the camp. He waved his bag to us, indicating that he too had had a successful morning gathering greens and the like.

I had enjoyed the morning with Raymond and his light-hearted banter but, if the truth was known, I had been thinking mostly of Ruth the whole time. As we walked back to camp, I gathered some wildflowers to bring to her. I imagined myself plaiting the flowers into Ruth's hair.

I was not ready for the sight that greeted me as we wandered back into the camp. There, no more than twenty yards from the campfire and Godfrey's palliasse, lay three motionless bodies piled on top of each other. They were lying in a surrounding pool of congealing blood.

<h1 style="text-align:center">31</h1>

Both Raymond and I were initially paralysed with shock at what we beheld.

Godfrey's corpse was lying uppermost on the pile of bodies. The wounds on his back, shoulder and head had all burst their stitches and had opened up, draining him of what precious blood had been left in him after his combat. His left hand gripped a thick lock of Benedict's hair while his right hand still held a knife, which was embedded in Benedict's neck, having pierced the great vein there. Beneath Godfrey and Benedict, I could see the top half of Ruth's face and hair. Blood stained and filled every crevice and crease of her face and her hair was matted with congealing blood.

Hadar's arrival at the campsite a few moments later brought Raymond and I back to our senses and, for me, a disturbing feeling of loss, shock and horror. My legs and knees began to tremble and I thought for a moment that they would buckle beneath me.

'Come, lads, we must lay them out as we try to determine just what has happened here. Let us lift Godfrey away,' said Hadar in a hesitant tone. It was as if he did not wish to know the truth.

Raymond gently unclenched Godfrey's hand from Benedict's hair and from around the knife that was still embedded in Benedict's torn and lacerated throat. As we lifted Godfrey's body away from Benedict's, the true horror of what had happened was revealed. Beneath Godfrey, Benedict's buttocks were exposed where he had drawn up his cassock in much the same way as he had forced Ruth's tunic up around her waist below him.

Realising the enormity of what Benedict had done flooded me with a wave of rage and anger. I grabbed the knife from Benedict's neck, wanting to stab and stab and cut at him as if I could still somehow defile his corpse as he had defiled Ruth's body. It was Raymond who stayed my arm and pulled me away before I could do any damage. I broke down and started sobbing, crying, 'Ruth... Ruth... Ruth.' I knelt by her body and gently swept the blood-matted locks from her face.

Suddenly, one eye opened and stared at me as a small mewing sound came from her throat.

'My God! She's alive,' I cried.

Immediately, the three of us grabbed Benedict's inert form and unceremoniously flung it as far away from Ruth as we could. I pulled Ruth's tunic down as best I could in an attempt to cover her modesty. I tried to hold her but she screamed wildly and pushed me away. Her face was a picture of terror and confusion. She screamed again and then began to sob hysterically.

'Let her go, Ippolito. Leave her. Step away now,' said Hadar gently. He was standing right behind me.

I was once again hurt and confused but did as Hadar bade me.

'Look at me, Ippolito,' ordered Hadar, taking me by the shoulders and staring into my eyes. 'Ruth has not only been raped but has had two men bleed out and die whilst lying on top of her. She is in a state of emotional shock and who knows what is going on in her mind. You and Raymond step back there where she cannot see you.'

I reluctantly did so and watched as Hadar remained close enough to Ruth to prevent her from harming herself but far enough behind her so she could not see him.

Ruth continued to sob and cry, wrapping her arms around her knees and rocking back and forth with such a look on her face that I too could not hold back my tears for her.

Gradually, the sobs and sorrow-ridden cries quietened to be replaced by a soft mewing sound.

Hadar softly spoke behind her, 'Ruth. Ruth. It is Hadar.'

Ruth stopped her rocking and looked around to see Hadar sitting behind her. His opened hands and arms were held out in front of him in the time-honoured sign to show he meant her no harm.

Ruth looked at him in puzzlement and began rocking herself again.

'Ruth. Ruth. It is Hadar,' he said again. 'Go to the stream and wash. Wash yourself in the stream, Ruth. Wash him away from yourself. Wash in the stream. Wash the blood away,' Hadar's voice had a soothing soporific tone to it yet had an insistence on the word 'wash'. He continued gently repeating the mantra.

Gradually, Ruth stopped her rocking and seemed to understand Hadar's injunction to wash. Slowly, she stood up, clutching her torn and bloodied clothes around her as if ashamed of being seen and shuffled her way to the stream where she stepped in, fully clothed. She began sobbing and crying again as she looked down on the diluting blood rinsing away from her clothing. Then she sat down in the stream and began the process of cleansing herself.

'Caspar and Edward are returning,' said Raymond quietly to alert us.

'Run to them and keep them out of Ruth's vision for the time being,' ordered Hadar. Raymond quickly took off.

'Ippolito. Go to Ruth's bags. Find her some spare clothes. Find something that will serve as a towel and bring them here to me.'

When I returned, Ruth was still washing herself, rubbing sand over her skin to remove the dried blood. There was a frantic obsessive quality to her actions. It was as if she thought she could never be clean again. I moved behind Hadar.

Hadar quietly stepped forward and placed the clothes and towel on the bank while Ruth had her back turned.

'Ruth... Ruth,' called Hadar quietly. 'You are clean. You are clean. You have washed him away. You have washed him away. The blood is gone. The blood is gone.' Hadar used the same soothing tones and simple mantra as he had before and it seemed to work. With only her head and shoulders showing above the water, she turned in our direction.

'We are moving away. Right away. There is a towel on the bank. Use the towel. Dry yourself, Ruth. Dry yourself. You are clean. You are clean. You have washed him away. He is washed away.'

I somehow knew that it was not all washed away and that Ruth was deeply scarred by what had happened. I felt foolish about the thoughts I had earlier in the day. How could Ruth ever love a man again after what had happened to her? Tears started to well in my eyes.

Hadar and I stood apart from Ruth and looked the other way. We could hear the occasional sob of anguish coming from her. About fifty yards away to our right, Raymond had brought Caspar and Edward to a halt where they stood holding the reins of their horses, looking concerned.

'Ruth,' called Hadar gently. 'Are you dressed?'

There was no response.

After a few more moments, Hadar called again. Again, there was no response.

'Ruth. I am going to turn around,' advised Hadar and slowly turned around to face Ruth.

'May I come nearer to you so I can see that you are alright?'

I heard no reply from Ruth as I was still facing away from her but she must have nodded her head as I became aware of Hadar moving towards her.

As Hadar was attending to Ruth, I moved slowly to where Raymond, Caspar and Edward quietly waited with the horses. I noticed a young deer buck slung behind the rear of Caspar's saddle. Somehow the prospect of the good meal we had all been seeking left a bad taste in my mouth after what had happened to Ruth. Even so, we set about dressing the meat in preparation of a meal.

An hour later, Hadar joined us while Ruth remained sitting beside the stream, her head down and held between her hands. She was quietly sobbing and gently rocking back and forth again.

Although Ruth had not spoken a word to Hadar, he had put together a picture of what had happened for us.

'It would appear that Benedict has attacked Ruth while she was attending to Godfrey and dragged her away from the campsite by the hair. There are drag marks through the grass and she has a raw spot on her scalp where a large lock of hair has been pulled out. Benedict must have used a degree of violence upon her as she has a swollen eye where a blow was struck and one of her teeth is chipped. There are also bite marks on her neck and shoulder. There are bruises on her neck in such a position to suggest that Benedict tried to strangle her. She must have put up quite a fight. This is all I was able to examine.

'There is no doubt from the evidence that was revealed before our eyes that Benedict had also raped Ruth. I think it reasonable to infer that Godfrey must have heard the assault and despite his precarious state of health, has risen from his cot and taken his knife to investigate. Upon discovering Benedict, he has launched himself upon him and driven the knife into Benedict's neck. Apart from Ruth's teeth marks on Benedict's hand, this is the only wound upon the vile priest. Sadly, the exertions Godfrey put himself under to save Ruth opened up his wounds and he lost what little blood was left in him to die on top of an already dead Benedict.'

'On top of the horror of rape, Ruth has also endured seeing the death of two men at exceptionally close hand – their dying faces only inches from hers. The blood from Benedict's neck and Godfrey's head wound poured all over her own. All she could do was lie there as she was unable to release herself from under the weight of two dead men. I suspect she was in this position for a number of hours.

'She is in a state of shock at the moment and with that, has gone her volition to speak. She understands what is said to her but cannot, or perhaps, will not, respond. She is also quite understandably somewhat... ah... "man shy" at the moment and I ask all of you to give her plenty of space and time, announce yourself and tell her what you are doing before going near her. I will build her a campfire and prepare her sleeping arrangements on the bank of the stream.

'Now I am going back to sit with her while you are going to make the best meal of what we have hunted and gathered. Despite what has happened, pursuing normalcy in our routines will be very important.'

I was wracked by Hadar's revelations of the day and wished so much to take Ruth in my arms, tell her it would be alright, calm her fears and hurts and somehow – I knew not how – to make everything well again.

'May I speak with her?' I asked as my voice broke and feared tears would disarm me yet again.

'Not yet, Ippolito. Fear not. You will be very much a part of her cure,' said Hadar sympathetically.

32

We buried Godfrey the next morning with as much ceremony and honour that we could bestow in the circumstances. Caspar and Raymond somehow half-dressed him in his mail and armour and placed his sword in his hand so that it lay diagonally across his chest. It had to be this way as rigor mortis had set in. I cleaned his face, neck and hands and did my best to make him as presentable before the Lord in Heaven as best I could. Just before we covered him in the soil of the meadow, Ruth came up to the graveside and gently placed some wildflowers she had gathered upon his chest. There were silent tears in her eyes for Godfrey.

It was Edward who decided Benedict's fate.

'I'll not give that one the dignity of a burial. I say leave him for the dogs, the birds and the other vermin and may he roast in hell.'

'I agree,' I said, wanting to launch a kick at Benedict's balls but then thought better of it.

I spat on the corpse instead. Hadar looked at me in some surprise at this.

Ruth was still silent and had a hollow, haunted and faraway look about her. She still responded to Hadar's gentle directions and seemed to trust in the avuncular manner he took with her.

'Ruth. Are you listening to me?' Hadar asked.

Ruth slowly nodded her head.

'Do you feel up to riding a horse?'

Ruth shook her head in definite 'no'.

I realised that the saddle would be an uncomfortable reminder of what had happened to her.

'Do you feel up to walking?'

Ruth nodded.

'Would you like Ippolito to walk with you?'

I felt a sudden pain in my heart that Ruth would reject me as company. She looked uncertainly at Hadar and then at me. It was as if, despite her pain and trauma, she saw into my heart. It seemed for a moment the slightest smile came to the corners of her mouth but was then just as quickly gone in a breath.

She slowly nodded her head.

'I am glad, Ruth,' I managed to say before tears could overwhelm me.

Ruth and I did not share any conversation that first day. It was enough for me to know that she still wanted me to be close. I think it was the same for her. Occasionally, she would look up at me as we walked and it was as if she wanted to say something that the look in her eyes could not give depth or meaning to.

I was sitting with Ruth by the fireside that evening when a piece of wood exploded in the fire and sent a small coal flying at Raymond and down the front of his tunic. Raymond leapt up and immediately started to dance and prance about, urgently 'ooohing and ahhing' as he tried to remove the tunic and shake the coal free. The whole episode was so comic to watch that despite Raymond's discomfiture, we laughed at his antics. I looked across at Ruth and noticed that she had her hand over her mouth. It was her eyes that told me she too had found a glimpse of simple human happiness in the darkness that currently filled her horizons.

Our progress over the next two days was limited to a walking gait as Ruth and I set the pace of our progress. I had started to talk to Ruth as we travelled, even though she was unable to respond. I told her of things I had not shared with her before. I knew she had never been to Acre and I told her much about my memories from my early years in the city. I told her of Maria, our family nurse, who had helped invest me with a desire to heal. I told her of the fabulous wonders and inventions hidden away in Papa's storerooms and of Urbino's books and the day he had knocked a shelf of scrolls over in the bookshop when he discovered a lost copy of *The Sibylline Prophecies*. Ruth had made a small chortle in her throat about this and I had looked across at her to notice again the beginning of a smile on her face that again was gone as quickly as it appeared. It was at that moment that I felt Ruth gently slip her hand into mine and give it a little squeeze. I looked across at her again and this time the small smile on her face remained in place.

Once again, my heart skipped a million beats.

The next day, Ruth indicated that she would ride and we saddled her horse for her. As he had when our journey began, Raymond thoughtfully placed a sheepskin over the saddle to help cushion any discomfort it might cause her. She smiled and nodded at Raymond in thanks for his quiet consideration. As my feelings for Ruth were again becoming more assured, so did my feelings of camaraderie and friendship toward Raymond strengthen as a result of this simple gesture.

It was on the fifth day after the violence that we saw the city in the distance.

'I believe I know exactly where we are now,' commented Hadar. 'Judging by those minarets, I would say that we are approaching Shiraz. I was here when I was a younger man and travelling with Usama through these parts. We should have no problems with communicating as it is an Arab settlement and garrison city.'

I looked at Ruth, wondering how she was going to feel and react in such close proximity to so many people, particularly men that she did not know.

33

We were now far from Outremer and it seemed the complex political and militaristic business of the Crusades was some other potentate's worry. We could be honest and open about the 'whats, wheres and why-fors', as Hadar had put it, for our presence in the city and our mission.

The guards at the city gates of Shiraz were nothing less than thorough. Each of us, with the exception of Ruth, was briefly interrogated regarding our business and destination. Aside from the interrogation, we were obliged to unpack all our belongings for the guards' inspection and submit to a brief body search for concealed weapons. Religious obligations prevented them from any more than a brief scan of Ruth to determine that she carried no weapons. Little did they know about the slim throwing knife she kept strapped to her upper arm.

'Physician travelling with two apprentices, one a mute girl, and three guards, one barely old enough to sport a beard, who are travelling to Hind to find some miracle cure for their leprous king. If it were not for all these vials, jars and packages of supposed medicines and cures in your baggage, I would refuse you entry to the city for being likely frauds or criminals,' said the guard in charge at the gate and then paused as if suddenly considering something.

'As things stand right now, your presence here in Shiraz may be very opportune. Are you aware that the city is only just recovering from a contagion of the bloody flux?' asked the guard.

'No. We are not,' responded Hadar with some caution.

'Many hundreds within the city died of it. The few physicians, healers and quacks in Shiraz are either dead of the flux or have fled the city to safety somewhere else. I believe the Emir may be interested in your services.'

'So...' began Hadar even more cautiously. 'What is it that you would have us do?'

'I think we might pay a call on the court chamberlain and let him decide if you can help. Pack your gear and we will make our way to the palace.'

We made our way through the crowded and busy streets of Shiraz to the palace. Our guard led the way, casually waving his sword in front of us to clear a path through the crowds of people going about their daily business and we were not hindered in our progress by the throng.

Eventually, we arrived at a walled compound within the city. Guards at the gate immediately halted our progress. Our guard spoke quietly to one of them and we were waved on.

We entered into a large forecourt that fronted the palace proper. It led up to the palace entrance where again a squad of guards delayed us. After some further discussion, we were allowed to proceed. We followed some corridors lined with rich hangings that reminded me of King Baldwin's court. It was not long before we arrived at an anteroom where we were advised to wait and were left under the scrutiny of yet more palace guards.

After what seemed like an hour or more, the guard returned in the company of a courtier introduced to us as the first secretary to the royal chamberlain. His name was Ali ibn Rashid. After we had introduced ourselves, he turned and dismissed the guard.

An hour later Hadar, Ruth, Ali and I stood before the great doors of the Palace Court. Caspar, Edward and Raymond expected that they would have to wait in the anteroom, but Ali instructed all of us to follow him and his lead in all things. We were to speak only when spoken to. It was much like the rules and protocols of the court of Jerusalem. We only had to wait a few short minutes before the doors opened inwards and we stepped forward, following Ali.

I had been impressed with the opulence and grandeur of Baldwin's court, but it paled beside that of the Emir's. Everything was bigger, brighter, shinier, more colourful. From the jewels worn on the courtiers' fingers to the wall hangings to the flowing robes to the vases of fruits and flowers, everything was an explosion of colour. I heard Ruth gasp in awe as we respectfully made our way to the bottom of the dais that the Emir's throne sat upon. Following Ali's lead, we fully prostrated ourselves by lying face down upon the floor before the Emir.

It was only on hearing a deep-throated voice say, 'Arise,' that we were able to stand before the Emir and his advisors. The Emir showed us a benevolent smile and had a very pleased-looking expression upon his face. I noticed that his eyes lingered on Ruth more than I liked before he turned his attention back to the group of us.

Ali spoke first. 'Oh, grand and gracious Emir, Star of Islam and light of the faithful, may I present Hadar, physician of Jerusalem and his two apprentices, Ippolito of Acre and Ruth of Jerusalem.'

Hadar bowed his head in deference and our party followed his lead.

Coming straight to the point, the Emir asked, 'What exactly is your mission? I have heard from my guards that you are seeking a cure for the Christian king's leprosy. Is this so?'

Hadar detailed our mission, stressing its urgency and our desire to be on the road again if his eminence would be so pleased to release us.

The Emir appeared to consider this and turned to whisper

something to one of the black-cloaked advisors standing behind him. He turned back and smiled before continuing. 'I believe I have a proposal that will be advantageous to us both. I can shorten your journey by many weeks. The trade winds are propitious at the moment and my trading fleet will shortly disembark to sail to the trading ports of Hind. I am willing to offer your party safe transport there for... shall we say... a small consideration on your part.'

I was not sure I liked the way he smiled at this part.

'May I ask,' said Hadar cautiously, 'what that small consideration might be?'

'This... ah... contagion, as you call it, has left my harem depleted of a corps of essential eunuch guards. They need to be replaced. Added to this is the fact that the Caliph is expected here in Shiraz next month. The tribute the Caliph expects this year is one hundred eunuch boys. I understand some are bound for his harem and others to constitute a new personal bodyguard.'

I noticed a slightly pained expression creep across Hadar's face as I too saw what was coming.

'You are, of course, aware that the recent contagion has left Shiraz depleted of physicians and healers. My offer is this. Perform the necessary castrations for those boys going to the harem and the lesser castrations for those boys selected to join the Caliph's bodyguard. Do this for me with only minor loss of life and I will not only provide you with speedy transport to Hind but also reward you well in gold to assist you in your mission. Think about it, Hadar. You will not only make up the time you have lost but also arrive in Hind ahead of your original expected time. What say you to this?'

Briefly, Hadar had the look of a cornered animal who saw no way out but then spoke up. 'May I consult briefly with my apprentices on this, Your Eminence?'

'Do so. You may retire to the back of the court to consult.'

'Thank you, Your Eminence,' said Hadar, bowing, and he motioned Ruth and I to do the same and then follow him.

I was puzzled by Hadar's uncertainty in this matter. I expected him to immediately accept the terms of the Emir's offer.

'This is a difficult decision for me,' opened Hadar.

'Why?' I asked respectfully.

'Principally, for two reasons. The first relates to the fact that, although I question many issues of creed and belief in all the faiths, I am still a Jew and the injunctions in our scriptures against castration are evident in many of the books. Secondly, as a physician, it does not fit well with my beliefs and practices to do no harm in the practice of healing.

'There are other considerations in this as well. The first is that should we deny the Emir his request, our mission risks failure due to time lost on the journey. Second is the fact that should we deny him, he will only be able to draw upon the crude practices of those charlatans and quacks that inhabit his city and the loss of life amongst those boys will be considerable. What are your thoughts on this? Both of you.'

I looked at Ruth. She gestured with her hands that said she did not feel anything one way or the other about performing the surgeries. I gathered Ruth's mother had not had much time to instruct her in matters of Jewish religion.

I had an idea.

'Hadar. You do not have to perform these cuttings. Ruth and I can. All you need do is supervise our activities to make sure that no lives more than unavoidable are lost under the knife and afterward. That way you are not violating any of your religious beliefs or professional ethics and we arrive in Hind earlier than expected.'

Hadar looked immensely relieved at my proposal and said, 'Thank you, Ippolito. This is indeed an acceptable answer to my dilemma. Let us inform the Emir.'

We walked back to the dais and informed the Emir of our decision.

'Excellent. Excellent,' exclaimed the Emir, plucking a deep-fried lamb's testicle from a nearby platter and placing it in his mouth.

34

Hadar negotiated with the Emir for two days to prepare for the mass castrations. This was to help us ensure the greatest safety for the boys who were to go under the knife. Ali arranged for us to have a quick inspection of the boys, which was, in reality, a simple walk-through of the separate pens and cells where the boys were detained.

Many of the boys had been taken as captive slaves by the Emir's army during raids and skirmishes with neighbouring states and cities. The remaining boys were the children of impoverished families sent to Shiraz in the hope that the life of a eunuch in the palace or harem would be better than the suffering and short life awaiting them in the poverty and deprivation of the Shiraz slums and the dirt-poor rural villages.

After our tour, Hadar requested that Ali provide us with four uncastrated male lambs.

'I gather that the lambs are for our training and practice before we begin on the boys,' I commented to Hadar and Ruth.

'Correct,' stated Hadar. 'The anatomy is a little different around the penis but the principals of the surgery remain the same.'

Later that evening, we were seated on cushions in our rooms.

'There are four adversaries we will have to face in carrying out these procedures. The first is shock. Sometimes the body reacts in ways we don't expect, particularly when what is happening to it is unexpected. Signs and symptoms of shock are many and varied and may or may not include any of the following: pale, cold, sweaty skin, a weak rapid pulse, thirst with little urine flow, irregular breathing, profuse sweating, dilated pupils in lacklustre eyes along with confusion, anxiety and irritability. Naturally, all this combined can lead to death.'

Ruth and I nodded our heads at the gravity of this.

'Those boys who are only having their testicles removed are relatively unlikely to experience complications. It is those boys who are having both testicles and penises removed that are at most risk of dying from their experience.

'To combat the likelihood of shock I will give each boy a draft of poppy milk and tincture of hemp an hour prior to the procedure, which will hopefully put them to sleep and eliminate any consciousness of pain. A further draft may be given if there is pain after the procedure. I will look after this myself.'

'Hadar,' interrupted Caspar. 'Aside from my military duties with the knights, my other duties included maintaining the apothecary. I am familiar with the poppy, its preparation, administration and effects. I can manage this for you.'

'That is good. Thank you, Caspar. The second enemy of our endeavour is blood loss,' Hadar continued. 'This should not be an issue for those who are destined for the palace and just the removal of their testicles. Tying off or cauterising two moderately sized blood vessels should reduce the risk of haemorrhaging.

'It is the removal of the penis that presents the greatest bleeding hazard. It is a highly vascular part of the body and will bleed profusely once severed, no matter the amount of pressure bandaging placed around the stump. It is how most candidates for the harem guard are lost.

'There are two possible methods of preventing blood loss. The first is to cauterise the blood vessels with a red-hot poker.

This, needless to say, causes a lot of post-operative pain and may also risk irreparably damaging the vessel that carries the urine from the bladder to the outside. It is for this reason that I wish to use spiders' webs to assist in the clotting of blood and wound closure along with bandages soaked in turmeric and vinegar to also lessen the bleeding and help prevent contamination setting in.

'The third enemy that we face is that of urine retention caused by damage to the vessel that carries urine to the outside. That is why the Emir's gold and silversmiths are now fashioning fifty of these,' he said this as he removed a slim silver tube from his pocket. 'It will be necessary to insert one of these tubes into the vessel that carries the urine from the bladder and to insert it to at least the length of this marker on the side of the tube. This will prevent the vessel that from closing up or becoming blocked and allow urine to escape freely from the body. You will need to insert it before the penis is removed from the body. In my surgical kit is a curved blade that will enable you to quickly slice the penis and remove it from around the tube.'

It was Edward's turn to offer some input to our discussion. 'Hadar, I have seen the desert tribesmen gelding their herds. They use a black pitch to cover the wound, which, when it quickly cools, prevents further blood loss and prevents contamination. The hardened pitch peels off when the wound is healed. It would also remove the risk of further damage to the area caused by cautery. They should have plenty of the black stuff in the Emir's stables.'

'What an excellent idea!' exclaimed Hadar. 'We can make arrangements to have a brazier and a bubbling pitch pot in the surgery with us. Well done, Edward.'

Hadar cleared his throat and then continued. 'The final threat to the successful castrations of all our would-be eunuchs is that of contagion and fevers. We have many curatives and preventatives in our supplies and I know you are both familiar with all their applications and usage. I will be there to assist and advise in this matter.

'Now, down to the practical matters of castration. The lambs are upon the table.'

35

We needed the extra day Hadar had negotiated to further plan the logistics of the operations in full to minimise the risk for the boys, maintain our comfort and needs and ensure that every contingency was prepared for. Ali negotiated the provision of a disused barracks as a hospital, providing us with the space to prepare, operate upon and post-surgically care for the newly-made eunuchs.

At one stage in our preparations, Ruth disappeared. I was just beginning to worry about her when she returned carrying an unusual-looking chair. It had shorter legs at the back, allowing for a semi-reclined position and the seat was shaped like a horseshoe, supporting the rear of the buttocks and upper thighs.

'Ah!' exclaimed Hadar. 'A birthing chair. An excellent idea. Where did you find it?'

Ruth pointed to the walls of the palace harem.

The birthing chair would allow Ruth and I easier access to those parts being removed from the boys' bodies whilst also allowing us to sit as we performed the delicate procedures, thus maintaining our comfort and ability to focus on the task at hand.

Ruth then pointed at the birthing chair and held two fingers up to indicate there was another such chair in the harem and she left immediately to retrieve it. It struck me as somewhat ironic that these specially designed chairs used to assist in the labour of birthing women were now to be used in a specialist manner for the prevention of pregnancies.

Hadar requested that Ali make some small alterations to the chairs, one of which was to place small wheels on each of the chair's legs. This would facilitate the easy transport of the boys from the pre-operative area to the operative one and then onto the post-operative care in the beds of the barracks proper.

We were fortunate that Caspar's Hospitaller training included working in the knights' apothecary. He was familiar with preparing tinctures, their administration and the signs of overdose upon patients. Caspar had the boys waiting in the courtyard of the barracks under the watchful eyes of the Emir's guard to prevent any last-minute rioting or panic. Caspar would admit the boys one by one to the anteroom of the barracks, tell them to strip naked and wash from waist to knee with a rinse Hadar had devised of myrrh, capsicum juice and crushed golden seal. Hadar explained this would reduce the likelihood of a miasmic contagion setting in after the procedures.

Once cleansed, Caspar would administer the poppy milk and hemp tincture to the boys. The boys would then settle down on one of the two birthing chairs as the fog of the poppy caused them to drift off to what we hoped would be an uninterrupted and painless sleep whilst undergoing their transformation into what some have called the 'third sex'.

Once asleep, the boys were wheeled in their chairs to an area we had cordoned off at one end of the barracks where, under Hadar's supervision, Ruth and I would begin the 'transformations'. When the procedure was completed, the boys were wheeled into the barracks proper and transferred by Raymond and Edward to a cot or bed where their post-operative recovery could be closely monitored.

We decided that we would begin with those boys destined to be palace eunuchs and only required the removal of their testicles as this was the simpler procedure. I won't go into the details of the operations but suffice to say Ruth and I felt the same 'oneness' of thought and action we had experienced treating Godfrey's wounds. It was as if we were four hands directed by a single mind speaking with two inner voices. This union of thought and action doubled our expertise and efficiency.

We managed to complete all fifty partial castrations in one day without the loss of one life, a fact that Hadar praised the two of us grandly for.

Hadar had also sensed and seen the union Ruth and I underwent as we worked together. 'I could not observe the two of you when we worked on Godfrey but what I observed today has me truly astounded. Never have I seen two people more called to the healing arts and sciences than the pair of you working together. You both achieve a level of expertise seldom seen. It makes me wonder how this can be in ones so young and new to the calling. It also makes me very proud to be your teacher and mentor.'

Ruth and I looked at each other. She flashed that smile I first saw in Hadar's apothecary. Inwardly I rejoiced at this. It meant she was healing as well. Hadar saw it too and he laughed as he put his arms around both our shoulders.

The next day was not as successful, nor the one after that. The total castrations were much more complex and we were beset on numerous occasions by uncontrolled bleeding from the stump, difficulties of inserting the urine tube or our patients waking up and jerking in pain whilst we went about our work. It was fortunate that Hadar was present and on more than one occasion, his intervention helped to keep the boys alive. However, at the end of the second day, we had only lost one newly-made eunuch who had simply bled and bled and no amount of cautery or suturing could stem the flow. We later lost another eunuch who failed to pass urine at all despite the tube into his bladder. A regime of poppy milk kept him comfortable during his final days.

Needless to say, the Emir was highly pleased with our success rate.

'My best surgeons and physicians usually lost at least a quarter of the candidates and you tell me these two "apprentices" of yours have only lost two,' he said with some amazement. 'I would very much like all three of you to stay in Shiraz and become court physicians. However, I am indebted to you, and as a man of honour I must do whatever I can to assist you in your mission. The last of my trading caravans to the coast is leaving in a few days to link up with this season's trading fleet bound for Hind. I will ensure that you get all the assistance you need and any comforts you may desire in reaching your destination.'

36

The journey from Shiraz to the coastal harbour city of Rey Shahr would take us a week. We were persuaded by Ali to abandon our horses and mules as they were unsuited to the terrain over which we would be travelling. Instead, the Emir provided us with eight camels, one each to travel upon and two as pack animals, and we joined the last caravan leaving for the coast before the trading fleet sailed from the harbour city of Rey Shahr.

The caravan included over a hundred camels along with their owners, mostly merchants and traders, their families, employees and other assorted travellers. As the Emir had made a large investment in the trade goods being transported, he had thoughtfully provided a squad of twenty cavalrymen mounted on camels as protection against the bandit packs that infested the isolated hills and valleys we would traverse on our journey to the coast.

I had seen camels in the markets and souks of Acre and Jerusalem but had never had much to do with them up until this time. I will be grateful if I never have much to do with them again. I was given a stubborn and surly male aptly named *Darta al-shitan*, which meant 'the Devil's fart' in Arabic. Not only could the wind from his tail end disperse a caravan but he also had the vile habit of throwing up, and out, the contents of his stomach in sticky boluses of green vegetable matter at any who displeased him or threatened him with a whip or goad. He was constantly complaining in the form of moans and groans and disturbing deep, throaty bellows of obstinacy when being coaxed into service. Worse than this, he could deliver a tearing bite with his large front teeth. No man, or other beast for that matter, was safe from his cud-chewing maw.

I could never tell if *Darta*, for that was what I called him – it just meant 'fart' – had a stupid or belligerent look about him. His small ears, arched nose, wide thick-lipped mouth and receding jaw made him look like a hardened criminal. Yet, at the same time his large brown eyes, surrounded as they were by double rows of thick eyelashes, gave his face a gentle beauty suggestive of a wide-eyed doe.

What I disliked most about *Darta,* or any other camel for that fact, is their pacing gait. When travelling, the camel moves its front and hind legs on the same side at the same time. This causes the camel's body to pitch from side to side in a swaying motion that reminded me of being at sea in a large swell. After just a short time on a camel's back, one can see why it is sometimes named 'the ship of the desert'. I was fortunate in that I do not get seasick.

Our first day out in the caravan had something of a festive air about it. Excited children ran squealing and laughing up and down the line, playing games of chase or flying gaily coloured kites. Two musicians, one playing a two-stringed instrument I learned was called a *dotar* and the other a goblet-shaped drum known as a *tonbak,* seated on their camels were able to provide merry and lively tunes to those around them whilst other travellers passed skins of wine, water or fruit juice to each other.

Hadar insisted that Ruth and I resume our lessons with him each morning. After our recent experiences, Ruth and I were keen to know more about the different conditions that would require surgical intervention as opposed to herbal or curative treatments. Hadar obliged us with the details of numerous conditions and procedures that required 'the knife' for treatment.

Each evening after we had settled into one of the many caravanserais along our route, I resumed my lessons in swordcraft with Edward while Ruth and Caspar went to find a convenient tree or palm to practice their knife-throwing skills.

The caravanserais of the route were placed at distances of approximately one day's journey apart. If the terrain to be travelled was mountainous or difficult, the caravanserais were anywhere between six and twelve miles apart, whilst those down on the easily traversed coastal plain were around twenty miles apart. Each caravanserai was placed just outside a regional centre or village, and they were all of very similar design. Most were a walled square or rectangular shape and were entered through a large gateway, which was kept closed after sundown. Once through the gateway, there was an open courtyard with verandaed, well-appointed rooms occupying the inner sides of the walled yard. These rooms accommodated all kinds of travellers along with the merchants, their servants, animals and merchandise. In some of the caravanserais were special enclosures known as *Khana-e-Padshahi* or King's Houses that were solely for the use of government officials and other travelling dignitaries.

Most caravanserais supplied areas for hot baths and the hygiene needs of all faiths and sexes. Cooks located around the courtyard provided meals acceptable to travellers from other non-Persian cultures. Our medical skills were not required during this time as each caravanserai was supplied with its own treating physician, clinic and staff. Various other employees of the caravanserai offered other services, some of a more intimate nature. Troupes of acrobats, jugglers, entertainers and musicians strolled through the crowd, offering other diversions to weary travellers. Needless to say, there were also guards who manned the walls night and day for the protection of guests and, more importantly, their merchandise.

The courtyards were lively places that were used as marketplaces for the merchants and for local traders with special permission to do so. Most interestingly for all of us was that these courtyards facilitated interaction between people of different cultures, languages, customs, faiths and ideas as well as providing sources of news and information. It was a welcoming environment and lit in the warm glow of the many torches and braziers burning in and around the perimeter.

On the morning of the seventh day of our journey, we descended from the undulating hills and valleys of Persia's midlands. In the distance, we could see the dry coastal plains that bordered a stretch of water the caravan master told me was called *al-khalij al-farsi*, which translated as the Persian Gulf. Far away in a south-westerly direction, we could see our destination, the harbour city of Rey Shahr.

'All being well, we will reach the city gates late this afternoon,' the caravan master informed me.

'All being well,' I thought to myself, wondering what the darkening line on the far-off north-western horizon was.

It was not long before the caravan master called for a faster pace than the usual ambling gait we had grown accustomed to.

I learned from one of the caravan outriders the darkening line on the north-western horizon was the approaching front of what he called a *khamsin* wind. The *khamsin* was a fierce desert wind that carried and drove dust and sand with a flaying and suffocating strength and intensity.

The caravan master was desperately trying to hurry the caravan to the protection of Rey Shahr before the killing wind struck his train of goods and charges. Unfortunately, poorly secured goods and merchandise soon bounced free from the humps of the faster-moving camels and progress to the city was regularly interrupted.

We could see the walled ramparts of Rey Shahr only a few miles ahead of us. The *kamsin's* front was also only a few miles away to the left of the city. The difference was the *khamsin* was rapidly moving towards us, not sitting stationary as the city was.

The front was a towering cloud of grey, brown and yellow sands and dust that seemed to reach up to the very heavens in a boiling and billowing wall. The wind around us had been freshening and getting stronger when the caravan master called a halt and directed the caravan to form up in spiralling formations of about twenty camels. There were five spiral-shaped groups. He then directed that pairs of camels within each spiral be hobbled in a chevron shape with their rear ends and flanks facing into the front of the *khamsin*. This allowed for two to three individuals to take shelter between the bodies of the two kneeling camels.

As a result of pure chance, our party wound up in the outer circuit of the spiral we were allocated to. Ruth and I occupied the centre of our group with Hadar and Caspar to our left and Edward and Raymond to our right, filling the tail position of the formation. Our camels were all surprisingly agreeable and non-aggressive throughout the process of forming up. They had probably been well-trained in this defensive manoeuvre.

The wind was rising steadily and whipping grains and dust before it as the actual wall of the *khamsin* grew in size before our eyes. Ruth and I burrowed out a cavity between *Dartha* and her camel, *Aisha*, laying a saddle blanket underneath us while pulling another over us making a reasonably protective cavity. Before crawling into our shelter, I checked left and right to see the others were similarly engaged in their burrowing in. I waved to them and called, 'Good luck.'

The others responded similarly with Raymond adding, 'See you soon, my friend. Behave yourself under there.'

The light was fading rapidly and the roar of the wind had reached such an intensity that any further conversation was all but impossible as I secured the covering blanket over Ruth and I as best I could. As we settled into our protective little burrow, I felt Ruth push something against my side. It was one of her veils and I knew she was telling me to cover my face as well. I did so. She then snuggled up to me and placed her head on my left shoulder as she lay curled up by my side. Never had mortal danger felt so marvellous.

Then the *khamsin* struck. Despite all our protective measures, sand and dust quickly found its way through every small gap and space we had inadvertently left. It found its way very quickly into our ears, nostrils, eyes and mouths as well as finding its itchy way beneath our clothing. Both of us coughed, snorted, sneezed and choked on the air as we struggled to breathe. I could not imagine any living thing surviving the holocaust of wind and sand outside the small world Ruth and I occupied. I hoped the others were safe.

The noise and wind went on for several hours with no abatement in its intensity. At one point, I heard Ruth gasp as her body suddenly jerked beside me. A moment later I understood the reason for her discomfiture. *Dartha* had let a string of his noisome farts go, which instead of being blown away in the wind, had drifted beneath our covering blanket in a disgusting and smothering effect worse than all the sand and dust. I thumped his side in retaliation. In response, the beast let another string go and I swore what was normally a deep-throated and threatening roar of defiance became a deep-throated chortle of amusement and satisfaction. I did not hit him back this time as I was too wary of getting one of his tearing bites in retaliation. Oh, how I hated that beast.

It was then I noticed that Ruth was seemingly shaking beside me. I initially thought she was having some kind of spasm and was about to do my best to check on her when I realised she was having a deep belly laugh. This, in turn, started me laughing as I realised the absurdity of our situation; deadly flaying winds beating outside our small burrow and a smell like rancid death insinuating itself into every space within it. Ruth placed her arms around me as we lay there together alternatively laughing hysterically or gasping for air. How strange the blocks on which the house of love can be built.

At some stage, despite the noise and discomfort, Ruth and I had drifted off into separate and unsettled sleep. When I awoke, the noise of the wind had abated and the darkness seemed less obscuring. Mercifully, there were no more of *Dartha's* lingering offerings. Suddenly our covering blanket was whipped from above us in a spray of sand and dust to reveal a distraught Raymond standing above us.

'Quick. Help me. I can't find Edward.'

37

'It was as the *khamsin* struck when the sand started to blast and it became too dark to see clearly. The noise was so great I could not properly hear him. I think he said something about a child crying and then he disappeared from under the blanket into the dust outside,' reported a distraught Raymond. He then turned away to alert Hadar and Caspar of the emergency.

'Help me. Help me find Edward,' he said as he shook the blankets and sand from Hadar and Caspar's refuge, alerting them to the crisis at the same time.

Ruth and I began urgently sweeping sand or kicking into the drifts of sand surrounding our end of the defensive spiral. A small-sized dune had formed in the sand just behind our camels. Ruth and I kicked and swept our way as fast as possible into it. We were joined by Hadar while Caspar and Raymond went to work on another drift. Around us, other travellers were emerging from beneath their shelters, shaking themselves of sand and dust and checking their goods and camels.

Suddenly a woman's scream rent the late afternoon silence that followed the *khamsin*. She followed this with sorrowful shrieking and wailing as she called the name Omar over and over. She was the wife and mother of a large family travelling on three camels immediately behind us in the caravan. Her husband and sons and daughters were desperately searching the sand drifts.

Hadar went over to the group and spoke briefly with her husband as he wildly shovelled sand with his cupped hands.

'It is my youngest boy, Omar. In the wind, darkness and terror, my wife and I each assumed that he was safe with the other. He was not with my eldest sons either. Oh, Allah have mercy on us. Help us find him,' cried the man.

'We too are looking for one of our own,' informed Hadar. 'Perhaps they are safe together. Let us combine our search.'

This seemed to reassure the father somewhat although his desperate bailing of sand did not diminish in determination and speed.

The sandscape had changed in the hours of the *khamsin*. New drifts of sand had piled themselves against the backs and sides of the camels all around us and small dunes and mounds lay in the areas between the arms of our protective spiral of camels that had not been there before.

Other travellers in the caravan soon joined the search, cupping and kicking sand into the remnant wind that still blew around us.

Suddenly a voice called, 'Over here. Over here.'

Ruth and I turned and ran to where a youth was furiously sweeping sand away from what appeared to be an arm and a shoulder. By the colour of the tunic, I knew it to be Edward. The youth, a brother of the missing child, stepped aside as Ruth and I began cupping and sweeping sand from the inert body. It was only a few moments before we had exposed Edward's neck and face, one side of which was bloodied and raw from the abrasive effects of the whipping sand blown by the *khamsin*. He seemed to be lying in a protective foetal position. He was obviously dead.

Hadar, Caspar and Raymond joined us as we slowed the pace of our excavation out of respect for his deceased form. Raymond was quietly weeping and said, 'I should have gone to help him.'

'And then we would probably have two dead,' offered Caspar, placing his arm around his younger companion's shoulder and pulling him close in consoling comradeship.

Around us, other travellers and outriders were still flinging sand aside in their frantic search for the missing boy when the caravan master rode up to the search site.

'The boy is dead and lost to us,' he announced loudly for all to hear. 'Cease your searching and ready yourselves and your animals to ride out. We only have a couple of hours to reach the Rey Shahr caravanserai before the sun goes down. We leave in half an hour.'

Raymond was gently sweeping the last of the sand from Edward's face as the rest of our party cleared sand away from his body. We would at least lay him straight in the sand with his sword beside him and say a few words before we covered him in again. We could see Rey Shahr in the distance and would catch the caravan up once finished with farewelling our friend.

Suddenly Ruth gave a squeak of surprise and began urgently pulling at Edward's tunic. With a sudden tear, the garment ripped apart, revealing a small child wrapped in Edward's arms inside the protective folds of his tunic. I raised his lifeless arm and Ruth pulled the child from the protective cavity Edward had created.

Ruth laid the child on the sand and immediately lifted the boy's tunic and placed her ear over the left side of his breast.

'Quiet,' I ordered those talking and making noises around us so that Ruth could listen for the precious sounds that would indicate that the boy was still alive.

Within a moment or two, Ruth had raised her head and her smile told us the boy was alive. She immediately rolled him on his side and with her finger, began clearing the sand and muck from his mouth. The child spluttered, coughed and then vomited as he jerked into awareness and then began a gravelly wailing as his tears washed the sand from his eyes.

Ruth promptly and joyfully handed the boy back to his mother who had come running up to us. They stood together laughing and hugging, the child still gustily wailing and held between them.

A crowd had gathered around us, laughing and cheering in amazement. Even the taciturn caravan master, who had ridden back down the train to see what was unfolding, gave a loud cheer.

I looked back to Raymond, sitting on the sand and holding Edward's head in his lap, stroking his head and hair. Tears were now streaming openly down his face.

38

The sun had set in a blaze of different colours and lights that reflected off the sand and airborne dust from the *khamsin* when our small party eventually re-joined our caravan and the others outside the city walls of Rey Shahr.

Given Edward's selfless heroism, we had decided to inter him in his full Hospitaller uniform. This task was principally given over to Caspar and Raymond. Gently and with great care, they removed the sergeant's clothing and used the precious contents of their water skins to wash Edward down. Then they began the awkward task of dressing Edward's body in its uniform of mail coif, helmet, aventail, hauberk, sergeant's surcoat, chauses, greaves, boots and gauntlets – no easy task, particularly as rigor mortis was setting in.

Raymond's tears continued to quietly fall. The love and care he showed his fallen comrade told me something of the nature of the relationships these knights had with each other, both in their loyalty to each other and their commitment to the mission of the Order to which they belonged. Nearby, Hadar, Ruth and I scraped out a shallow grave in the sand and found two small wind-seared branches from a desert shrub with which to fashion a makeshift cross for the grave.

It was over an hour after the caravan had moved out that we laid Edward in the grave we had prepared. Both Caspar and Raymond spoke briefly of their friend and their admiration for him before leading us in the Lord's Prayer for this hero of the Hospitaller Cross. Finally, the two knelt beside the grave and reverentially placed Edward's sword in his hand and shield by his side.

It was with great sadness that we cupped and pushed the sand back over the body and shaped the sand into a respectable mound. No desert flowers had survived the *khamsin* but Ruth had found a piece of ribbon in her baggage and had penned in charcoal 'Edward of London' upon it. She tied it to the small cross.

'We must go before darkness is upon us,' said Caspar.

In silence, we mounted up, and in silence, we rode toward Rey Shahr. Even *Darta* was silent with no offerings from either end of his gangly body. I told myself it was an after-effect of the *khamsin* but was grateful for it nonetheless.

The evening call of a ram's horn announced the closure of the caravanserai gates as we dismounted in the inner courtyard and re-joined our fellow travellers. We were greeted very warmly and with consideration for our loss by other members of the caravan; in particular, the family of little Omar. The caravan master also made a point of visiting our small billet near the stables to give us his condolences.

The whole day had been exhausting and distressing for us all, particularly for Raymond and Caspar. It was no surprise that after a small evening meal in the common, we took to our billet and then to our beds.

The next morning, the caravan master informed us that the trading fleet for Hind was ready in the harbour and would depart tomorrow once all the goods and merchandise carried by our caravan from Shiraz were lade aboard. Even though the day was dark with overhead clouds threatening to burst in a drenching downpour, we had a day to explore Rey Shahr.

Both Caspar and Hadar chose to stay in the caravanserai as they were keen to learn from other travellers heading to Hind just what to expect in this land.

Ruth and I had to encourage Raymond to come with us to explore the harbour city. Eventually, he decided to put his grief aside and agreed to join us.

Like Acre, Rey Shahr was a maritime and trading harbour city. It was home to both the mercantile and military maritime interests of the local Persian and Arab elite. As in Acre, hostilities between the forces of Islam and the Cross did not appear to affect the trading interests of either side. We made our way through the streets, lanes and souks of the city passing traders and travellers from all over the known world. Dark-skinned and strongly muscled Ethiopians made up much of the stevedore workforce. They laboured alongside lighter-skinned traders and porters from lands further to the east. All were busily lading the ships with trade goods bound for cities along the coast between Persia and Hind.

The souks of the city were as colourful and noisy with the tongues of many lands and as fragrant and scented with spices and perfumes as those of Acre. Unlike Acre, there were no European faces and I noticed that our fairer skins were attracting the attention of some of the harbour city's inhabitants. In one souk, we encountered a group of smaller yellowy-skinned people with almond-shaped eyes. All wore their hair long in ponytails, which hung down the middle of their backs. Many were dressed in richly hued silk clothes. Their wares varied from bolts of silk cloth, jewellery and small pieces of occasional furniture to unusual preparations of exotic plants and animals' parts. I later learned that many of these were of medicinal use to those in the east. Hadar would have found these of great interest.

The harbour of Rey Shahr was immensely larger than that of Acre. Over a hundred mercantile and military vessels either sat at anchor in the harbour or were carefully making their way to or from the dockside. The vast majority of trading vessels I learned were called *jalbuts*. They came in a variety of sizes but all conformed to a general shape that enabled the high loading of goods with minimal deck space for crews and passengers. There were several vessels from the Persian navy lying further out to sea. They were of either two types of vessels. Most of the galleys, like their Byzantine counterparts, were called *dromons* and consisted of two rows of oars with one or two masts. The largest vessel at anchor was called a *harraga*. At the bow were two spout-shaped devices that I later learned were for showering enemy vessels with Greek fire, a substance that burned on water. All were manned by slaves, many of whom were only now being herded along by whip-cracking masters to board their different vessels and continue their lives of misery and slow death below decks.

Raymond, Ruth and I settled down to a lunch of hot flatbread, spiced beans and chicken, which we ate sitting along the edge of the harbour mole watching all the activity going on around us. The weather was unsettlingly hot and humid and we were all sweating heavily in our clothes.

'A swim would be good right now,' offered Raymond, wiping the sweat from his brow.

'I do not see anyone else in the water beyond those engaged in work,' I replied. 'I'm not sure that splashing and swimming around down there would be welcome right now.'

'I think you are correct, my friend, but I would give anything to be a little bit cooler.'

Overhead, thick dark clouds had been slowly gathering. They had bloomed in the west and were growing in size above us. Suddenly, a great crack of thunder assaulted our ears, followed by a drenching downpour that left the three of us soaked to the skin in just a few minutes.

'I think you got your wish,' I said with a laugh as we splashed our way across the puddles rapidly forming on the pathway of the mole.

I looked over at Ruth who was merrily dancing and spinning around in the rain with her face to the sky and letting water run and splash all over her. Her laughter was a joy to hear and the smile on her face was the same as that day in Hadar's apothecary when we first met.

I felt a bittersweet pain in my heart. My only wish was to hear her speak and say my name.

39

The next day was all chaos in the harbour and along the mole as seamen, merchants and travellers jostled with each other to lade last-minute goods or gain the best berth available for their journey. Our party was fortunate in that all of this had already been taken care of by our caravan master who was under orders from the Emir to secure the best possible vessel and berths for us. *Reh Allah*, 'The Wind of Allah', the vessel we were to travel on was a two-masted bireme galley with an enclosed deck that provided protection from the weather and sea for goods that would otherwise be spoiled by water. The enclosed deck also provided sheltered accommodation for the handful of wealthy or, in our case, worthy passengers, travelling to Hind. The deck also reduced the stench of human suffering arising from the oar decks below us.

Most of the vessels in the harbour of Rey Shahr were trading dhows of different sizes with either one, two or three masts. Nearly all were open decked and had bales and bundles stacked well above their transom lines making them appear dangerously top-heavy on the water. Only a small handful of trading vessels in the harbour were bireme galleys like ours. Standing further out to sea was the trading fleet's escort, a line of six Persian war galleys. They were the biremes, either the *dromons* and the lone *harraga* we had seen yesterday. On their decks, we could see soldiers and sailors standing around and waiting for the orders to get underway.

Once onboard, and having stowed our belongings into the small cabin space that would house the five of us for the coming weeks, we wandered up on to the deck to watch all the activity below on the mole and in the harbour. Ruth, Raymond and I stood side by side leaning on the gunnel when our attention was caught by a group of gaily costumed entertainers making their way along the mole. In the lead, a small group of musicians beat and blew out a comic tune with multiple leaps between high and low notes, abrupt changes in melody and the steady pulse of two drums emphasising an off-beat. The musicians tripped and stumbled along in a comic fashion that reflected the humorous themes and tempos underlying the musical score.

Behind the musicians came a troupe of obvious entertainers. They too, like the musicians, feigned tripping and stumbling along in time to the music but were also demonstrating their varied skills. Where space allowed, a group of children moved in and out of the crowd, doing acrobatic tumbles and walking on their hands. One child led a group of small fluffy dogs standing on their hind legs and dancing along to the music with similar canine trips and stumbles. Ruth laughed and clapped her hands in delight over this. Further back, two jugglers walked along either side of the mole, tossing balls back and forth to each other high over the heads of the crowd, making their way along the dockside mole. Periodically, a fire-breathing older man launched bursts of smoke and flame into the air.

'I don't know how his beard does not burst into flame doing that,' ventured Raymond, having never seen anything like it before.

Following the fire-breather came two carts; the first was pulled along by two men, the second by six. On the former sat the skinniest man I have ever seen who was contorting his body into various poses that quite simply seemed anatomically impossible. On the latter, reclined on numerous cushions, was a heavily sweating woman of the most immense proportions I had ever seen. She had an extremely saddened expression upon her face. She was cooling herself by waving a small ostrich-feathered fan around her face and upper body. Beside her pranced a man whose face was painted in a comic grin and wore a collection of bright veils and ribbons attached to a tunic he wore underneath. He too stumbled and tripped to the music but between his steps, he splashed water over the large woman, presumably in a bid to keep her cool.

The procession made their way further along the mole to where a dhow painted in a host of bright colours with a similarly coloured sail sat gently rocking beside the mole. It was here the music ceased and the procession made its way onboard the dhow.

'I'm not sure what that was all about,' said Raymond, 'but I am glad we had a chance to see it.'

We returned our attention to the crowds moving along the mole. Above us, the sky was again filling quickly with dark rain clouds as the monsoon wind started to rise from the west. It was only a matter of minutes before large heavy drops of rain started slowly plopping on the deck around us and then burst into a full-scale downpour that had us all drenched before we could find suitable shelter. Except for Ruth.

Ruth, as she had yesterday, stood gently twirling and turning herself around on the deck, her arms were bent at the elbow with her palms upwards and her head was tilted up to face the sky. She was laughing and her face had the most beatific look about it. Suddenly, she whipped the veil covering her hair from her head and let her long black silky locks fall down her back to rinse themselves in the purity of the rain. She ran her fingers through her hair and shook her locks with her hands. Her clothes, designed to hide the feminine form, began to cling to her body revealing shapes and curves that were meant to be hidden from the eyes of men.

I looked around and noticed that all work on the galley had

ceased and that seamen and passengers alike were staring open-mouthed at the apparition that was revealing herself before them. I gave thanks that the crowds on the mole could not see what was happening above their heads on the ship. There would have been a riot.

Ruth's performance was cut short as Hadar ran to the centre of the deck where she stood twirling herself and threw his cloak over her sopping form. He then appeared to beat her about the head several times before dragging her off to what was our cabin.

I was shocked, and even more so, furious with Hadar for treating Ruth in this manner. My emotions overcame me surprisingly quickly.

I strode angrily after him.

Ruth was still laughing when I entered the cabin and Hadar had an expression of exasperation rather than anger upon his face. It did not matter. I was still angry with Hadar for what I thought I had seen him do to Ruth.

'Hadar! How dare you? I can't believe what I have just seen. Hitting a defenceless girl,' I blurted without thinking, my fists balled akimbo at my side and my anger rising even more so.

Ruth immediately leapt between us, shaking her head from side to side and waving her hands at me. Unexpectedly, she slapped her hands deftly and ever so lightly about my head and face, pointed to Hadar and then herself. She then slapped me again in a similar manner, laughed again and pointed to Hadar and then herself. She had not hurt me in any way.

It suddenly dawned on me that Hadar had not hurt Ruth at all. He had been trying to protect her.

'Ippolito, I did not hurt Ruth but I had to appear as an angry and outraged guardian for her behaving in such a manner. Ruth was risking public humiliation, punishment or worse for her immodest display. I had to end the performance as quickly as possible, and, as befitting her elderly guardian.'

I immediately understood and my anger vanished as quickly as it had arisen and I suddenly felt ashamed for thinking that Hadar was capable of harming or hurting someone. I said so and begged his forgiveness. He gave it readily. Then he hugged me.

Ruth joined us before looking at us both and silently mouthing what appeared to be 'sorry' to both of us.

'Ruth,' Hadar said. 'You need to be more careful. As we all saw today, you are no longer a girl. You have become a very desirable and attractive young woman. This is something I have neglected to talk to you about as I guess I am used to older women talking to younger women about such things and not a tired old man having to take on this role.'

40

The next six weeks were among the most relaxing and enjoyable times of my life. Our days at sea were spent speeding over and through the waves whipped up by the monsoonal winds that also filled our sails. The wind drove us to a cruising speed that was exhilarating. The mast and ship's timbers groaned and creaked in obeyance to the wind's demands. At various times the sails whipped and cracked to changes in the wind's direction or the wild squalls that came lashing white horses across the surface of the water.

The hot and humid weather was relieved by the wind in our faces and hair. Every afternoon, the dark clouds would line up on the horizon only to overtake our fleet, drenching everyone and everything in beating showers of large drops. Then the monsoonal downpour would pass, the clouds dissipate and the broiling sun would again appear in the sky above us causing clouds of steamy vapour to rise from wet clothes, hair and any other rain-drenched surface.

We passed our days in a variety of ways. As had been our routine earlier on our journey, Hadar insisted that Ruth and I spend time with him in our cabin each morning, instructing us in medical matters.

Ruth and I also had plenty of time to enjoy each other's company. For the most part, I did all the talking with Ruth either nodding or shaking her head, making a facial expression of disdain or delight or using some other gesture to indicate an opinion. Over the length of our journey, we developed this form of communication into a convenient sign language that Ruth could use to communicate with me and I with her. By indicating the phalanges, those short bones making up the fingers and ascribing a letter of the alphabet to each one, Ruth could spell out words and phrases to me. Over time, we elaborated on this simple digital spelling technique to develop other hand signs, eye movements, face-pulling and body gestures to indicate whole words and phrases. I might not be able to hear Ruth's voice but at least we could communicate with each other more meaningfully.

Hadar commented most favourably on this new development, saying that it was yet another sign that I was helping Ruth's mind to heal. Caspar, Raymond and Hadar encouraged our 'language development' by learning the basics of what Ruth and I had developed and by the cruise's end, all five of us were able to communicate to each other without making a sound.

Sometimes, after our lessons, we would pass our time dangling lines over the gunwale of the dhow and try our luck at fishing. This was a new past-time for all of us in our party and we would join those crew members not actively on duty in attempting to catch our daily meal. Hadar was the most successful of our group when it came to landing a catch. He did, however, get the shock of his life one day when he was pulling in a good-sized fish that wriggled and writhed on the end of the line as he was pulling it in. He was just reaching out to grab the fish when suddenly a razor-toothed monster rose out of the water, snapping the fish in half and returning to the depths where schools of menacing dark shadows trailed and swam between the ships of the fleet. Their dark fins lazily cutting through the surface of the water were a constant reminder that should anyone fall overboard they would be savagely mauled and eaten – not drowned.

Later in the day, Caspar would coach Raymond and I in sword and shield play. As Raymond and I were similarly aged and of like build we were well-matched in our combat training. I had always felt that Edward's tuition was imbalanced by his size and strength over me, something that I did not feel with Raymond and which made our training with each other all the more competitive. It was also entertaining as the crew would often gather and place bets on who would win the day's duels. Raymond and I would sport a variety of bruises and abrasions from our efforts but there was never any heated blood or ill will in our efforts. Most often one of us, on the end of a telling blow or thrust, would yield or collapse and then we would slap each other on the back and laugh good-naturedly. Caspar would then begin an analysis of our swordplay, showing us where we had failed to counter a stroke or block the blow that had knocked us down.

Caspar was satisfied that he had passed onto Ruth all the skills and knowledge he could in teaching her how to throw knives. While in Shiraz, he had purchased six very thinly pointed knives that were perfectly balanced for throwing. He had also arranged for the palace seamstress to sew a cunning array of sheaths for the knives that were stitched together in such a way as to make a purse-like arrangement for holding the knives. This was attached to a belt that ran diagonally across her chest and kept the purse hidden beneath her clothes but always at the ready if needed.

Ruth had applied herself to mastering the throwing knife and could pierce an apple from thirty yards on nine out of ten attempts. Caspar was satisfied that her eye and accuracy were at a point that would benefit from a further refinement of skills. At the stern of the dhow, he had set up a small wooden target that swung from some ship's twine with the rocking and swaying of the ship. A moving target was a new challenge to Ruth and she rose to it accordingly, hitting the target and making it spin even more so before landing another knife in it.

I was quite amazed. Ruth, armed with her knives, was becoming decidedly deadly.

41

If our days were busy with tuition and the learning of medicine, weapons training, fishing or just quiet times between Ruth and I, many of our evenings were spent ashore, exploring and enjoying the sights of the numerous trading harbours and ports along our route. Night sailing was a risky business and one which was to be avoided, if possible, especially when we passed by rough and rocky shorelines. Fortunately, this was the exception rather than the rule and more often the smaller vessels would be run ashore while the larger vessels anchored off-shore if the weather looked to remain relatively calm.

Mostly we would find moorings in the bays and harbours that dotted the coast. The arrival of the trading fleet in any of the coast's numerous habitable locations was one which was greeted with a festive atmosphere by the locals and was always cause for celebration. Once anchored or moored, vessels would immediately commence unlading merchandise for sale onto the small boats or fishing boats that came out to greet and assist the fleet in its trading operations. Once ashore, either in a harbour town or along a beach, stalls would be hastily erected and goods displayed alongside the food and drinks stalls operated by local vendors. For many of the inhabitants of these locations, it was the twice a year chance to purchase goods and merchandise not normally available at their local markets.

Once the initial noise and chaos that accompanied the

commencement of trading had settled down to a quieter hubbub the sounds of music would drift across the water as the musicians on board the *Dhahka Allah*, or 'The Laughter of Allah', as their vessel was named, began their comic tunes. Slowly and with care, the musicians would continue their playing as they boarded the small rowboat towed from the stern of their ship and kept playing as they were rowed ashore. Once ashore, they would perform their concert as an inevitable crowd would gather, eager to enjoy the entertainment on offer. This continued as the rowboat went rapidly back and forth bringing the entertainers ashore. The only exception to this rule was the large woman we had seen on the mole at Rey Shahr. She only came ashore when their vessel was moored alongside a mole or a pier and she could be wheeled down a sturdy gang-plank in her cart.

There existed a great sense of fun and humour amongst the members of the troupe, and it was inevitable that Ruth, Raymond and I would gravitate to members of their company. There were fourteen performing members, six musicians, six children of various ages, a captain helmsman and his mate aboard the *Dhahka Allah*. Most of the performers and musicians were also able to double as deckhands when called upon such as in heavy weather or entering ports. Most of them lived, cooked and slept on the half-deck under old sails and canvases.

Ishaan, the troupe's leader, and his wife, Opal, had a small cabin as did the captain helmsman at the stern of the dhow. Ishaan and Opal had twin teenage boys, Arjuna and Anish, who tumbled, juggled and clowned. The oddest couple were Meera – the hugely obese woman – and her husband, Jay, who was the thin and bony body contortionist. It must have been a loving marriage as four of the children aboard were theirs. Other key performers were Ravi, the fire-eater, Asha, the sword swallower, Bili and Dili, the male and female dwarf clowns who were also the parents of the other two children aboard. Others onboard their dhow included Kali the magician and conjuror, Aarush, the strongman and two acrobats, Madi and Avani. All of the acts were accompanied by comic and lively tunes played by the musicians.

Raymond found himself gravitating to Bili and Dili, the dwarf clowns. In their company, it seemed that the grief he bore over the losses of Edward and Godfrey melted away. Not having a language in common and only using mime and gestures, the three negotiated some of Raymond's ideas and suggestions into their performances. It was only a matter of time before Raymond too became a small part of their show. I won't go into detail. They called it 'dwarf-tossing'.

For reasons best known to herself, Ruth gravitated to the company of Meera and Jay and their children, particularly the youngest, Shaila, who was only three. Meera, despite her enormity, was an extremely maternal and caring woman. I think she sensed the trauma still buried deep inside Ruth that prevented her from speaking and she was instinctively protective towards her. For Ruth, Meera provided an oasis of female comfort and understanding which her male travel companions could not provide. Ruth expressed her thanks to Meera by giving her massages in the evenings to relieve the pain of her swollen ankles and feet.

As for myself, Kali, the magician and conjuror, saw my interest in his skills and was soon teaching me what he called some little tricks requiring an extraordinary degree of dexterity that utilised finger and thumb manipulations. Using a simple playing card, I spent hours and hours practising how to make it disappear from my hand and then make it miraculously reappear again as I pulled my hand from behind someone's ear or, as Raymond suggested, from my own backside. My first performance before the other members of the troupe received a round of applause and a good laugh.

42

Late one afternoon while turning one of Kali's cards between my fingers, I looked to the shoreline and saw that the beaches had vanished and were replaced by rocks, shoals, tall rocky cliffs and turbulent white water. There would be no evening ashore as the fleet would have to anchor off-shore and pray that the night would be calm. The two small communication dhows attached to the naval vessels escorting the fleet were moving down the line of trading vessels to communicate the same message. This was no simple operation as the fleet travelled in relatively close formation and the timing of furling or lowering sails, shipping oars and anchoring was critical if collisions were to be avoided.

I looked across the forty or fifty yards to the *Dhahka Allah* and noticed the captain looking to the nearest naval vessel for the flag to cease oars and or lower sails. At the helm of our vessel, our captain was looking in the same direction for instruction. I followed his gaze to the leading galley and watched for the flag that would signal all vessels to slow. Within a few minutes of the messenger dhows returning to their mother vessels, a long red pennant was unfurled from the mast of the leading vessel. I watched as our crew lowered the sails of our galley and the oars ceased movement and then slid onboard. I looked astern and saw it was the same on down the sailing line.

Suddenly, I heard the sounds of shouts immediately followed by the wrenching sound of timber being torn apart. I turned back to see the *Dhahka Allah* being mounted and torn apart from the stern by the ram mounted on the large galley that had been underway behind her. The galley appeared unharmed by the collision but all was panic and destruction aboard the smaller vessel. The small rowboat that had been towed by the entertainer's dhow was crushed between the two vessels. There was no way for the troupe and crew to escape the doomed and already sinking dhow.

Caspar's voice rang out across our deck, demanding we release our own small loading barge and attempt a rescue of the stricken vessel's occupants. This was going to take several precious minutes. I was joined by Raymond and Caspar as we ran across the deck to assist the crew in untying the ropes that secured the barge to our deck. Hadar and Ruth had emerged from our cabin and were both looking in consternation at the drama unfolding across the water from us.

I briefly looked up from our frantic attempts to untie and lower the barge to see the stern of the entertainer's dhow was now underwater and her bow pointed at about forty-five degrees into the air. A handful of her passengers were already in the water either struggling to stay afloat or clinging desperately to any piece of floating debris. The crew of the ramming galley were frantically hauling in the dinghy towed from the stern of the galley or attempting to throw ropes and lines to those in the water. It seemed most of the troupe and crew were still aboard the doomed vessel and were clinging to the ropes and rails in a panicked attempt to stave off the inevitable disaster that was revealing itself before our eyes.

At last, the securing ropes were freed from the barge and with a great heave, we turned the vessel upright and dropped it over the side in a great splash of water. Those of us who were closest descended the ropes hanging from our side and swung ourselves aboard the barge. Immediately we unshipped the oars and commenced making our urgent way across the water to where the *Dhahka Allah* was now more than half underwater. Across the water, I saw that the crew of the galley had boarded their dinghy and were making their short way to where the people in the water were frantically floundering and struggling to stay afloat. Two of the musicians using their drums as floats were the first to the side of galley's dinghy and were quickly hauled on board. Others still in the water were clinging to water butts, oars and other flotsam and jetsam and trying to propel themselves toward the galley's rescue dinghy. It seemed all were wailing in fear and desperation.

'To the side of the dhow. The other dinghy can save those in the water we must try to save those still on board,' came Caspar's urgent voice from behind me.

As we drew near to the side of the dhow, the first of those on board began to leap into the water and thrash about, calling us over to save them. A great splash announced that Meera had hit the water and I saw she was clutching Shaila to her body, one hand held tightly over the child's mouth and nose. Her great mass brought her straight back to the surface where others started to clutch and cling desperately to her floating form, threatening to drown both her and Shaila. Other people were landing in the water all around our loading barge. Their cries and screams filled the late afternoon air.

It was then I saw the fins travelling at a speed I thought impossible, coming straight for us from different directions. Within seconds, dozens of fins were twisting and swirling in a frenzy amongst those floundering in the water or desperately trying to scramble aboard one of the two rescue vessels.

Meera was floundering amongst those trying to cling to her in the water and doing everything she could to keep Shaila's small face above the water. Our eyes made contact and I instinctively reached out to take the child from her hands when a set of razor-sharp teeth ripped the child from her hands and sped away under the water. There was only time to hear the briefest of heart-torn shrieks from Meera before she too disappeared under a frothing pink and white turbulence. All around us, those still in the water were being ripped apart and pulled under by these savage monsters of the deep.

I was shaken from a state of shock by Raymond's urgent plea. 'Help me Ipp.'

I turned and immediately grabbed the free hand of a pale and fearful Kali whom Raymond and I unceremoniously jerked aboard in one quick and violent action, causing his head to crash against one of the oar benches. Apart from that, he was miraculously unharmed.

We tried desperately to grab others in the water nearby but just as each of our hands made contact with another reaching up from the water a rapidly moving fin tore it and its owner away and under the water.

Just then a panicked, 'No!' sounded across the water from the other rescue boat. Too many people had clustered to one side and in their attempts to clamber on board were in danger of capsizing the vessel. It seemed as though some sort of collective feral intelligence passed through the frenzied sharks in that moment. As one, the larger sharks began attacking the boat itself in unison by ramming the sides with their blunt snouts. At the same time, two of the largest sharks leapt from the water and threw themselves over the gunwales snapping and biting at those on board. The combined effect was to see the overloaded dinghy pitch violently to one side and capsize sending all onboard screaming and wailing into the water and the certainty of a bloody and gruesome death below. The water exploded in a violent pink and red frothing turbulence of blood, body parts, fins, tails and the blood-maddened black and grey skins of the sharks.

For a few moments, all was quiet in the water around our boat as the sharks that had been there had speedily moved off to the nearby feeding frenzy. Those of us on board were grateful for the respite and could only look on helplessly at the terrible carnage unravelling before us across the water.

I could not get the image of little Shaila being snatched from Meera's hands out of my mind and a few minutes later suddenly had to be sick over the side. It was as I was wiping my mouth that I saw the monstrous black shadow under the water speed with a loud thump into the side of our boat, causing it to rock dangerously in the water.

'Quick, get your oars out and get this rig back to the ship. The bastards are attacking the boat,' called one of the crew.

Two more destabilising thumps from the same side confirmed this.

We ran the oars out and pulled desperately. The sharks were cunning and attacked our oars as if trying to rip the means of our escape from our hands.

'Bastards,' yelled Raymond as his oar handle was suddenly ripped from his hands and jerked upwards, smashing into his chin.

Cold fear ran through my entire body as I noticed more fins moving away from the now quietening frenzy around the capsized dinghy and heading towards our boat.

'Row, you fuckers!' came the call of the same crewman as before.

We needed no encouragement to do so.

It was Caspar who saved our skins that day. He had been wearing his seax, a shorter sword than the conventional long battle sword of the knights, when the crisis began to unfold. He suddenly began rapidly plunging the sword into the shadows moving around below us in the water. They were so densely packed that within a few seconds, he had scored a hit on one and followed it up with three or four more quick strikes that drew blood from the monsters. As quickly as they had turned on our boat, the sharks now turned on each other – frenzied by the blood of their own kind.

Caspar was too slow in withdrawing his hand and seax from the last stab and suffered a shearing bite to his forearm that tore skin and flesh from his wrist and hand as well. He thrust the injured limb beneath his armpit to try and stem the bleeding. His actions saved the day for us as they enabled our little boat to make it to the side of our galley without being upturned by the sharks who were now finishing off their comrades below the water. Ropes were already hanging over the side to assist in our ascent up the side of the galley.

The sharks had begun to circle our little barge again as Raymond and I finished tying a rope around Caspar's waist and he was unceremoniously hauled up the side. Raymond and I followed just as quickly, hanging on to the ropes as those above us pulled us frantically on board. Saving hands hauled us unceremoniously over the gunwales where Raymond and I tumbled onto the safety of the deck.

I went to stand up only to feel my knees buckle and my legs go from under me and I tumbled down once again.

The next thing I knew, Ruth had her arms around me and was holding my head to her breast. She was sobbing uncontrollably and making the kind of keening sound often heard at funerals. Through the strands of her hair, I could see Raymond still lying on the deck. His lips were moving in what I took to be a silent prayer of thanks and deliverance. Behind him, Hadar was rinsing Caspar's injured arm and hand in water from a butt. Around them, other members of the barge crew were either still lying on the deck, slowly getting to their feet or standing using the gunwales for support. Everyone on board, the barge and the galley were shaken in some way to the core of their soul by what they had seen and heard that afternoon.

Except one.

As Ruth slowly settled and I gently extricated myself from her wonderful embrace, I noticed a dripping Kali sitting not far from me. He turned to look at me. His eyes were wide with a fevered animation. I could not believe what came next.

'Oh, my goodness! By Shiva's blue balls! That was exciting,' he exclaimed and joyfully clapped his hands.

43

The 'butcher's bill' from that dreadful afternoon was twenty-seven dead men, women, children and crew from the *Dhahka Allah* and six from the galley's rescue dinghy. Caspar's wounds to his sword arm were mercifully mostly superficial and Hadar was confident he would regain full combat usage of it in a few weeks.

'In all the battles, skirmishes and engagements I have had with the Saracens,' reflected Caspar later that night in our cabin, 'I have never known the kind of terror that took hold of me this afternoon. I would rather be stark naked and facing a horde of hashish-crazed assassins than go through that again.'

For some reason Caspar's imagery made us laugh and I felt something of my residual terror wash away from me. Ruth was sitting beside me with a protective arm around me as if she were scared she might lose me again. Her head was on my shoulder and I held her free hand between both of mine, gently stroking hers. It was Ruth's closeness that was doing the most to settle my aftershock and I relished the intimacy of it. We were one again.

Perhaps the most unexpected outcome of the day was the adoption of our party by Kali. He seemed unperturbed by what had happened in the water that afternoon and busied himself with tending to our needs by way of preparing our evening meal, assisting Caspar in his one-handedness, tidying the cabin and helping out in whatever way he could. It was a side of him I had not seen before. I had only known the showman magician who had kindly shown me some sleight of hand tricks and liked to project an air of wizened mystery about himself.

Kali looked to be about the same age as Hadar. His head and facial hair were silvered while the lines around his mouth and eyes were wrinkled and creased in what were well-etched lines of laughter. He told us that he had originally come from Kashmir in the north of Hind and at the foot of a mountain range he called the *Himaliyas*. He maintained, with a note of pride, that Kashmir was the most beautiful and heavenly place on earth and hoped that someday he could take us there. He told us how as a child he had learned his craft from a similar showman magician who used to visit Kali's village regularly to take the mountain air, enjoy the heated springs and entertain the locals. Kali had travelled through most of Hind as well as Persia and Arabia and like so many travellers spoke a number of languages and dialects. His association with the entertainers had begun ten years beforehand when Ishaan had seen Kali entertaining children with his 'magical' tricks on the docks of Calicutt – our fleet's eventual destination.

We had decided that until we knew Kali a little better, we would say nothing about the exact nature of our mission to Hind and settled upon the near truth that we were indeed a physician, his two apprentices and a Hospitaller knight and squire who were simply seeking knowledge of cures unknown to westerners and the opening of trade in these goods.

We did not need to press Kali for information about Hind. Kali was most forthcoming on just about everything we would need to know. He had us in some consternation telling us of Hind's deadly animal and insect life. I had seen the lions of Outremer with Raymond on our journey from Acre to Jerusalem but the big cats of Hind, the tiger and the leopard, supposedly had a worse reputation as man killers. The same was true of the black and brown bears from the mountains of Kali's homelands. I had heard of Egypt and Africa's crocodiles but was unaware that they inhabited just about every river and lake to be found in the warmer more tropical parts of Hind. The same was true of elephants who could suddenly stampede in fear and run a man down, crushing him to death underneath the enormous weight that these beasts carried. Even so, I was keen to see one.

Kali was keen to make clear the danger of wild dogs. He said these creatures roamed in packs that often invaded villages, snatching small children and babies. Worse, he said, was that just a small bite from a diseased dog could bring on symptoms of uncontrollable violent movements or inability to move parts of the body plus a fear of water, eventually leading to loss of consciousness and finally death.

Hadar offered that this 'dog disease' was also known in the west and was called rabies or hydrophilia, the 'fear of water'.

I felt Ruth crawl with a sense of horror as Kali stressed the importance of shaking all bed linen out before use and never leaving clothes or footwear on the floor. This he said was to remove any nesting insects such as the giant black scorpion or its equally deadly partner, the red scorpion, whose bites were inevitably fatal. Apart from these ground insects, Kali informed us that the bites of several giant wasps and bees had been known to kill people or at least make them seriously sick.

Just as Kali's summary of Hind's deadly animals caused us some consternation, his description of Hinduism – the principal religion of Hind – was one that drew my interest as it did Hadar. He told us many tales of the Hindu gods' adventures and misadventures along with what were their personal attributes and aspects. This variety, he said, was reflected in the infinite number of ways Hindus practised their worship based on family, community and regional traditions. It was a religion that saw one true god in everything from the smallest mote of dust to the stars and planets of the night sky, yet it was populated with countless lesser gods and goddesses who represented different aspects of this one true god.

It was a week after the shark attack and our journey was coming to its end. In the distance, we could see a harbour city with vessels of all kinds making their way in, out and around the harbour including those from our fleet. Our galley was anchored in the sea lanes offshore from the city awaiting harbour master approval to enter the harbour and unlade its cargo and passengers.

Kali, Hadar, Ruth and I were standing to the steer board side of the galley, enjoying the gentle sea breeze that helped relieve the oppressive tropical heat and humidity of southern Hind. Kali was telling the three of us what little he knew about Hind Ayurvedic medicine and health practices. It was here that he unintentionally dropped the axe on all we had been about.

'Obviously, Ayurvedic practitioners cannot cure all the diseases and ailments of mankind. Take that island off to our right,' said Kali, pointing out an offshore island that seemed to have a cordon of yellow buoys sitting off its shore and surrounding it. People were sitting and lying on the sand of the beach. All seemed heavily draped despite the heat.

'Those poor wretches living there have been exiled there to a life of quarantine from the rest of the population lest their disease infects others. There are similar colonies of sufferers all over Hind.'

'And just what is their disease?' asked a suddenly worried Hadar, realisation dawning on him.

'Why, leprosy of course. It is everywhere in Hind.'

44

Hind. What a land. What a culture. So many people. So many colours. So many beliefs, temples, festivals and gods. I could not begin to count the number of gods, avatars, demons and spirits on a hundred hands of fingers. Let alone all the people of that many coloured land.

And, the heat.

And, the humidity.

It was like walking into a wall of solid air when we disembarked from *Dhahka alleh* and moved away from the cooling air of the southern monsoon winds that were sweeping their way down the Hind coast at that time of year. Sweat immediately began to pour down our bodies. It stung its way into our eyes and burned over every raw scratch and sore we had acquired on our journey. It made its way into our clothes to appear as large, dark, damp spots that clung clammily about us.

'I think,' said Hadar, mopping his brow, 'the first thing we need to purchase is some of the local clothing. Cotton is lighter and will help us stay cooler than the woollen clothes we are wearing. It will also help us blend in and attract less attention.'

Kali led the way through the busy docklands and warehouses to a large public square he called a *'chowk'* which was surrounded by stalls and public buildings around its perimeter. The stalls were all erected on platforms each about a half-yard high off the ground. At the front of the stall and over the platform was a shaded covering Kali called a *'verandah'*. It was upon these shaded platforms that the traders displayed their goods and commodities. Buyers stood on the ground below to buy what was on offer. Most of the stalls appeared to be a uniform ten feet wide and about twenty feet deep. Behind many of the stalls were either private residences or warehouses.

Ruth made her sign for attention and pointed to several stalls where brightly coloured fabrics and robes were displayed upon the stall *verandahs*.

Kali laughed and smiled. 'I believe Ruth has spied something of interest to her already. Ippolito, I think you and I will be needed to help translate Ruth's needs and preferences in this transaction.'

Ruth clapped her hands and then smiled brightly in anticipation of buying new clothes.

An hour later, she was still trying on different clothes and fabrics while the rest of us sweated under a hot and sticky afternoon sun. It was Hadar who drew this to Ruth's attention. Ruth disappeared into the back of the shop and fifteen minutes later emerged looking very much like the daughter of some well-to-do Hindi merchant. She was wearing a length of a pale blue cloth draped about her. Ruth signed it was called a *sari*. The lower part of the cloth was shaped like a skirt below her waist with the top part thrown over her shoulder and coming back to form a veil over her head. The borders of the cloth had been embroidered in a gold and red stitch that rippled and wound its way through the folds of the *sari* wrapped around her. Underneath the *sari* she was wearing a tight-fitting and shape forming bodice of the same colour. Around her wrists were some brightly coloured metal bands Kali called *bangles*. The effect was transforming; particularly as the wife of the trader, who had shown Ruth how to fashion her *sari* in the local style, had also thought to add a small red dot she called a *'bindi'* just above the space between Ruth's eyebrows for decoration. That was not all about the *sari*.

Ruth went on to show us how the *sari* could be pulled up between her legs to make a pantaloon arrangement suitable for riding or walking over difficult terrain.

'You have chosen wisely, Ruth,' said Hadar. 'It has been worth the wait.' He rolled his eyes in playful mockery.

Hadar, Caspar, Raymond and I made short work of our clothes shopping. We all purchased a pair of *'dhotis'*, which were basically an unstitched cloth that was wound around the waist and knotted at the back and like Ruth's *sari* could be hitched up between the legs if needed. Hadar insisted we also purchase a pair of men's loose pantaloons with cuffed ankles called *'shalwars'*. He said this was to look more respectable should the need arise. Completing our outfits were long tunics Kali named *'churidars'*, which hung down to just above the knees of our *'shalwars'*. Hadar, as leader of our expedition, also purchased a turban that had some jaunty and colourful birds' feathers set to the front of it and an embroidered waistcoat. The four of us were done and newly and coolly attired in less than an hour.

Ruth made her sign for attention and then the one for hunger, a gnawing need we were all beginning to feel, and we set off with Kali leading the way to find a food vendor.

'Do not be fooled by all the enticing and exciting fragrances and aromas of the foods you see,' offered Kali. 'Many vendors use spices and herbs to hide the fact that their food is spoiled. Such food may cause you to fall ill or die. Unless you can be sure of the freshness of any meat in Hind, do not eat it. It is the heat that ruins the flesh. Your safest options are to stick to vegetarian dishes. They are just as spicy and fragrant as the meat dishes and will please your palates. Oh, and never, never ask for pork or beef; they are forbidden to the Hindus and Moslems. Ask only for lamb, goat, chicken or fish as a meat dish. But only if you know it is fresh.'

Half an hour later, we were seated by a small street vendor's kitchen and enjoying flatbreads made of chickpeas and herbs with a rich and spicy lentil sauce with either minted yoghurt drizzled over the top or a spread of a pickled fruit called *chatni*. It was delicious and restorative.

Our next concern was to find some suitable accommodation where we could rest up, escape the heat and make some plans out of the wreckage of our mission to save the leper king. Kali advised not seeking any beds in any of the local dockside 'serais' as they were expensive, unclean and the haunts of criminals working the underside of the 'city of spices' as he called the port of Calicut.

Calicut was a city of waterways, backwaters and lagoons fed by rivers further inland that snaked their way in and around the populated and built-up areas of the harbour city. Kali took us to a riverside where a small pier ran out into the waterway. We only had to wait a few moments before a long and thin flat-bottomed passenger barge pulled up next to the pier we were standing on. It was poled by a young man wearing just a *dhoti* and sweating heavily.

Kali negotiated a fee for the passenger service as we loaded our bags aboard and then settled back into the hold of the barge to take in the scenery and sights of the harbour city. Away from the buildings and busy streets, the waterway was ablaze with colour. Brightly coloured birds swooped and called from branches in the trees and exotic flowers bloomed swathes of colour amidst the treetops and gardens. As we moved upriver, I noticed a settlement of very run-down and tattered-looking huts, hovels and awnings populated by equally run-down and tattered-looking people. Many were missing limbs and used a variety of crutches or wheeled themselves in small carts of various descriptions.

I asked Kali if this was another leper colony.

'No. It is a special camp set aside for the injured and wounded veterans of the king's armies. It is not much, but they have a better life than the armies of beggars who must live on, and haunt, the streets of cities all over Hind for a living.'

Just then Ruth made an excited-sounding squawk of sorts and pointed ahead to a bend in the waterway. There in the shallows were three of the largest animals I had ever seen.

'Elephants,' said Caspar, recognising the animals for their long trunks that they were using to spray themselves with water. Around the beasts was a group of children who were happily splashing and playing with the animals. One young boy had managed to climb on the back of one of the beasts and was standing up taunting his friends when a large spray of water from the elephant's trunk knocked him from his feet and sent him tumbling into the water below. He quickly re-emerged, laughing with innocent joy. For a fleeting moment, I envied the children and their carefree state.

The serai that we arrived at was more like a large inn than a caravanserai. There were no protective walls, no central courtyard, no market area or extensive stabling yards. Instead, it was a very large house with several dormitories, communal areas, two kitchen and dining areas and several huts or cabins, called *bungalows*, all with cooling *verandahs*, dotted around the grounds and the riverside of the property. It was to one of these *bungalows* that we took our accommodation.

'No noisy dormitory of farts, burps and grunts for us.' Raymond winked, evoking memories of the night we had shared bed bugs and other vermin at an inn in Bethinople whilst travelling from Acre to Jerusalem.

Instead, we all lay awake for different periods of the night, trying to blanket the incessant cacophony of night birds, crickets, cicadas, grasshoppers, beetles, mosquitoes, bats and frogs that filled the Hindi night all around us.

45

After we broke our fast with flatbread, fruit and yoghurt along with cups of a heavily sweetened and milky tea called *chai*, Hadar called us all together for a meeting. He said it was to make new plans given the failure of our mission in Hind. Kali joined us as well. Hadar filled him in on the details of what we had been about.

'I had thought your reaction to the news of leprosy being everywhere in Hind was overdone but now I understand your shock and disappointment,' commented Kali upon hearing Hadar's summary.

'It seems,' began Caspar, 'that we must bide our time for a few months while we wait for the monsoon winds to turn around and we can catch sail back to Outremer with the outward-bound trading fleet. The question is, do we just sit here in Calicut twiddling our thumbs till then, or not?'

'Speaking for myself, and I hope, Ippolito and Ruth,' said Hadar, nodding to the two of us, 'I would like the opportunity to learn more of the *Ayurvedic* practices of medicine and healing. I learned a little in my travels as a younger man and would not like to waste the opportunity for us to learn some new perspectives in the treatment of disease.'

Ruth and I nodded our heads in agreement with these sentiments.

'I see much merit in this plan, Hadar,' replied Caspar. 'But why should you and your young companions be the only ones to benefit from such learning? Raymond and I are both Hospitallers. Any proven skills and knowledge we can bring back to our knightly order would be highly valued.'

'Forgive my oversight,' begged Hadar. 'I forgot that your order is not just one of knights and warriors but also one of healers and helpers. It would seem the five of us can act in unison and together seek out sources of healing knowledge here in Hind. Are we all agreed?'

We were.

Kali had been sitting, silently taking in what he could as we had been speaking mostly in the lingua franca of Outremer.

'Kali,' said Hadar, switching to Persian. 'What do you know of Hindi wisemen and physicians from whom we can learn some of their healing skills?'

Kali had been listening to what we had said earlier and had a patchwork idea of what had been said.

'Let me see. First, are you all healers and physicians?'

'Yes,' we responded as one.

'You have come a long way to Hind to find a possible cure for leprosy and now you know there is no cure?' he said, making his statement a question.

'Yes,' came our mutual response again.

'And now you wish to learn something of *Ayurvedic* medicine before returning to your homelands?' Again the statement was a question and again we responded in the affirmative.

'I do not wish to offer you false hope but there may be a cure or treatment for the lepers' disease. I do not know. I only know of stories that circulated in the villages of my youth in Kashmir. They could be fables or superstitious falsehoods or it could be that there is a grain of truth within them.

'The stories tell of monks who live high in the *Himaliya* mountains that overlook Kashmir. It is said that these monks spend their time in esoteric practices that give them the attributes of the gods. I have heard of monks who sit near-naked in the snow yet do not suffer the cold nor die of overexposure to it. They are rumoured to be able to elevate themselves and float in a meditative trance of communion with their One God. There are also stories of their prowess as unarmed warriors able to fight and defeat fully armed adversaries without a single weapon of their own to bear.

'Other stories tell of the monks living to great ages and that they have conquered the diseases that plague the rest of humanity. Within the halls of their mountainous monasteries are said to be scrolls thousands of years old that contain the secrets and mysteries of the ancients. It may be that in these scrolls is the answer you seek.

'To seek these monks and their knowledge out would be a very dangerous thing to do. Their monasteries are high in the mountains and often perched precariously onto the side of their slopes. To travel there one would have to face the adversaries of the intense cold, deadly blizzards, the mountain illness as well as avalanches and crevices that can suddenly open up and swallow a human being into their depths.'

Kali finished and looked around at us as if to say, 'Do you really want to do this thing?'

His only answer was the silence of our individual considerations.

It was Hadar who broke the silence.

'It seems we may be able to complete our mission after all.'

'And,' signed Ruth with some animation, 'learn the wisdom of the ancient healers.'

46

Over the next three days we made plans and purchased goods we would need for our journey. Kali advised that we would traverse all sorts of terrain and climates and that purchasing too much ahead of time may be a mistake as conditions could vary a great deal as we went north.

Our biggest problem proved to be finding transport for ourselves and packs. The military of the region was ramping up for a campaign to the north and just about every mountable and packable animal in the region had been commandeered by the army under the reigning prince's orders. In the end, we had to settle for a well-used but sturdy hand cart that would carry all our goods. It had large wide wheels that would make the pulling of the cart easier than others with smaller wheels, a wide flat-bed that could accommodate a man lying down in the back if needed and two sturdy tow bars at the front with which one or two people could haul the cart. It was Kali who suggested attaching an awning to the cart to provide a little protection against the elements if required.

Once the awning was in place Kali stood looking at our little covered cart, scratching his chin, deep in thought.

'I have an idea if you would care to hear it,' he said cautiously and not very sure of himself.

We all looked at him as Caspar said, 'Well, let's hear it then.'

'While we are travelling to the north it would be good to have some sort of external cover or purpose that will help us to blend in rather than being simply travelling strangers who might attract unwanted attention from dacoits and thieves.'

'Just what are you suggesting, Kali?' asked Caspar.

'That we name our cart the *Dhahka Allah*, "The Laughter of Allah", paint it in gay colours and designs and continue Ishaan and Opal's tradition of being travelling entertainers,' responded Kali.

'And just what sort of entertainment will be on offer?' asked a sceptical Caspar.

'I, of course, would be the magician, who is ably assisted by my apprentice in magic, the young Ippolito. We can work on the "tricks" of our show as we travel.'

'One act does not make a show, Kali,' said Caspar.

'And that is where you and Raymond come in. You two will put on a show of amazing swordsmanship, acrobatics and clever comedic tricks while supposedly fighting a duel to the death. Nobody gets hurt, no one suffers. It is simply a matter of learning various steps, poses, thrusts and parries that are orchestrated to look like a serious duel to the death.'

Raymond and Caspar were looking at each other in consideration of what Kali had proposed. Then they both smiled simultaneously, indicating their acceptance of the possibility of the idea.

Ruth interjected by signing, 'And what about me?' which I translated for Kali.

'You, young mistress, will be the star of the show. I have seen your skills with those thin and slender knives you throw. I have many ideas about how we can showcase your skills and abilities.'

Ruth flashed that winning smile of hers and I could tell she was pleased about taking the centre stage of our show.

A cough from Hadar indicated his interest in just what his part in our little circus would be.

'Why, you will be demonstrating and selling our miracle cures, of course.'

Hadar nearly exploded in what was a real coughing fit. He finally ceased his coughing, got his breath back and spluttered, 'I am no quack charlatan selling snake oil to unsuspecting customers, Master Kali. There will be no miracle cures on sale, only the proven and bona-fide cures and treatments that I, Caspar and my two young apprentices prepare ourselves.'

'That is of course, what I meant,' responded Kali, stammering with some surprise at Hadar's indignation over the 'miracle cures' comment.

'It is a good plan, Kali,' said Caspar. 'As you said, it gives us a suitable cover to be travelling under and will not attract unwanted attention.'

'Thank you, Caspar. If you are agreeable, I offer myself as entertainment director to help you all develop your individual performances.'

Later that morning, Kali, Ruth, Raymond and I set about painting the awning for the cart. Kali had managed to procure several different-coloured paints along with some rather old brushes that were still serviceable.

We stood before the awning looking at each other and wondering just what it was that we were going to paint. We looked to Kali who said, 'I'm not sure now that "the canvas" is before us.'

Ruth signed for attention and then quickly made the signs and fingers for a long list of easily drawn natural images: rainbows, clouds, the sun and moon, the stars, birds in flight, butterflies, flowers – the list went on and as quickly as Ruth signed them, I translated for Kali and the others who could not keep up with

Ruth's rapid pace of signing. Finally, she slowed her signing, ending with, '… all against a background of dark sky blue.'

Ruth was not finished and went over to a smouldering cooking fire nearby and retrieved a short but well-blackened stick. She then went over to the cart and began sketching her ideas and their design on the awning. I was amazed at how she could make accurate representations with just a few bold strokes of her charcoal. I had no idea that she had such an artistic ability. It was yet another revelation about her.

Hadar and Caspar had spent the day organising and doing their best to restock our 'travelling apothecary'. Hadar had requested that he have a small booth that could be set up with curtains or blankets for use as a small clinic for the lancing of boils, teeth extractions and other quick but minor procedures.

By the end of that day, we were all set to take our magical and marvellous travelling medicine show to the people of Hind.

47

Kali led us along coastal roads and tracks, always heading in a northerly direction. It was the most direct route to Kali's Kashmir gateway to the mountains, which was as yet far, far away. The route also afforded us the luxury of being close to the sea breezes that helped to relieve the energy-draining heat and humidity of the inland areas away from the coast.

As we were travelling on foot and towing our cart behind us, we only averaged about ten miles a day. Sometimes more, sometimes less depending on the terrain. We would start our day with the dawn cacophony of songbirds greeting the day and be on our way within an hour and travel till mid-afternoon when we would pitch a camp or find a nearby inn or serai. Evenings were spent either perfecting our performance skills or learning Hindi from Kali. Ruth, Hadar and I were particularly attentive during these sessions and Kali was pleased with how quickly we picked up the new language.

After two weeks on the road, we had our acts pretty much together and in a small coastal village named Mangalpandi, we gave our first performance. We were able to use the rear of the cart as a stage, which also gave our audience a good view of the show. First up was Kali and his magician's show. It began with some colourful flares of smoke and sparks from two braziers into which Kali discreetly threw some powders that he and Hadar had made from crushed rocks they had gathered along the route of our journey. Inevitably it drew 'oohs' and 'aahs' from the crowd with the occasional squeal of fear from a frightened child or infant. Kali would then begin the appearing and disappearing tricks, which were all abetted by the dozens of pockets sewn inside the cloak and sleeves of a long coat he had put together for this purpose whilst on our journey. Magically, he would make bunches of flowers, statuettes of the gods, picture cards and other items appear and disappear from his hands, all the while keeping up a lively banter.

It was after this that he would invite his apprentice, me, to join him on the stage. Kali and I had worked my part in the show into a comedic routine that saw me performing magical tricks but all ones in which something went humorously wrong. One trick involved placing what seemed to be scented flowers inside a turban but when placed upon my head, it 'magically' turned into water, giving me a thorough dousing. Another trick involved my *shalwars* falling down revealing my *dhottis,* which had been dyed with yellow and brown splashes at the front and rear. I was not fond of this trick but Kali insisted it got a good laugh, which it did, and I relinquished my misgivings for the sake of the show.

As soon as Kali and I finished our show, a loud argument would start in the front row or line of the audience. It was Raymond and Caspar. Comments quickly grew to insults and before anyone knew what was going on, the two had drawn their swords and commenced fighting. Hadar had coated their sword blades with the same powders he had made from crushed rocks and each time the swords clashed, there would be bright sparks of blue, green, yellow and red. Inevitably, this led some in the audience to believe that it was two avatars or demons fighting in front of them. Caspar and Raymond had worked acrobatic ducks, rolls and leaps, timed perfectly to avoid the slashing swipes of each other's sword. At some stage in their duel, the two managed to ascend to the back of the cart while maintaining their swordplay. It was at this point that the two of them would start to exchange humorous insults with each other.

'You son of a wormy elephant's dropping.'

'And you who smell like one.'

'No doubt like the taste on your very brown tongue.'

And so the trade in insults would grow into a ridiculous and humorous badinage between the two. When they had the crowd guffawing and hooting with glee, the two combatants, by now sweating heavily after their exertions, would appear to suddenly slash each other in a deadly swipe that would see the two of them stumbling and staggering about in their simultaneous death throes before falling in a heap upon each other. At this, the audience inevitably exploded in cheers and applause for the two entertainers.

As the applause settled down, Kali would emerge from the back of the cart and call for silence before quietly settling down on crossed legs and pulling out a small flute which he began to play. He would begin with a strange haunting tune that evoked night-time and all its terrors. The crowd remained silent, wondering what the sinister-sounding melody could be portending. By this time Hadar, Raymond, Caspar and I had positioned ourselves at different, but planned, locations within the audience. Each of us had several small wooden discs, about a foot in radius with a face painted upon it. These were mounted on small handles. Once we were all in place, Kali would pause and simply say, 'Ladies and gentlemen, I give you the demon… "Rooti".'

As Kali recommenced his haunting melody, Ruth would burst through the drapes at the rear of the cart in a dramatic pose and make the closest sound to a vicious snarling that she could. It worked. Many women and children in the audience shrieked in terror of the demon before them. Ruth would wear her blue *sari* hitched up at the back to allow for the freedom of movement she would need for her performance. Her skin was painted a very similar blue to her *sari* with the addition of some blood-red drops painted around the edges of her mouth. Crossing her chest were two belts with carefully sewn sheaths containing twenty long and slender throwing knives that Kali and Caspar had made up in Calicut by a local smith. The smith had used one of the original knives as a cast to keep the weight and balance of each knife as true to the original as possible.

Kali would begin another tune once Ruth was on stage and had finished her dramatic posturing. Slowly, Ruth would commence a dance that was both graceful and sinister. At pre-arranged signals from within Kali's tune, one of us within the audience would raise one of our discs into the air above and shout, 'Die bloody demon,' or some similar sentiment. As the cry echoed, Ruth would deftly snatch a blade from one of her belts and send it flying over the heads of the crowd to land between the painted eyes on the face of the disc. Ruth accomplished all of this whilst not missing a step in her dance. Those of us holding the painted faces would turn them around for all in the crowd to see Ruth's awesome accuracy. This would be repeated several times at different distances and places within the crowd.

The next part of the show would see Raymond, Caspar or myself moving at a fast walk through the crowd, holding up the painted discs which upon the shouted threat, would suddenly receive the piercing thump of a blade somewhere around the eyes. And still, Ruth's dance would go on without missing a step or a beat. At this point, Kali would increase the tempo of his music so that it sounded more like a gay village tune or dance. At the same time, the three of us would begin skipping and dancing around and through the crowd holding up a disc. This time, Ruth's targets were not only moving but going up and down in time to our prancing and skipping dances. Again, the slim blades would flash through the air above the audience's heads to pierce the faces upon the discs.

The crowd would roar their appreciation of 'Rooti's' deadly knives while she quietly kept up her dance which had now slowed as Kali tempered the tempo and melody of his tune. Raymond, Caspar and I would then move through the crowd to some prearranged places each twenty feet behind the other but slightly offline from each other so that Ruth could clearly see us. We would then place a piece of fruit carefully upon our heads. Caspar was the closest and would have a papaya upon his head; Raymond was next in line with a mango balanced upon his head while I stood the furthest away with only a small apricot balancing upon my head. Those in the crowd who realised what we were about to do moved away from the path, lest they be hit by one of the knives.

We would stand motionlessly while Kali slowed his tune as Ruth simultaneously did the steps of her dance, which still continued. Suddenly, she would commence a twirl and in one deft motion, would draw one her knives and fling it first at the papaya and then repeat the movement splitting the mango with deadly accuracy. All of this whilst continuing to dance. Again, the crowd exploded in appreciation of Ruth's skills.

At this point, Kali's tune would change again to one, which helped to build tension, and 'Rooti's' dance would come to a complete halt. It was here that she would turn and face away from the crowd. Kali would cease his music and the crowd become deathly silent. The tension quickly mounted in what was only a few seconds before Ruth suddenly whirled around and flung her knife the sixty paces required to split and knock the apricot from my head.

I would start to breathe again. My love and faith in Ruth the greater for it.

<h1 style="text-align:center">48</h1>

After our performance, while the crowd was still gathered, Kali would announce that the services of 'The Divine Dhanvantari Hadar' were now available to those who required them. A *dhanvantari* was a physician in Hindi medicine who knew and could prescribe more than three hundred cures. The title was named after the Hindi god of *Ayurvedic* medicine, Dhanvantari. After a show with so many amazing and magical feats, the crowds would flock to Hadar's humble awning and apothecary in the hope of some miracle cures. Caspar, Ruth, Kali or I would greet the patients, assist Hadar with translations, dispense remedies or assist in minor procedures. Raymond would set about sharpening knives, grinding Hadar's coloured rocks and minerals to a powder and getting the show ready for its next performance. Our show lasted a little under an hour; some of Hadar's clinics went for hours and by the end of a long day or evening we were all exhausted – and considerably richer.

News travels quickly in Hind and our reputation for showmanship and healing had soon spread far ahead of us. It was after several weeks of travelling that we found ourselves at a medium-sized village a day's journey from the large harbour city of Goa. As had become usual for us by then, a large crowd had gathered in the village square to await our arrival.

As we were setting up for our performance, the crowd was startled by the arrival of six mounted, armed and armoured warriors who simply sat upon their horses and watched our preparations from the back of the crowd. The gathered people quickly settled as the warriors showed no signs of hostility and sat almost immobile upon their mounts. I noticed that their armour was a long-sleeved tunic overlaid with a composite of metal and leather scales that would resist the torsion of a heavily slicing cut of a sword but not very effective against piercing weapons such as a spear or stabbing knife. Upon their heads were a variety of helmets and all faces, except the eyes, were covered in a thin veil – a protection against the dust of the coastal plains. There was something unusual about the warriors but I could not put my finger on it so I continued with my preparations for the performance.

The warriors were still there mounted and immobile when the performance and clinic were finished for the day. One of them, their obvious leader, turned and said something briefly to the others and then motioned his horse towards us, followed by the other warriors a horse length behind. We were all standing at the rear of our cart having ceased what we had been doing and cautiously watching the approach of the silent warriors.

The warriors stopped their horses a few yards in front of us and removed their helmets and protective face veils.

The leader of the warriors was a not a man but a woman, as were the five warriors behind her. It was hard not to hide our surprise.

The leader was the first to speak. 'I am Narmala, Captain of the Queen's Horse. Which of you is the leader?'

Hadar and Caspar stepped forward at the same time and both said, 'We are.'

Narmala smiled. 'I am pleased to meet you. But, why are there two of you leading?'

'I, Hadar, govern the mission. Caspar,' and here he indicated Caspar by his side, 'governs its defence.'

'Your reputation has travelled to the northern Gujarati Court of Anhilwara Patan and reached the ears of our beloved queen, Naiki Devi. In particular, she is interested to meet your two sword masters and the demon "Rooti" who I see is not as terrifying as her reputation.' A smile crossed her face as she said this and she turned to look at Ruth directly.

'I did not believe the stories reaching the court but after watching your performance this evening, I now know them to be true. It is an honour to meet you and will be for our queen as well. Gujarat has need of your... talents.'

At this point, Kali broke in and said, 'Hadar. Caspar. This is good news. This will bring us closer to Kashmir much more quickly and in safety with the aid of an escort of warriors.'

'Yes, Kali. But why should a queen we have never heard of want our... talents?' he said this last while looking at Narmala.

'She will tell you when she welcomes you to her court,' replied the captain.

'How far away is this court?' asked Caspar.

'With a change of horses every day, we can be there in about a month.'

'A month! How far away is this Gujarat?' asked a surprised Caspar.

'About six hundred of your western miles.'

We gave our hand cart with its painted awning to the village headman the next morning, loaded and packed our saddlebags and each of us mounted up behind one of the female warriors, Narmala insisting Ruth ride behind her.

Each night of our journey north through India was spent in a royal serai where couriers, diplomats, courtiers and others on the business of the many royal and imperial courts of India were able to enjoy the best of food and accommodation on offer to travellers in India. There was also a change of horses available to all on royal duties. We left Goa the next day with each of us riding our own horse.

Each day of our journey brought new surprises to our eyes. Everywhere we went there were temples to any one of the hundreds of deities on offer to the Hindis. Many reached high into the sky and were covered in sculptures depicting scenes from the life of the gods, great battles fought by kings, local legends and other stories. Festive lights and garlands often surrounded these temples, and in some places, members of the local village had painted their faces and bodies or covered themselves in coloured dusts.

Every major town or village had its local masses of beggars. They were ubiquitous and very demanding. Kali told me that quite often the mothers from the poorer castes, or classes, would often bind, break, bend or distort their children's limbs into disfigurements so that they could join the army of beggars and hopefully make a living they otherwise may not have been able to. I thought this terribly sad.

In some of the villages and towns, large congregations of beggars and the poor lived in the most appalling ramshackle poverty. We passed near some of these as we made our way through the different cities and towns on our route. The smell arising from the unwashed squalor of these camps was often appalling. The sight of little children scrabbling and playing in the dirt looking for worms, bugs and beetles that could go into a cooking pot was particularly distressing to those in our party. Kali and the warrior women seemed indifferent to these scenes. Kali said it was simply the result of a divinely planned class and caste system designed by the gods of India.

As we passed one of these camps one evening, Kali drew our attention to the activity of its inhabitants. Everyone in the camp was standing stock still and not moving the least little bit.

'What is going on?' asked Raymond. 'Why is no one moving?'

'Look to the ground at their feet and you will see why,' responded Kali.

We did so. The ground appeared to be in motion with rippling and undulating waves of grey, black and brown moving between and around the feet of the stationary inhabitants of the camp. As our eyes came into sharper focus, we realised it was not the ground that was moving but thousands upon thousands of rats.

'It is an evening migration of rats from the camp to the nearby riverside. The beggars know that to move is to invite an attack from the rats. Bites from these filthy creatures can be fatal, particularly to the young. The beggars remain still and simply let the rats pass around, over and between their feet. The migration will not last long and then the beggars will return to their normal routines.'

The sudden terror filled shriek of a child's scream followed by that of another grief-filled female wail told a sad story.

49

There was only one other incident of major note on our journey north. We had been travelling along the coastal plains of southern Gujarat and were nearing the harbour city of Surat. As we entered the outskirts of the city, we became aware that some disturbance was taking place by the appearance of smoke above the rooftops ahead of us and the movement of crowds both towards and away from the smoke. Those moving away appeared fearful whilst those moving toward the smoke were angrily shouting, many of them carrying clubs, knives and farming or trade tools.

Narmala and her warriors drew their swords in readiness of trouble as did Caspar, Raymond and myself. I noticed Ruth fondling the belt of sheathed knives across her breasts and concealed beneath her *sari* as she too prepared for any danger of attack. Narmala motioned for Kali and Hadar to take a protected position in the middle of our group. She tried to usher Ruth with them but received such a withering look from Ruth that she immediately desisted and nodded her approval.

We progressed slowly along the road until we came to a temple and grounds dedicated to the god Vishnu. The temple was burning along one side and at its rear. People ran in and out of the edifice carrying precious cloths, golden and bejewelled ornamental statuettes and effigies. Outside, fierce fighting was taking place, apparently between two groups, but without the savagery and massive bloodshed of expensive swords and other military hardware. Instead, participants lay upon the ground with cracked and wounded heads, shattered teeth and broken limbs. Some were dead from their wounds; others were trying to limp or crawl away from the melee.

'It is another raid by Saivists against the Vaisnavists and the temple of Vishnu,' said Narmala. 'Keep moving past. But be on your guard.'

To illustrate Narmala's call for caution, one of the protagonists started yelling and shouting while at the same time pointing in our direction. In response, Narmala raised and waved her sword above her head and then uttered a loud ululating cry, which was immediately repeated by her troopers and then ourselves. It was enough. Almost immediately, half the combatants melted back into the jungle surrounding the grounds and temple while those remaining set about trying to douse the flames now beginning to engulf the entire temple.

Two brave souls had covered themselves in animal hides and ran into the burning temple. The pair emerged some minutes later dragging a golden statue of Vishnu on one of the hides clear of the temple whose roof came crashing down just after they emerged. The superficially burned and smoking pair were greeted as heroes by their co-religionists who began to dance and sing around the statue as the temple collapsed behind them in an explosion of sparks and flames. No one seemed to care about the temple; it was the statue of the god that mattered to the worshippers.

We rode on.

'What was that all about back there?' I asked Nirmala as we rode. Ruth was by my side and Raymond and Caspar were just behind us.

'It is a disease of our great and many-faced religion,' replied Nirmala with a sad look on her face. 'There is so much that we all have in common in our religion. So much opportunity to get along with each other and enjoy peace but along comes some supposed holy man who says something different than before and attracts a new band of followers and devotees. Frictions develop, usually started by the priests and holy men who have been dispossessed of the worshippers and followers that they need to keep themselves fed and in business. That ugliness back there was between Saivists and Vaisnavists. It is all over whom they consider the more supreme god – Vishna or Shiva. To make matters worse and even more complicated, there are a host of schools of thought and interpretations of the scriptures within each group.'

I was reminded of the conversations I had had with Usamah and Saladin about the similar problems facing Islamic unity. What Rudolphus had told me about Paul's motives in creating some of the New Testament texts also came to mind.

'My warriors and I follow a different path to those two – hence we did not wish to get involved back there,' continued Narmala. 'Our path is in the steps of the Mother Shakti in all her different forms, be it the gentle and protective Durga or the violent and fearful Kali or, any other form the Mother takes. We are named Shaktas after the Mother.

'Other paths within Hinduism can be with the Smartas. I quite like them as they treat all our deities the same and do not involve themselves in the kind of fracas we saw earlier. It is non-sectarian and worshippers can decide for themselves the nature of the god they wish to principally worship as well as which other deities they might wish to turn to at any time they feel the need for that particular god's gifts and patronage. It has a large spiritual element.'

This time, a memory of Abubakhar dancing naked in the desert to the spiritual voice of Allah and ignoring the man-made strictures and laws governing the behaviours of other Islamists came to my mind.

'There are others such as Suryaists, Ganapatists, Shrautists and Kaumarams – the list goes on and on. Strangely enough, there is one thing that unites all these different Hindu sects.'

'Which is?' asked Hadar.

'Our dislike of Jains, Christians, Buddhists and now we have these damned Islamists with their agenda of invasion and conquest over Hind.'

'Has this Islamist invasion something to do with our being summoned to the presence of your queen?'

'It has indeed, Hadar. War is coming to Gujarat and the fate of Hind is in our hands.'

50

Ten days later, we got our first glimpse of Gujarat's war preparations and they were massive. We had left the coast as it turned westward and were now travelling inland but still in a northerly direction. Our party had just crested a range of low foothills revealing a long and wide river basin and plain below us. A river – Narmala called it the Saraswati – bisected the plain and upon its banks sat Anhilwara Patan, the capital of the Gujarati Kingdom. Occupying the banks of the Saraswati River and the plains surrounding it was the encampment of the largest army that Caspar, Raymond and I had ever seen.

There were the usual rows upon orderly rows of tents with the occasional oversized pavilion of a senior officer scattered throughout. The majority of these were to the north of the city while to the south, east and west were vast herds of elephants, most being tended by their handlers and warriors assigned to the elephant army. Further out on the plains, teams of horses tethered to brightly coloured war chariots raced in tight formations. A constant line of carts pulled by oxen, horses and people were bringing the vast supplies of hay needed to feed the army's large four-legged weaponry. Other carts carried grains, pulses, legumes, vegetables and rice whilst young children drove goats, pigs and sheep before them to feed the human members of the army.

Narmala seemed somewhat pleased by the sight and offered,

'I see the banners of the Raj of Narwala flying around that large troop of elephants on the eastern bank. Over there on the western bank are the clan banners of the Naddula Chahamana, the Jalor Chahamana and the Arbuda Paramara clans. At least they have come to Gujarat's aid. But there should be more banners.'

Ruth leaned across from her horse and placed a consoling arm across Narmala's shoulders and then made a circle of her thumb and forefinger to reassure Narmala that it would be all right. For some reason, I felt uneasy about this gesture by Ruth.

We descended the foothills down onto the plain and joined the mass of busy, dusty and dirty warriors setting about their preparations for war. I was quite amazed to see the number of armed women amongst their numbers and without fail, they greeted Narmala with respect and friendship as our party made its way toward the city gates.

As we were making our way through the city to the royal palace we passed by an unusual construction, which is probably the wrong word as the structure went down – not up. Narmala noticed the curiosity with which we viewed the edifice.

'That is the *Rani ki vav* or Queen's Stepwell. It is a tiered stepwell that goes down seven levels to a ground-water well from which the city gets its water.'

From where I stood, it looked like an inverted seven-storied temple with hundreds of carvings and sculptures upon its walls and columns depicting gods, demons, avatars, kings and heroes.

'Those women with jars on their heads are making their daily trip down and then back up the well to get the water they will use for washing and cooking. They only have to go down four levels where there is a water tank that they can collect their water from. The holy men and physicians tell us that the water at the seventh level is sacred and blessed by Vishna. They say it has curing properties. Many medicinal herbs are grown around the water at that level.'

Hadar's eyes widened with interest at this piece of information.

'The well was dug and built just over a hundred years ago by another widowed queen, Udaymati, in honour of her late husband King Bhima.'

'I can't believe the amount of digging and work that must have gone into this,' I said.

'Then think on the tunnel work that lies beneath our feet. It connects a gate at the bottom of the well to the town of Sidhpur which is nearly twenty miles away,' responded Narmala. 'It is an escape route for the court and any who can follow after should the city ever fall to besiegers.'

I was quite stunned when I considered this feat of engineering.

We turned our horses away and continued to make our way through the city toward the royal citadel and palace.

As with the royal courts and pavilions of Baldwin, Saladin and the Emir of Shiraz we were greeted by a troop of royal guards when we arrived at the palace. Again, I noticed the presence of women in the troop, mostly by their overall size and build as their armour hid most facial and obvious body features. They surrounded a palace that clearly rivalled and surpassed those royal houses we had seen in Jerusalem and Shiraz. The Gujarati palace was ten tiers high and ornately carved statues and sculptures covered its exterior. Around the lower five levels were battlements upon which were stationed the now ubiquitous warriors of Gujarat. They were everywhere I looked. The Gujarati capital of Anhilwara Patan was clearly on a war footing.

Before entering the palace proper, Narmala directed that we gather the 'tools of our entertainment' as she called our swords, knives, painted discs and fruits.

As with our interviews with Guy de Lusignon, Saladin and the Emir of Shiraz, Narmala, as our guide, directed us to follow her through the court corridors and hallways, up richly ornate stairways to the two-story high doors of the grand court. There, as in the other courts, Narmala asked that we follow her lead when we entered the court; prostrate ourselves when she did, rise when she did and speak only when spoken to.

After having seen the squalor of the beggars' camp, the poverty of the rural towns and villages and the tragedy of children maimed and disfigured by their parents limping or crawling in the streets, I found it hard not to show my disdain at the display of wealth before me in the royal court. Gold, silver and precious stones were on display in or upon every feature of the queen's court. I will not dwell upon it for my words could not describe it with justice.

As before, we bowed and then prostrated ourselves before the throne and rose when indicated by Narmala.

Before us sat a very large woman with a small boy child sitting at her feet, obliviously playing with a toy spinning top. Around the queen were her heavily armed royal bodyguards; all were women. I noticed Narmala discreetly nod her head to a few.

'Your royal highnesses, Queen Naiki Devi of the Gujarati Kingdom and Crown Prince Mularaj II,' began Narmala. 'My mission has been successful and I have returned with the westerners I was sent for.'

The queen looked up from playing with her son and said in a gravelly voice, 'Well done, Captain Narmala. You may introduce them to our royal personages.'

I studied the queen briefly while this went on. She was large, there was no doubt about it, but it was not fat. I could tell from the contours of her arms and body shape that she was one of the most heavily muscled women I had ever seen. Her face was not attractive in any sort of feminine way instead it was heavily browed above a bulbous nose hanging over what looked like a downy moustache. Her smile, however, was a counter to this overall masculine appearance. It was reassuring, warm and friendly despite the serious nature of Gujarat's current situation and the busyness of the court going on around us. The smile was, of course, mostly reserved for the small child playing at her feet.

'May I present,' began Narmala, 'Hadar, physician of Jerusalem in the land of Outremer and Sir Caspar del Calabria – leaders of this group.'

Hadar and Caspar nodded their heads to the queen at this.

'With them are their protegees and apprentices Masters Raymond de Toulouse and Ippolito de Medici of Acre.'

Raymond and I both bowed our heads at our introduction.

'They have been assisted on their journey by our Kashmiri neighbour Kali the conjurer.'

Kali bobbed his head.

'And lastly, but by no means least'—Narmala was smiling at this and then continued—'the blue demon "Rooti".'

The queen looked at Ruth, an expression of surprise on her face.

'This girl child is the death-throwing demon we have heard about?' asked the queen incredulously.

'She is,' replied Narmala, turning to smile reassuringly at Ruth. 'Yet,' she continued, 'she is unable to speak, your highness. You will need to have her signed responses to your questions translated through her interpreter, Master Ippolito.'

'An interesting situation for a demon to be in,' replied the queen with a wry smile and chuckle at her wit.

Ruth and I looked at each other and then smiled at the queen before nodding our heads in agreement.

'We can dismiss the conjurer's show but I would see these two swordsmen and this demon "Rooti" perform before my court at a royal dinner this evening.'

Kali looked slightly indignant.

51

Our audience was ended with the invitation to the court dinner that evening. Narmala bowed deeply to the queen with us following her lead and then we walked and shuffled backwards from the presence of the queen to an acceptable distance before turning and exiting the hall.

'Unfortunately, the presence of the Raj of Nirwala and over half his royal court has created some accommodation problems for the royal chamberlain, let alone so many unexpected elephants! She has no rooms in the immediate palace environs to offer you and has requested that I make our best quarters in the men's and women's officers' barracks available to you. I apologise to you, Ruth, about separating you from your friends but the presence of a female in a men's officers' barracks would offend both local custom and religious teaching. It would also place you at some risk as I cannot vouch for the moral integrity of all our male officers. As captain of the Queen's Bodyguard, I have the best suitably appointed quarters and I offer to share them with you during your stay here in Anhilawara Patan... if this is acceptable to you.'

Ruth immediately nodded her head and smiled in acceptance of Narmala's offer. I was a bit disappointed as this arrangement would limit the time that I would have to share with Ruth during our stay. I accepted Ruth's decision graciously without comment or show of disappointment. I recalled some of Hadar's advice about not crowding Ruth with male company and accepted that after all her travails, she might just prefer female companionship for a while.

Narmala showed us to our barracks and then she and Ruth departed, Narmala saying they would be back within half an hour to allow us the preparation needed for the evening's entertainment.

And what an evening of entertainment we gave the royal guests.

Narmala had told us that no arms – knives, swords or daggers – would be allowed into the dining hall. Only she and the queen's bodyguard would be wearing weapons and she would word her guardswomen about what to expect from our performance. Secondly, so Narmala informed us, that despite the queen's outwardly fearsome appearance she had an acute sense of humour and would love to see some of her guests a little bit 'undone' by our performance. She drew an illustration of how the dining hall would be set up and indicated which tables and dining couches were to be especially 'entertained'.

The dinner was more a feast and was well underway when suddenly the doors to the dining hall burst open to reveal two swordsmen, Caspar and Raymond, in what appeared to be a heated duel. So hot in fact that red, yellow, blue and green sparks flew from their swords with each clash of steel. Hadar's dusting of powdered rocks and crystals on their blades was proving particularly impressive. Diners all around the room either stopped eating, stood up before realising they, themselves, were unarmed and then sat down again. Some in the crowd screamed or looked to the bodyguards to intervene. The guards did not move. Caspar and Raymond went through their routine of rolls, jumps, ducks and twists while still maintaining the sparking clash of their swords. The two fought upon dining tables, couches, through drapes and curtains, around and over guests in what was an even more amazing display of swordsmanship than any show they had put on before. Those who weren't horrified and hiding behind, under or in something watched in rapt appreciation of the two duellists. And of course, the dialogue of colourful and degrading insults was carried on between the two throughout the swordplay. The 'special' entertainment the queen had requested involved the slicing in half of a particular prince's ostrich feather that sat too high in his turban for the queen's liking, the overturning of dinner plates into the laps of two grandees who were dressed a bit too sumptuously, again, for the queen's liking and another two or three other unexpected stunts.

The queen laughed and guffawed throughout these episodes, slapping her thighs and clapping her hands. When the two combatants reached the finale of their entertainment, having apparently slain each other, the vast majority of guests rose in a roar of applause and cheering, even those who had received salutary lessons in sartorial restraint. Raymond and Caspar leapt up at the same time, bowed first to the queen before doing so to the guests and then the two skipped gaily from the hall holding hands, blowing kisses to everybody around them. This brought another round of applause and laughter. At the high table, the queen was clearly pleased as was the infant prince upon her lap.

As the hubbub settled down and the guests resumed their dining and drinking pleasure, we quickly prepared for our next 'entertainment'.

An hour later, as the guests were slowing down their consumption, the haunting sound of a flute slowly made its way through the buzz of conversation and the guests began to look around the hall, wondering where the music was coming from. Once the noise had settled somewhat, the sound of the flute took on a more sinister melody. Suddenly, there was a flash of blue fire accompanied by blue smoke from one of the braziers by the entrance to the dining hall. Out of the smoke stepped the blue she-demon 'Rooti' and began a slow sinuous dance around the tables.

Narmala had added one or two touches of her own to Ruth's

makeup, which included more kohl around her eyes to emphasise a skull-like depression to her eyes and two ivory toothpicks placed in her mouth to look like fangs. The red drops of painted blood at the corner of her mouth were still there. It completed a definite demonic effect on Ruth's appearance and startled and frightened some of the guests yet again. The little prince on the queen's lap looked decidedly fearful and ready to burst into tears. Raymond, Caspar and I too had painted our faces and limbs blue so that we appeared as though we were the demon's familiars. We, too, sinuously and slowly danced and turned as best we could to Kali's sinister piping. Even Naiki, the queen, sat silent and watched with anticipation at the same time as trying to reassure the young prince.

Then Kali picked up the tempo and 'Rooti' began to twirl more rapidly, arms waving in time with the music as the three of us moved about the room in our bobbing and skipping dance, taking up locations according to Narmala's illustration of the seating arrangements. Suddenly, Ruth stopped twirling and threw one of the knives directly at a guest who only had time to open his mouth in terror before Caspar's disc flashed in front of his face as the knife buried itself in the wood of the disc. In the space of a second, Ruth had ceased dancing, thrown her knife and then continued her demonic twirling. A few moments later, the routine was repeated and Raymond's disc flashed over the heart of another guest as a spinning knife again buried itself in the wooden disc. Hearts, heads, eyes and even two backsides were chosen by Ruth as targets for her flying steel. Naturally, the vast majority of guests were diving for cover under tables, behind chairs and drapes wondering just how far the queen's entertainment was going to go and whether any of them had been earmarked for an entertaining assassination. At the high table, the queen and her little prince were laughing loudly at all these antics. When Kali ceased his piping, Ruth her twirling and the three of us our bobbing dance, she rose from her throne in applause – a gesture repeated by every guest in the room, no matter how unsettled and put out they had been by the performance.

Our small troupe bowed and acknowledged the applause of our audience when the queen loudly announced to the throng, 'Muhammed of Ghorr will shit himself with terror when he meets our secret weapon – Rooti, the blue demon of death.'

This was news to all of us.

<h1 style="text-align:center">52</h1>

We were not to know exactly what Queen Naiki Devi had in store for us until the next morning when Narmala and Ruth came to the men's barracks.

'We are summoned to an audience in the royal presence,' signed Ruth before Narmala could announce the same message. Ruth's face and arms had been washed of her blue paint, but kohl had been reapplied to her eyes and a rich red paint was upon her lips. Her hair was freshly oiled and hung in ringlets down her back and upon her shoulders. She was dressed in a beautiful green *sari* embroidered with birds, flowers and insects that appeared to be alive as the *sari* rippled with her body's movement. A red *bindi* decorated her forehead as did numerous *bangles* upon her wrists and forearms. From the *sari's* slight over-size appearance, I presumed she had been loaned it by Narmala. She looked more beautiful than I had ever seen her before. I wanted to tell her this but she kept smiling at Narmala and not looking at me. The moment was lost when Narmala insisted we get ready as quickly as possible.

An hour later, the seven of us stood in the presence of the queen. The little prince was on her lap once more and enjoying a very juicy apricot that was running all over his fingers and onto his lap. Neither he nor the queen seemed disturbed by the sticky mess he was generating on skin and clothes.

'I cannot believe,' said the queen, looking at Ruth with approval, 'that this beautiful creature before me is the same demon that haunted and terrified our guests last night at dinner. It was a stupendous show and a mischievous reminder of court protocols for some of the guests. I am grateful for that.'

'Yeeaah,' said Prince Mularaj and clapped his hands. 'Again.'

'Thank you, Your Majesty,' said Caspar, speaking for us all.

'Thank you,' came the reply. 'But that is not why we are here. Captain Narmala, would you outline the current situation in Gujarat for our friends?'

'Majesty. We have spies in just about every court that borders or is near Gujarat. For some time now, we have been receiving reports from our agents in the Ghaznavid court to the northwest that the Moslem ruler Muhammad of Ghor is planning on extending his influence and power in the region and has set his eyes upon Gujarat, in particular, Anhilwara Patan, as a prize. He has allied himself with the Turushkas, or Turkish peoples. They are wild horsemen from the eastern steppes and his army is now one of the biggest ever seen in the region. He has declared *jihad* against the Hind nation and promised the wealth of the royal kingdoms and religious places to those who follow him.

'On our own, Gujarat could not hope to defeat Muhammad of Ghor,' continued Narmala. 'However, the queen's diplomacy has won over many of the Chalukya clans to our side as well as the Raj of Nirwala and his elephants. Whilst this has been positive for us our combined forces are still considerably less than Ghor's. In fact, he is so confident of his numerical superiority he has boasted that no army, let alone that of a woman and a child, can defeat him.'

'News has recently come that Ghor has taken Multan to the north and is setting about to take the nearby fortress of Uch. This will currently place his armies about a month's journey from Anhilwara Patan. The speed with which he has moved against Multan has been unexpected. Fortunately, his passage across the Thar Desert coming south to Gujarat will of necessity have to be a slow one due to constraints of water supply, terrain and climate. I don't think his Turushka allies will enjoy this part of their alliance – nor will the large number of elephants he is reported to have in his army.'

Here, Narmala paused and looked to her queen.

The queen nodded and then began, 'Thank you, Captain Narmala. The ministers and commanders of my war cabinet agree with me that Gujarat has little chance of defeating Ghor on the plains around Anhilwara Patan. For this reason, we are going to bring the battle to him but on the ground of our choosing. We have selected a battleground where we can have the advantage of the upper terrain and one of which our enemy will have little knowledge or experience.'

The queen took a sip from her glass while Narmala placed a map upon the low table between our group and the queen.

'Six days journey to the north-east lies the locality of Gadaraghata,' she said, placing a finger upon the map. 'It sits beside Mount Abu near the village of Kasahadra. The terrain is rugged and features many narrow hill-passes that can be used to our strategic advantage against the enemy.'

The queen looked down and considered us, looking at us individually one after the other.

'My proposal to you is this. Gujarat has already saved you many weeks of travel on foot and should you accept my proposal and we defeat Ghor, we will save you many more weeks of travel time by providing you with a mounted escort to your Kashmiri destination. What I ask of you is this; give me and Gujarat your expertise in arms, healing and'—here she smiled and looked directly at Ruth—'the ability to summon a very fearful and deadly demon.'

The queen laughed at her joke, which made the little prince upon her lap drop his apricot and begin to cry.

'How do you see us contributing our expertise in this... proposal?' asked Hadar when the prince ceased his crying after the queen had handed him another apricot.

'You, Hadar, would naturally assist in operations behind the conflict at the aid and medical stations. I believe a combination of your western perspectives and our *Ayurvedic* practices will work well to save the wounded and injured. I do not like to leave wounded and brave warriors to bleed out on the battlefield when they can be saved.'

'I would like to have my apprentice assistant Ippolito with me for this,' replied Hadar.

'I have other plans for Ippolito. You will need to train your conjuror for the role.'

Kali pointed to himself as if to say, 'Me!' with a look of shock and horror on his face at the prospect of having to assist in a medical situation.

'Sir Caspar and Squire Raymond, you have demonstrated your expertise in a new and different kind of sword fighting that is unfamiliar to my armies. I understand that you both belong to an elite force of warriors in your homeland. My request to the two of you is to train a small corps of shock troops to be used as a backup and breakthrough force in the upcoming battle. You will find a variety of weapons in our arsenal. Any other ideas you may have to assist Gujarat will be welcome.'

'I have already sworn to fight the Saracen enemies of God in the west and will continue to do so here in the east,' said Caspar.

'I, too,' added Raymond although he was yet to take his oath as a knight of Christendom.

'Ruth and Ippolito,' began the queen after a pause, 'my court astrologers have advised me that your destinies are inextricably linked and that any separation of the pair of you in the forthcoming war would be to challenge fate and the will of the gods. It is my hope that you will both accept my proposal and agree to undertake some... special training for the offensive I am planning against Ghor.'

I readily agreed to this if it meant that Ruth and I would be inextricably linked to one another and nodded my head to the queen. I looked at Ruth as she smiled and then nodded her head to the queen.

'Captain Narmala. Take our guests to their stations. We have a month to prepare. It is time to get to work.'

53

And get to work we did.

Narmala led us from the royal court along various corridors and hallways in a convoluted route that was difficult to remember. Eventually, we arrived at a beautifully gardened and cool courtyard where various people reclined on couches or sat in well-cushioned chairs. Many were bandaged or looked unwell. Attendants moved around the space, offering cool drinks and snacks to the patients. In another part of the garden courtyard, wisps of steam and vapour arose from a heated pool in which other patients were reclining in a relaxed manner or were being massaged on couches around the perimeter of the pool. Directly opposite us was a three-storied building with large wide-open windows and balconies.

'This,' explained Narmala, 'is the Royal Hospital – the *Dhanvantari Maristan*. Hadar and Kali, if you would follow me, I will take you inside and introduce you to some of our more esteemed local physicians. They are expecting you. The rest of you may take your pleasure here in the garden until my return.'

It was nearly an hour before Narmala returned, which gave Ruth and I some time to talk.

'Despite her somewhat brusque manner, Narmala is a very kind and generous woman,' signed Ruth after I had asked her about her night in the female officers' barracks. 'It was she who gave me these clothes and jewels to wear. I like her. A lot. She has been kind and soft to me.'

I wondered exactly what 'soft to me' meant but kept my questions and reservations to myself and we signed about other matters such as how Hadar would cope with Kali for an assistant.

'He will work well as a translator between Hadar, the other physicians and the patients,' I offered.

'I bet he will pass out at the first sign of blood or run at the first sign of conflict,' responded Ruth and we both laughed.

Both of us were a little bit put out that we were not able to accompany and assist Hadar as the *Dhanvantari Maristan* would offer many opportunities for learning and practice.

Captain Narmala returned, somewhat irritated that introductions and questions had taken so long in the *Maristan*.

'Come. We must make haste,' she said, turning away from us and heading in another direction. We quickly followed.

From the hospital we made our way through the city and its western gate to the fields outside of the city where the army was camped. Like all military camps, it was well ordered in appearance and busy with warriors moving to and fro or engaged in mock fights, manoeuvres and individual contests of arms. There was also the smell. The odour was a blend of the open sewers that ran from the edges of the camp to the river Saraswati, thousands of sweaty under-washed bodies, stale ash from cold cooking fires and the ordure of horses and elephants.

Narmala led us up to a very grandly dressed officer whom she introduced to Caspar and Raymond as Bahadur.

'Bahadur speaks Persian, Arabic as well as Hindi. He will be your principal guide and liaison officer as well as translator,' said Narmala.

The three men greeted each other with a warrior's wrist grip of respect and welcome.

Bahadur seemed a friendly and genial personality and displayed a keen interest in his two new charges.

After Caspar and Raymond departed with Bahadur to the training fields, Narmala requisitioned a passing chariot with only a driver in the chariot. The driver took us slowly through the crowded western campgrounds to the open fields beyond the perimeter of the camp. Once there and upon Narmala's order, the driver lengthened the reins and gave the four horses of the chariot's team their head. The horses took their head with an alarming acceleration that saw me almost lose my footing and Ruth tumble backward into the arms of an awaiting Narmala who held onto her to prevent her tumbling from the chariot. The two of them laughed together. Ruth was smiling happily at the thrill of the ride and I was glad to see her joy, but why did I feel so unsettled at seeing Ruth enfolded in the protective arms of this Hindi warrior woman? My feelings were getting very confused.

As the ground became more uneven and broken up, the driver slowed the chariot and we gently cantered into the *Hathi Shahar* or the Elephant City – what else would you call a camp of over ten thousand elephants along with their *mahouts* or handlers, groomsmen, carters and cavalry? It was huge.

Narmala informed us that all the queen's chariot and cavalry horses had been exposed to, and trained around, elephants from birth and were not likely to shy away from them. We slowly picked our way through the masses of grey giants as they either chewed their way through pounds and pounds of hay a day or moved ponderously across their city to the plains beyond. If I had not seen it, I would have thought such a gathering impossible.

Narmala directed the driver to some pens that were situated to the rear of the elephant encampment and separated by a makeshift wall of rocks and stones about five to six-foot high.

'These are the royal pens where the largest and fiercest elephants are kept,' said Narmala. 'You will be getting to know the queen's personal mount. He is truly a giant among his own kind.'

And a giant he was. He was a good foot taller than his companions and seemed to have a head that was larger in proportion to the rest of his body than the other elephants. Perhaps this was to accommodate the massive tusks that protruded from the underside of his trunk and just above his mouth. Despite having had their tips removed, the tusks reached to the ground in a great sweeping arc and were longer and thicker than those of any other elephant in the pens. His great ears were lacerated and scarred in several places presumably from fights with other males during rut or gained in battle against the queen's enemies. Strangely, this massively eared and trunked huge head had eyes that seemed disproportionately small on either side of its trunk but still to the front of its head.

'Ruth and Ippolito. Meet *Bhagavan Ganesha* – Lord Ganesh,' said Narmala.

The great beast looked up from the pile of hay he was making his way through and looked each of us up and down with a discerning eye. He then raised his right foot from the ground and bowed his head as much as his tusks would allow, before resuming what must have been his lunch.

'This is a good start,' observed Narmala. 'The *Bhagavan Ganesha* has acknowledged you.'

54

That evening, we were all gathered in the male officers' barracks and eager to tell the others about our day. Out of respect, Hadar was given the first opportunity to tell of his day. He was very excited.

'What a day I have had. The *maristan* is not just a hospital that treats those who can afford the care but also provides medical care to the poor and homeless at no cost. The Hindi rulers seem to have the welfare of the people at heart. Aside from the excellence in care, the hospital is also a teaching college and has one of the largest libraries on medical matters there could be. If I had not seen it, I would not have believed it. Did you know that much of what I have learned from Arabic and Moslem physicians originated here in Hind and then drifted west with various scholars, traders and adventurers?'

Hadar was very animated by all he had seen, heard, discussed and read that day.

'Physicians are paid by the crown or by wealthy patrons, patients are fed and clothed and medications and treatments are provided daily. And all free of charge. Assistants, like my good man Kali here, give out medications and assist with the dressing of wounds and other lesions. For those who are severely unwell or injured, the assistants aid the patients with feeding and drinking as well as washing and using toilet facilities.'

'I am so looking forward to that part,' commented Kali sarcastically, which brought a smile to our faces.

'Tomorrow I will be assisting one of their principal surgeons with the removal of some cataracts from the eyes of the afflicted. They also have specialist practitioners such as bone-setters, urine and stool specialists amongst others. If it were not for the mission, I could be happy to spend the rest of my days practising and learning more medicine in a place such as this. Oh! Happy day.'

It was good to see the spark back in Hadar's eyes again. The labours of our mission had taken a toll on his years, which often left him more fatigued and slower than the rest of us.

'Do you think when we return to Jerusalem, we should petition the royal court to set up such a hospital for the poor of the city?' I suggested.

'An excellent idea, Ippolito,' replied Hadar even more excitedly. Ruth was nodding her head in animated agreement to this idea as well.

Caspar and Raymond were similarly excited by all they had seen and learned of Hindi warfare and military matters.

'There is much that the armies of the west could learn here in Hind,' began Caspar. 'Firstly, most of their infantry are competent in the use of a wide range of weapons that they carry with them to the field of engagement. A troop may go from being archers one moment to being fearsome close order fighters the next. Nearly all warriors will carry at least one type of sword; either the common curved cutting blade, they call it a *talwar*, or a *khanda,* a long-bladed *dandpattta* like our long swords, or a deadly *ulfiqar.* It is a heavily curved and serrated blade that grabs onto your foes. Each sword has its specialist uses and each soldier his, or her, own preference. They also have battle axes much like our own except their blade is rounded and has a spear point. I cannot think of its name.'

'A *tabar*,' offered Raymond, not wanting to be left out of the story. 'Tell them about the close quarters fighting, Caspar.'

'Ah. Yes,' said Caspar. 'They have two sorts of weapons for close order fighting. One is a *katyar*. It is designed as a punching knife. Imagine a handle with one to three blades projecting perpendicular to the handle and running between the fingers of a fisted hand. A good punch with one of these will pierce armour. What is the other called, Raymond?'

'"The tiger's claw" or *bagh makha*,' answered Raymond. 'It is like the *katyar* but with the addition of a blade connected to the handle, as in an ordinary dagger. When there is no room to raise or swing a blade in the press, these two weapons would be deadly.'

'Of course, they have knives, maces, bows and arrows and spears and tridents much like those we use in the west but they also have two other weapons the likes of which I have never seen before,' continued Caspar.

'What are they?' I asked, eager to learn more of the Hind art of war.

'The first is what I can only call a razor-edged throwing disc. I think it was called a *chakram*. These cunning weapons somehow seem to float on the air when thrown and experts can hurl them a hundred yards. Their advantage is not in a stabbing wound but a slashing one. Imagine fifty of these razor-sharp blades launched at a cavalry charge coming directly at you. These blades fly horizontally and upon striking the legs of a charging horse will sever muscles, tendons and blood vessels bringing down horse and rider for all of those coming behind them to stumble over and collide with. Just about every warrior will carry some of these cunning blades in their kit. Raymond was very interested in another novel weapon the likes of which I have never seen before. Please, would you tell the others about it?'

'It is called an *urumi*,' said Raymond, commencing his

description. 'Imagine a whip but instead of one cord being attached to the handle there are five to ten. Now imagine that instead of fibre or leather cords there are thin ribbons of razor-sharp steel attached to the handle. These can be five to ten feet long depending on the expertise of the handler. These weapons take years to learn and require perfect hand-eye coordination and concentration. The slightest miscalculation or mishandling results in the bearer being deeply slashed and lacerated by his own hand. What is even more amazing is that masters of the weapon can use them two-handed which gives them a wide range slashing and cutting weapon of death. In full flight, a skilled warrior can create a whirling screen of slicing death to his front, back and sides. No swordsman can get near to them unless they are heavily armoured from head to foot. Only throwing weapons or arrows have any chance of defeating a squad of these deadly *urumi* warriors.'

'It sounds like science, mathematics and warfare have all been in bed with each other. This kind of military technology is incredible. It makes me wonder what other kinds of death and destruction mankind can dream up,' observed Hadar drily.

'So. Ruth. Ippolito. What did you see and do on this day?' asked Raymond.

'Oh, nothing much,' I said, smiling at Ruth. 'Just a ride on a wildly charging bull war elephant.'

55

Ruth and I had watched as *Bhagavan Ganesha* was prepared for manoeuvres on the open plain beyond the pens. Ravi, who was introduced to us as *Ganesha's mahout* or handler and driver, first used a long-handled goad to persuade the beast to lower himself to his knees. This seemed a slow and difficult manoeuvre for the animal but eventually, with a few prods from Ravi's goad, the elephant got himself into the desired position. Attendants then placed thick blankets over the elephant's back, neck and sides which were cinched with leather reins around the beast's great girth. At this point, a wheeled crane-like construction, similar to ones I had seen on the docks of Acre and other ports, was moved up to the beast's side and the first coat of armour was attached to the hook of the crane.

'*Ganesha's* full armour is made up of over eight thousand individual metal plates and weighs over three hundred pounds,' offered Narmala.

The body armour was lowered into place and its fitting adjusted and pulled into place by the attendants before it too was cinched in place. Next came the neck and head armour, which was also lowered into place by the crane and fitted by attendants. After that, a protected box-like arrangement, termed a *howdah*, was similarly lowered and fitted upon *Ganesha's* back. It was the armed platform that rode on the elephant's back and which could carry up to seven warriors depending on its size.

While attendants worked at securely fitting the *howdah* with clamps and hooks to the body armour, other attendants were fitting *Ganesha's* armaments. Two large crescent-shaped swords, called *hathi talvars* or elephant swords, were then attached to the *Ganesha's* sawn-off tusks. The blades of these swords were gouged with a conduit, which Narmala told us was to carry and coat a viscous and sticky poison to the blades. By simply turning his head right and left, *Ganesha* would be able to cut a headlong swathe through the lines of enemy infantry. Around *Ganesha's* feet and just above his knees were attached metal cuffs that had outward-pointing blades designed to prevent charges of infantry trying to cut and slash at the elephant's vulnerable legs and underbelly. Finally, ornamental and heraldic drapes and pennants were placed over the whole affair announcing that the queen's war elephant was ready for battle.

Around us, other beasts in the elephant pens were being similarly armed and attired by their *mahouts* and attendants. While waiting for these beasts to complete their armouring, Narmala informed Ruth and I as to how these beasts could be deployed in battle.

'There are several options available to the war commander in battle depending on a host of factors. Firstly, they can be positioned and moved about as a kind of mobile control and command position. This also serves as a rallying point for troops under pressure or in disarray. At other times, they may form part of a unit that operates independently. Such a unit may have ten infantry, two cavalry and a war elephant or chariot. But by far the greatest use of the elephant is in the co-ordinated charge against enemy infantry be they in their lines or preparing a charge themselves. They can crash through seemingly impenetrable walls of enemy soldiers, crushing them underfoot and allowing the archers in the *howdah* to pick of enemy soldiers below them. At other times they may be used to quickly transport and dump soldiers in particular hot spots where the fighting is fierce and undecided. They can fight with their trunk, tusks and legs. Wherever they are used they instil terror and fear in the soldiers facing them.'

I looked at *Bhagavan Ganesha* in all his combative attire and deadly accoutrements. He appeared to be studying Narmala, Ruth and I with an appraising look. We caught each other's eye, and in that moment, I knew that this was not just a massively powerful beast but a highly intelligent one as well.

'To make the elephants more ferocious in a battle, their handlers usually give them a hearty drink of strong palm wine. An intoxicated elephant will wreak more havoc and destruction amongst enemy troops than a sober one. So will its *mahout*,' said Narmala and then chuckled to herself before adding, 'although we do have to be careful. We don't want our *mahouts* tumbling from the neck of their mounts before the battle even begins.'

I knew that soldiers in the west often fortified their courage before battle in a similar manner and said so.

'So do our own soldiers and warriors,' replied Narmala before continuing, 'but it is not just in battle that the elephants serve their queen. The elephants are virtually tireless in carrying heavy burdens over long distances. They assist in the carrying and placement of stones and logs in the construction of fortifications, bridges and other military installations. I should mention they are also equally adept at sweeping men from these constructions or simply acting as a battering ram and knocking city walls back down to a pile of rubble. We also use the elephants for clearing the way through heavy foliage on marches. They are also good swimmers and lead the fording of broad rivers whilst others can be protecting the flanks of an advancing army.'

Ruth signed to me, 'How do you stand against an army of these animals? How do you fight them?' which I relayed to Narmala.

'Good question. Heavy bladed axemen bearing *tabars* are perhaps the biggest worry to an elephant handler. They tend to rush the elephant in groups of three or four in the hope that one will avoid the arrows of the archers in the *howdah* and be able to deliver a smashing blow to the elephant's tusk. The pain of the broken tusk will drive an elephant mad and cause him to run amok, trampling our troops and wreaking havoc. It is said that when the Raj of Pallava's elephant had its tusk broken the beast, in its blind rage, carried the Raj from the battlefield. Of course, his troops thought he was fleeing the field and laid down their arms in surrender. It was an unfortunate way to lose a battle.

'Another offensive weapon to the elephant is the heavy iron javelin. It is most effective when delivered with a running thrust rather than a throw. Its narrow pin-point will pierce an elephant's hide again, bringing about a rampaging pain-filled rage in the elephant. Elephants will also panic and run amok with the use of fire-pots hurled by enemy soldiers at the elephant. The igniting oil quickly spreads itself over the elephant's hide and armour. There is nothing sadder than seeing one of these great and noble beasts screaming in terror and pain as it runs burning and smoking around the field of battle.'

Ruth made a face that told me of her distress hearing this piece of information.

An hour later, the squad was ready to commence manoeuvres. *Ganesha* presented his trunk to Ravi as a step and he quickly scurried up the trunk to take his place upon *Ganesha's* neck. An attendant handed him two goads, one for each side of the elephant's head. A rope ladder hung from the side of the *howdah*, which allowed the three of us to climb up and take our places in its protected box structure. Aside from benches to sit upon, there was also room for a large arsenal of weapons. Large quivers held arrows and javelins, clips and brackets clamped long pole spears and axes to the side panels of the *howdah*. These were for jabbing down at the enemy. There were also boxes and other places for the storage of different types of weaponry.

There were twenty elephants in our squad, each with a *mahout* and two or three soldier passengers seated in the *howdah*. Narmala raised her arm, looked up and down the line of formed up elephants and then lowered her arm to signal moving out. From the height of our *howdah*, we had an excellent view of the plains and camps around us and I understood the elephant's value as a command and observation post. The height also accentuated the swaying gait of the elephant's movement. It brought back memories of *Dartha*, my camel from Shiraz to the sea, and his 'sea sickening' gait. If it weren't for the comfort of the royal *howdah*, the ride could have been unpleasant.

We eventually arrived at a flat and unpopulated part of the plain. Narmala gave another hand signal that saw the squad form up next to each other with ten to fifteen feet between each elephant. Once all were steadied and in position, Narmala gave another signal and the squad slowly moved forward in a line. Gradually, and still keeping the line, the squad increased its speed to a point where we were jolted up and down and to the sides in an unaltering but hectic rhythm.

'How are you able to use and fire weapons when you are being bumped and moved around like this?' I said to Narmala.

'That is what you are both here to learn,' came the reply.

56

'Why the two of us?' I asked Narmala after we had caught our breath, released our grips on the sides of the *howdah* and settled down after the exhilaration of several charges. We were now ambling back in a disordered line to the pens at a pace set by the elephants.

'Our queen, Naiki Devi, is a brave and courageous warrior. She is loved by the people of Gujarat, respected and willingly followed by her armies and listened to by scholars, scribes and priests. She is also very superstitious and given to believe in portents of the future.

'It was about six months ago when word arrived from our agents in Ghazni of Muhammad of Ghor's plans to expand his kingdom into northwest Hind. It was not long before further news arrived of his alliance with the wild tribes of the Turashka horsemen. This has greatly increased his military might.

'The queen and the court were greatly troubled by this news and the whole of Gujarat has been on a war footing in preparation since then. The queen has exercised her diplomacy and statecraft and brought many of the neighbouring clans and kingdoms to her side although just as many are still uncommitted preferring a "wait and see" approach to the outcome. Cunning and duplicitous cowards the lot of them. It was during this time that the queen had the dream that she has since taken to her heart and, her mind.'

Ruth signed her curiosity about this to me, which Narmala also appeared to understand.

'In the dream, she saw the armies of Gujarat and those of Ghor clashing on the rough terrain of narrow hill and valley passes. From her description of the countryside, this was identified as an area around Mount Abu called Gadaraghatta just near the village of Kasahadra. Even now, advanced units of the queen's army are there reconnoitring the locale for advantageous positions, the laying of ambushes and the setting of traps.

'The queen dreamed she led an elephant charge against Ghor. Beside her in her royal *howdah* stood a female demon who was coloured blue and hurled bolts of blue fire at the enemy causing them to panic and flee. Beside the blue she-demon stood a male red demon who protected the queen and blue demon with two magical shining shields that deflected the arrows, knives and stones the enemy were firing at the queen and her bodyguard. The shining shields dazzled the enemy at the same time.'

Ruth made the facial expression of, 'This does not make sense,' and pulled out one of her throwing knives from the sheath beneath her *sari* to indicate it was a grey and silver knife and not a bolt of blue fire.

Narmala laughed gently and smiled at Ruth. 'When news of your travelling show reached the court, the queen despatched my squad to investigate. The queen believes that while the two of you are clearly not demons, your presence and outward appearance as her guardian demons will be the factor that turns the battle to her victory and the eventual rout of the enemy.'

'Bolts of blue fire. Magical shining shields. How are Ruth and I to accomplish this?' I said in growing disbelief of just what the Gujarati court expected from the two of us.

'We have put our best minds to this and believe we have a strategy. You will learn more tomorrow when your training will really start.'

The next morning, Ruth and I were escorted to the royal armoury where we were measured and fitted with a light body armour that allowed a greater freedom of movement and was more comfortable than the armour of the crusaders. The armoury had a great store of individual parts and types of armour and the whole process only took an hour before Ruth and I emerged looking like Hindi warriors.

From there we were once again charioted to the elephant pens on the plains where *Ganesha* and another tall and formidable elephant were rigged up and outfitted for battle. Ruth was escorted to *Ganesha's* side where he again raised his foot and slightly bowed his head in greeting and acknowledgement of her. I got no such greeting from *Bhari Pair,* which meant 'Heavy Foot', and he simply gave me an unwelcoming trumpet at close quarters, which hurt my ears. He was an unpleasant beast according to his *mahout*, Sanjay, but had never run amok or been panicked in battle. He was also the queen's executioner of which I shall say more later.

Narmala, Ruth and Ravi took *Ganesha* to another location leaving myself, Sanjay and *Bhari Pair* to ourselves in the middle of a broad plain.

'Master Ippolito,' said Sanjay, 'today you must learn how to stand in the *howdah* without holding onto anything whilst *Bhari Pair* is in full battle flight. You must stand like so,' and here, he placed his feet about a foot and half apart with his knees slightly flexed. I took the same stance and then he began a gentle bouncing motion with an alternating flexion and extension of his knees and hips. I copied this motion and within a few moments we were both engaged in what must have looked like a silly bobbing dance to anyone watching the two of us.

'Now the trick, Master Ippolito, is to match your motion to the motion of the elephant. It must become second nature to you very quickly. It will be something that you do not even think about when being carried into battle.'

Our dance upon the plains was over and we both mounted *Bhari Pair*, Sanjay via the trunk to sit upon the neck and I via a rope ladder to stand within the *howdah*. Sanjay prodded the beast and we moved slowly off at an ambling pace, easy to maintain my balance in. Sanjay noticed this and gave *Bhari Pair* another prod with his pointed goad and the pace suddenly quickened which placed me on my backside.

'Hold onto the side if needed at first,' called Sanjay over his shoulder.

I did so, my hand moving on and off the side panel of the *howdah* as needed to keep my balance and stay off my backside. After an hour of this, I was able to maintain my balance unaided by the side panel and not having to think too much about it. What I was thinking about was the growing discomfort in my inner thigh and calf muscles from maintaining this balanced bobbing stance. I commented on this to Sanjay.

'Okay. This is to be expected and I am prepared,' he said, halting the elephant and letting him graze. He then climbed back and over into the *howdah* to join me. He had a jar of something in his hand, which he handed to me, saying, 'This is a good *Ayurvedic* balm for complaints such as yours. Remove your leggings and massage this into the aching muscles. You will very quickly find relief. We must progress to a full charge before the day is out.'

'Really,' I said, thinking this was all getting a bit tiring as well.

Twenty minutes later, we were back at it again but at a faster speed this time and once again I was bounced around on my backside a few times in the *howdah* before getting the hang of maintaining my balance at speed. The sensation of speed whilst standing was exhilarating and I hardly noticed that Sanjay had quickened the pace to full battle charge until he told me that was the pace we were setting.

We kept the charge up for about another half hour when Sanjay expressed his pleasure at how well I had done.

He then added, 'Now, I want you to practice turning and twisting to the left and right as we travel at speed.'

Again, I was backsided in the *howdah* a few times but after an hour of this I was able to maintain my balance and twist and turn my upper body without falling over.

The afternoon sun was getting low when I noticed Narmala, Ruth and Ravi on the back of a charging *Ganesha* coming towards us.

Ruth was at the front of the *howdah*. She was not simply standing there keeping her balance.

She was dancing.

57

Despite her exhilaration at the ride and the accomplishment of dancing in the *howdah*, Ruth was looking tired and uncomfortable. She was walking a little bit like a duck. Narmala, unlike Sanjay, had not thought to bring any liniment for aching limbs and strained leg muscles. I handed Ruth the jar that Sanjay had given me and advised that she remove her leggings and massage the lotion into her legs. I was surprised when Narmala took the jar and told Ruth she would massage her legs for her. I had to restrain myself from grabbing the jar back and saying, 'No! I will do it.' Hadar's advice repeated itself in my head. I eventually walked away from the two of them. The giggles and laughter they were sharing were unsettling me in a way I definitely did not like.

What was wrong with me? Why did I feel shut out by Ruth? Why did hearing Narmala promise Ruth a hot bath, a scrub and another massage back at the female officers' quarters cut me like a knife? I had never had these feelings. They were hurting me and I did not understand it.

I made Ruth's excuses for not joining our group that evening and pleaded the same excuse of exhaustion and muscle weariness for retiring to my cot early that evening. Sleep, however, was a very long time coming to my troubled mind.

I threw myself into the training Sanjay put me through the next day as a way of putting my troubles behind me. We were late in starting as a long line of troops, horse and elephant cavalry, chariots, carts, wagons and camp followers made their way from the plains in a northwest direction toward the hills and narrow passes of Gadaraghata to prepare the ground for the coming battle.

Sanjay had organised for twenty troops to be present on the plain when he, *Bhari Pair* and I finally arrived. Sanjay put myself and *Bhari Pair* through a couple of warm-up charges before explaining what the day's activities would be.

'You have the basics of stance and balance for a standing elephant charge, Master Ippolito. Today you will perfect them further by holding two shields, one in each hand, and deflecting the blunted spears these soldiers will hurl at you as we charge by them,' explained a smiling Sanjay.

As he said this, I noticed the troops dispersing across the plain. Each was carrying five or six blunted poles on their shoulders.

'To make your experience more realistic, you will only be wearing a headpiece of armour to protect your head and eyes from any serious misdirection of a pole.'

Oh great, I thought to myself, yet more pain.

'Do not look so grieved, Master Ippolito. I have a padded surcoat for you as well.' Sanjay was laughing and smiling at this. He clearly enjoyed training raw recruits to the elephant corps. It did, however, make me smile in return and I appreciated the lightening of my mood as a consequence.

Our first charge against the soldiers was a relatively simple affair. They were all spaced about twenty paces apart and on either side of the route Sanjay took *Bhari Pair* charging along. This gave me about three or four seconds between each soldier throwing his spear at me as we charged by. Enough time to see, anticipate the throw and raise my shield to protect myself. I thought it was pretty easy at first as none of the spears hit me on our first pass.

Inevitably, Sanjay increased the difficulty of each pass. He did this in a variety of ways. First, he shortened the distance between the soldiers, thus decreasing my observation and reaction time to the hurling of the poles. It was at this stage that the first of the blunted spears thudded against my side. I was surprised at the pain of it and realised the strength with which the soldiers could launch their weapons. The next stage of difficulty involved two soldiers on either side of our charge launching their poles at me simultaneously requiring me to raise two shields on either side at the same time to defend myself. As the day progressed, the charges grew more difficult in intensity with groups of soldiers clustered in twos, threes and fours on either side of the charge.

'Master Ippolito. You must learn to duck your head more,' called Sanjay over his shoulder after two poles had almost simultaneously clanged their impact on either side of my headgear, making my ears ring and head spin.

As the day progressed so did my expertise at avoiding and shielding myself from the poles. The soldiers were good at their work and none of the poles went near Sanjay, the elephant's head and eyes or any other vulnerable part of its body. The hard work on my legs, the quick thinking and reflex reactions required acted as something of a catharsis to my emotionally troubled state. I did not mind the battering and bruising blows to my body. That was a pain I could understand and I almost rejoiced in each thudding hit as a distraction from my personal pain.

We stopped for a brief midday meal and refreshment during which the soldiers also offered further advice on being a *howdah* shieldman.

'A spearman standing still is not likely to launch his weapon as it will not have enough impetus to strike hard at its target,' advised one hardened spearman. 'You must watch for spearmen running or stepping in your direction. They are the ones getting ready to launch rather than lunge.'

By the end of the day, I had more than a dozen rounded and purpling bruises on my arms, chest, abdomen and shoulders. My arms ached from holding up the heavy shields and my legs were in a similar state to the day before. I did not care. The pain was good. It beat the other pain down.

That evening I collapsed onto my cot and immediately fell into a dreamless and untroubled sleep.

I had not seen Ruth all day.

58

Nor did I see Ruth the next day or the day after that.

'A messenger came this morning after you had left to report Narmala has taken Ruth and *Ganesha* to the foothills. She wants Ruth to gain experience on uneven terrain,' explained Hadar on the second day when I commented on Ruth's absence. 'They are camping there and will return before we strike out for Gadaraghata.'

Again, that pain sliced through my guts upon this piece of news. Why couldn't Ruth have come and told me this herself?

Hadar must have noticed my inner pain as he put his arm around my shoulders and said, 'This will pass, Ippolito. You must allow Ruth her time and her ways. Remember she has been through an ordeal that has crippled part of her on the inside. I sense your hurt. Do you recall Ibn Sina's treatise on the relationship between mind and body? Unconditional love, patience and time are your allies. You must freely show and give them, for in time, they, in turn, will be returned to you.'

I threw myself into my training with Sanjay as an antidote. Within a few days, I was barely conscious of my leg work; my arms would throw a defensive shield up at just the whisker of movement seen out of the side of my eye. Everything was reflex, reflex, reflex and I revelled in it. Sanjay made things more difficult for me by taking one of my shields away from me making the training more strenuous. Defending myself from the blunted spears required twice the amount of turning, twisting, ducking, raising of arms and of course thudding blows to my person and a whole new crop of purpling bruises upon my body. I did not care. Pain drove pain away.

I grew reckless as the days till our departure for Gadaraghata drew closer. I became adept at catching thrown spears in one hand, turning them in my hand and then hurling them back at my attackers whilst other spears thumped and banged against the shield in my other hand. I even persuaded Sanjay to remove the *howdah* and allow me to stand bare-foot upon *Bhari Pair's* back as we charged at our would-be attackers. At the end of each day, I was a sweating and bruised body that had sublimated its pain into the mastering of martial skills.

The final days of my training were spent with a full complement of seven troops on board the *howdah*. Ranged against us were over fifty other warriors. Two of us on board were shield defenders whilst the others were offensive archers or polemen with their extra-long spears for stabbing down at attackers. The attacker's arrows were blunted like our spears but still hurt like hell when they hit you as I soon found out. This was truly gruelling work. I wondered what the real thing was going to be like and then tried not to think about it.

I do not know just how many days had passed before Raymond spoke to me one evening as I returned to the officers' barracks.

'Ippolito. They are back. We are to join the line of forces moving up to Gadaraghata tomorrow. Ruth said to say she was sorry to miss seeing you. She will catch up with you in the morning.'

Raymond had been sensitive to my hurt over Ruth. He had not pressured me in any way but had simply been there as a sympathetic ear and a good friend on the one occasion I had mentioned Ruth and some of the confusing feelings I was having. Those feelings suddenly surfaced again and became all the more tumultuous with this news. I did, and did not, want to see Ruth. Both, at the same time!

I heard their arrival at our quarters early the next morning as I was finishing the last bit of packing my belongings into a saddlebag. My heart was in my mouth as I entered the communal area of the barracks. I was pleased that the first thing Ruth did was to give me a welcoming hug and sign to ask me how I was. I was not so pleased to see that Narmala was with Ruth but kept that to myself and offered her a perfunctory greeting and a smile as well. Ruth and I had but a few moments to exchange news of what we had been doing over the last three weeks before Narmala stated that the queen wished for Ruth to ride with her and that they were shortly expected at the palace mounting yards. Ruth gave me another quick hug and then she was gone again before I knew it. My eyes briefly followed them as they made their way across the courtyard then turned away as Narmala put her arm around Ruth's waist and she put hers around Narmala's.

My pain became white hot.

It cooled over the next week as I did not see Ruth again until we had arrived at Gadaraghata. She had been miles ahead of the rest of us in the endless train of military personnel, weaponry, supplies, carts and wagons, animals for consumption, offense and haulage, and the inevitable camp followers.

On the third day we left the plains of Gujarat and began a gentle ascent into a region of narrow valley and hill passes that branched like a fishbone from an old central river valley that was surrounded by hills. The valley had a narrow flood plain and meander belt and was the route that column gossip said Muhammad of Ghor was going to squeeze his massive army through. The vanguard of Ghor's army was said to be two days away while the tail was three. As we progressed through this region various divisions and wings of the army deployed away from the column to take up their allotted strategic positions along different side valleys for the upcoming battle. These sites were located in valleys behind the surrounding hills and were invisible from the river plain.

Eventually the five of us were directed to the royal compound behind one of the highest hills overlooking the valley. It was possible from this position to look down on the river plain and to the mouths of the hill passes and valleys that opened into it. It was from these 'mouths' that the various divisions would attack Ghor's hemmed in army in numerous and repetitive hit and run assaults. Each attacking mouth was defended by lines of archers to prevent pursuit of a division running after its hit upon the enemy column.

The five of us were directed to a tent on the periphery of the command compound that was both spacious and well-appointed with small cots, water basins, jugs and glasses as well as cushions for sitting and reclining. Shortly after settling in, Hadar and Kali were asked to attend the hospital compound. Hadar gathered up his belongings and supplies of medicines, treatments, instruments and bandages before he and Kali departed. Kali was not looking forward to his duties. Caspar and Raymond were likewise requested to attend a compound officer's meeting. Before leaving, I noticed they unburdened one of our pack horses of four large sacks, which they then carried between them to the meeting. I wondered what was in the sacks as they had not been a part of our original baggage.

I felt almost sick with anxiety when a request to attend the royal command tent arrived.

Ruth would be there.

59

The royal command tent was a hive of intense activity when I entered. Commanders strutted about in their finery issuing orders to junior officers and aides who quickly turned and left the tent to convey orders and instructions to the frontline troops hiding behind the screen of hills overlooking the river valley. All was buzz and movement everywhere I looked within the command centre. My escort moved deferentially through the host, halting to allow senior officers to pass by whilst bowing to and saluting others. At first, I could not see Ruth or the queen amidst the throng but then noticed them ahead in the direction my escort was heading. An initial rush of elation washed over me but then quickly soured as I spied Narmala returning to Ruth's side.

'Ah! Young Ippolito,' greeted the queen who, even in the midst of all this activity and preparation for battle, still had the time and inclination to be bouncing the young Mularaj on her knees. 'You are in time to hear the latest disposition summary from Commander Vikram.'

I started to bow but the queen interrupted, 'No time for that, Ippolito. We are on a war footing. Come over here,' she finished and pointed to a space beside Ruth and Narmala.

I moved quickly to sit beside Ruth who smiled warmly at me, took my hand, gave it a gentle squeeze in welcome and seemed to move closer to me so that our upper arms were brushing against each other while we stood to hear Commander Vikram's report.

She signed. 'I have missed you.'

I nodded in reply and then turned to hear the commander's report.

'All is just about in readiness,' began the commander. 'Our forward troops and spies report that Muhammad appears unaware of our disposition as yet. His army moves slowly along the valley largely due to the limitations of space and not because he is being cautious. However, the dust from his forward lines can now be seen and his vanguard is only a day away. Our spies and scouts report that Muhammed is overconfident in his ability to defeat our army and that he has not bothered to send out his scouts to reconnoitre the way ahead of him.'

'Foolish little man,' said the queen. 'He believes that a woman and a child will be no match for him. We shall see who has the last laugh.'

'We have,' continued the commander, 'however, captured several of his spies trying to leave the camp and forward posts. They are currently staked out and awaiting the heavy foot of *Bhari Pair* as their reward.

'Captain Ashan reports all valley and hill passes have archers covering their entrances and exits. The engineers have completed their pits and surprises and preparations for a dozen or more rocky landslides are almost complete. Captain Chandra has completed the deployment of both heavy and light infantry all along the complete line of battle. We are still moving the elephants into their different positions of attack. Part of the problem is keeping the ground watered enough to keep down the dust which would give our plans and our positions away. Captain Narmala's cavalry is the only highly mobile squad currently ready for an assault.'

Here, the queen nodded to the captain of her horsed bodyguard.

'At the rear are the chariot corps as reserves and rear guard should the uh... er... unlikely need arise.'

Commander Vikram looked nervous about mentioning the possibility of a defeat to the queen.

'Be not so nervous, Commander,' said the queen. 'I have two lucky cards up my sleeve.' At this, she smiled to herself. 'That is all, ladies and gentlemen. To your stations. I will be along shortly for the entertainment. Ruth. Ippolito. To me please.'

Ruth and I waited by queen's side as the commanders and captains dispersed.

'You are both no doubt aware by now of the faith I have in the portent of dreams and, in my astrologers' abilities to interpret them for me.'

Ruth and I both nodded.

'Sometimes dreams need a little help to make them become a reality. It is for this reason that I have had these small gifts fashioned for you tomorrow.'

She clapped her hands and four attendants appeared. Two carried a large disc each while the other two carried a box each.

'Ippolito. Sanjay has reported back to me about your progress as a shieldsman. He is very pleased with you, and, I might add, some of the other skills you have developed. I wish I had seen you shielding barefoot on a charging bareback elephant.'

She turned to the first two attendants. 'Bring those here.'

It took me a second or two to realise that the two discs were in fact shields but very different from any others I had ever seen. The first thing I noticed was that the shields were concave as opposed to normal shields which were flat or convex. The external surface of the shield was coated in faceted pieces of glass surrounding a highly polished disc of silver that sat in the shield's central section.

'Tomorrow,' said the queen, 'the battle will see us with the sun in our eyes. With these shields, Ippolito, you will be able to turn this around and direct the sun's light at any troops attacking the royal command position. Those tiny facets of glass are situated in such a way to direct the sun's rays to the central silver disc which reflects the rays against the enemy in a manner that will surprise and dazzle them, hopefully to our advantage. Come, let me show you.'

The queen led the way just outside the tent and had the two of us stand with our backs to the early afternoon sun. She then raised one of the shields and lifted it to face the two of us catching the sun's rays as she did so. I was suddenly blinded by a scintillated explosion of light that seemed to be all around us. The queen quickly lowered the shield while Ruth and I blinked trying to recover our vision.

'Give yourself a moment. The lights are small but very bright.'

Ruth and I stood there until the myriad of floating black spots disappeared from our eyes.

'The trick of it is in the small facets of glass around the perimeter of the silver disc. They break the sun's light up into thousands of tiny beams which reflect off the silver disc in thousands of tiny but very bright beams that scatter upon, around and over their target. It is much more effective than a single reflected beam but due to the small nature of each reflected beam of light are only useful within a limited range. It is with these two shields that you will help to fend off enemy soldiers seeking to attack the royal howdah.'

I picked one of them up in each hand. They were well-weighted and lighter than the heavy wood and metal shields I had been practicing with. They felt good in my hands and I whirled them around in a mock defence.

'Thank you, your majesty. I will use them well in your defence.'

The queen clapped her hands again and one of the attendants carried one of the boxes outside to us and opened it before us. Inside were what looked like long shards of a pale blue glass. It was only when the queen carefully removed one from the box that we realised exactly what it was. It was fashioned as a double-bladed throwing knife made entirely of glass and very, very sharp.

'You will need to wear one of these protective gloves when throwing these to prevent cutting the tips of your fingers. Here. Try it on,' instructed the queen.

Ruth looked a little perplexed as she donned the glove and then felt the weight of the glass blade in her hands. She smiled broadly in appreciation of its workmanship and then suddenly turned and threw it. The blade shot, spinning from her hand at speed and had the illusion of leaving a trail of pale blue light behind it. The blade embedded itself in a not too far away tethering post. The shock of the impact caused the rest of the glass blade to shatter in an explosion of blue glass that seemed almost supernatural.

'Sometimes,' said a very satisfied-looking queen, 'we have to help our dreams and visions a bit.'

60

'Tomorrow,' continued the queen, 'you will find over two hundred such blades in the royal *howdah* and Ippolito shall be your shield and protector.'

I liked the way the queen had said this. It made me feel better within myself.

Ruth looked up at me, an unreadable expression on her face and in her eyes.

Suddenly, I was not so sure of how much better I felt.

'Now, I have briefed you both on your roles in tomorrow's engagement, I must attend the executions. You are welcome to join me if you like.'

Ruth signed to me that she preferred not to attend the executions and that she wished to spend some time alone with her thoughts. I made her excuses to the queen and Ruth departed, leaving me once again in a state of turmoil.

'Will you join me, Ippolito?'

Perhaps it was the turmoil I was in. Perhaps it was morbid curiosity, but for what-ever reason, I agreed to join the queen to witness the executions.

Accompanied by her bodyguards, the queen, young Mularaj and I made our way over to an open area in the camp around which a large crowd was gathered. At one end of the arena stood

Bhari Pair with Sanjay upon his neck. At the other end, a dozen naked wretches were being subject to verbal and physical abuse by the crowd surrounding the pen in which they were being held. Many already had cuts and bruises upon their bodies and all looked decidedly miserable. One man stood out as different from the others. He was relatively unscathed compared to his companions and stood ranting at the crowd in the middle of the pen.

'Ippolito. Do you know what he is saying?' asked the queen, stopping near the pen.

The ranter was speaking a language I did not know although some words and phrases seemed familiar. I suspected it may have been Tarushkan. I told this to the queen.

'Do any of you speak Tarushkan?' said the queen, turning to her bodyguard.

A lone guard raised her hand and said, 'I understand some of what he says but not all, Majesty.'

'What does he say?'

'Majesty. He says things about you and the prince Mularaj I would prefer not to repeat.'

'Rani. Please, have no fear. What you say shall determine his fate.'

'Right now, he is speaking of your dugs as full of excrement and that the young prince dines whenever he can upon the feasts you provide him with.'

'Colourful,' said the queen.

'Now he speaks of your *yoni*, Majesty. Do I have to go on?'

'Yes. Do.'

'He says it is a whore's *yoni* that drips pus and poison. That it delivered a demon who is full of these same fluids.'

'That is enough, Rani. Thank you.'

The queen moved toward the pen and drew the curved *arival* from its sheath at her side. She waved her bodyguard back and stooped her way between the rails of the pen. She came up behind the ranter who was still delivering his diatribe and had not seen her when she delivered a sweeping kick of her foreleg to the side of his knee that dropped him on his side in a heavy thud. In one swift motion, the queen bent down, grabbed his head by the hair and forced his mouth open before plunging the curved blade into the cavity twisting and turning it as she did so.

A brief gurgled scream came from the ranter as blood and pieces of tongue, cheek and gum erupted from his mouth. The queen stood up and walked away as the crowd showed their approval of her justice in loud cheering and applause. The whole incident had taken less than a minute.

We made our way to a dais just beside where *Bhari Pair* and Sanjay patiently waited to perform their duties. The queen sat down and placed Mularaj on her lap to watch the proceedings. She then beckoned me to her side and motioned that I sit at her feet on the steps of the dais.

'The Moslem spies first, except that one,' ordered the queen, pointing to the ranter who was holding his mouth in pain and trying to stem the flow of blood from it.

'These spies were doing their duty to their rulers as ordered to,' called the queen loudly. 'Therefore, I order their deaths to be swift.'

She turned and nodded to Sanjay who prodded *Bhari Pair* with his goad. The great beast slowly lumbered to the centre of the arena where a large flat stone had been placed. *Bhari Pair* stopped just in front of the slab. The first prisoner was led to the slab and made to kneel before it with his head placed on its side upon the slab. At a nod from the queen, Sanjay prompted *Bhari Pair* to raise his right foreleg and place his foot upon the prisoner's head. Sanjay looked up to the queen and at the next nod, prompted the elephant to lean forward, bringing his whole weight down upon the leg resting on the prisoner's head. Within a second or two, a clearly audible *pop* was heard and pink, grey and white matter burst from under the elephant's foot. The prisoner's body slumped.

Two guards appeared and dragged the now lifeless body from the arena as two other guards hauled another prisoner to the slab and forced him to his knees. The whole process was then repeated seven times with remarkable efficiency.

The queen then announced that the execution of the five traitors was to proceed as planned. 'These men have betrayed the trust I placed in them and have betrayed you, the people of Gujarat. Their crime is greater for it. Proceed but'—and again, she pointed to the ranter—'save him till last.'

The first traitor was brought before *Bhari Pair* and at a signal from the queen, Sanjay gently tapped his goad three times on the elephant's head. It was the signal to the elephant to gently wrap the end his trunk around the neck of the prisoner who suddenly soiled himself. Sanjay moved backward to sit on the elephant's back and shoulder region before once again tapping the beast gently upon its head. Immediately, the elephant raised his head and began shaking it side to side and up and down. The prisoner's body was flung around in all directions with a great deal of violence until with a loud slurping sound and a spray of blood the body detached itself from its neck and head which were still held by the tightly curled trunk. The body flew through the air, spraying more blood and as it thumped to the ground the crowd cheered its appreciation. *Bhari Pair* released the head from his trunk and it fell to the ground. Guards once again removed the detritus and brought a new prisoner, similarly soiled to his predecessor, before *Bhari Pair*.

The same style of execution was repeated four times, the only difference being the amount of time it took to shake each prisoner's body from its head.

It was now the turn of the ranter. The guards brought him from the pen and instead of placing him before *Bhari Pair,* staked him out face down upon the ground. He was ranting again but there was no making any sense of what he was saying as having no tongue and a mouth issuing gobs of flesh and blood made his speech incomprehensible. Sanjay prompted *Bhari Pair* and he ambled up to the prostrate form before gently placing his great right foot upon the hips and lower spine of the prisoner who loudly screamed despite what was not in his mouth. Very gently and very slowly, *Bhari Pair* moved his foot back and forth upon the prisoner's lower back and buttocks as if massaging them but all the time slowly increasing the downward pressure. The ranter was truly screaming when a cracking sound announced the breaking of his spine and pelvis. Still, the elephant continued his massaging even as the screams became louder. Suddenly a grey and pink fleshy snake covered in feaces burst from the anus of the ranter as his bowels and their contents exited his body.

Bhari Pair slowly raised his foot from the partially crushed and eviscerated body and moved backward away from the prisoner.

A still rapidly rising and falling upper body, but no screaming, announced that the ranter was still alive.

'He will be dead by sunset,' said the queen as little Mularaj clapped his hands and cheered along with everyone else.

<h1 style="text-align:center">61</h1>

During the night and with only a sliver of crescent moon for light the remaining queen's forces; commanders, officers and troops moved silently up and through the lines to take their positions for the coming battle the next day. The executions had stirred blood lusts and given new courage to the warriors who all seemed keen to greet the dawn and everything it would bring.

Caspar and Raymond did not return to our tent. Hadar concluded they were with their assigned unit somewhere in the network of valleys and hill passes the army was using for camouflage and ambush. I wondered again what had been in the bags they had taken away with them.

'I truly wish you were to be with me and not by the queen's side,' said Hadar in the pre-dawn darkness. 'Not only will I not have your skills with blades, clamps and stitches but you will be missing out on valuable lessons in anatomy for it is often in war that the physician gets to actually see what he, or she, has only seen or heard of in texts.'

Ruth had been absent as well, presumably, with Narmala in her tent.

A cough from outside the tent announced a messenger who informed us I was expected at the queen's pavilion. I hastily grabbed my coat against the pre-dawn chill when Hadar suddenly clasped me to his chest in a hug, saying, 'Stay safe today, Ippolito.

Keep Ruth safe as well. Our story is not yet over.'

He released me and we said no more before I followed the messenger across the command compound to the queen's pavilion. As we entered the pavilion, attendants were putting the last touches to Ruth's make-up, watched closely by the queen. Except for a helmet, the queen was already fully armoured for the day ahead. Little Mularaj was by her side and attired in a miniature suit of armour.

'Bring those horns to a more defined point. Have them directed a bit more to the side rather than straight up,' ordered the queen as her attendants sought to bring the locks of Ruth's hair mixed with a blue clay into the desired shape.

Ruth looked even more the part of a fearsome blue demon once again. Under the queen's artistic direction, she now had two horns, a third eye in the middle of her forehead as well as a blue skull-like face with fangs that appeared to drip blood. Even when she smiled at me in greeting, she looked horribly sinister.

'Ippolito. Behind the screen is your costume. Please. Quickly change.'

I stepped behind the screen to find loose-fitting *payjamahs* and a *kurta* as a body covering. They were the same matching red in colour. I quickly changed and came out from behind the screen.

'To your seat there,' ordered the queen pointing to a low settee. 'Mindi. Nala. The red paint to face and arms. Same skull-like features and fangs but just a single red horn standing in the middle of his head. Quickly now, there is not much time.'

I sat down in the chair and the attendants went to work on my arms and facial complexion. The paint was the same colour and hue as my outfit. I looked across at Ruth seated in another chair and whose transformation was complete. She seemed intrigued by my own and smiled a sinister smile at me.

Half an hour later, as the western sky began to adopt a pinkish hue, the queen, holding Mularaj's little hand and followed by her blue and red demons, exited her pavilion. Narmala and her squad of bodyguards were waiting outside and escorted us to the royal elephant pens.

Ganesha awaited us and looked resplendent in his armour and ornamental draping. He bowed his head slightly and bent the knee in acknowledgement of the queen as she came up to him. He then did something unusual in that his trunk meandered its way to Ruth's hair and then mine. He was sniffing us and if an elephant can have a quizzical look, he certainly had one. He ceased his inspection of the two of us and then nodded his head twice as if to indicate his approval before lowering his trunk for Ravi to clamber up and take his position.

The royal *howdah* was already occupied by four warriors; two fully armoured long-pole spearmen and two archers who stood to attention. It was not until we were on board the *howdah* that I realised they were women from the bodyguard. The queen took up a position on a cushioned chair at the front of the *howdah* and placed little Mularaj on her lap. I had to hide my shock at the realisation that the queen intended to take her infant son into battle with her. I hoped that at least the strong iron mesh along the front of the *howdah* was strong enough to deflect any arrows or spears directed at the royal family.

The queen indicated some sacking at the rear of the *howdah* under which I found my two shields and a heavy box of blue glass throwing blades. The bodyguards placed the box in front of where Ruth stood directly behind the queen. I took up my position behind Ruth from where I could protect her with my shields. On each side of me stood the two long-pole spearwomen and behind me, the two archers protected our rear.

At a command from the queen, Ravi goaded *Ganesha* and he began his lumbering gait making his way past and through hundreds of other armoured and unarmoured elephants to take up position on a gently inclined hill running down to the river valley below. From there we had a view down the entire distance of the river valley.

Two miles away, under the gradual lightening of a dawn sky, the army of Muhammad of Ghor was making its final preparations.

62

Far in the distance, we could see that some skirmishing had begun, probably as soon as dawn's light had allowed. The queen's cavalry was striking the enemy line ad hoc in what were both sudden and deadly hit-and-run raids before retreating to the protection of the branching valleys, which were all heavily defended by archers and elephant corps. Closer to us in the middle of the enemy line was an elephant corps that by its size and colourful trappings must have been Muhammad's command centre. A larger elephant with a green awning over its *howdah* pinpointed his exact location. All down the enemy line infantry, archery, cavalry, chariot and elephant corps alternated in groups, suggesting that Muhammad had deployed his troops in a classic defensive ploy. The tactic would allow the rapid deployment of any specialist forces required to deflect the hit and run skirmishing our forces were orchestrating against the enemy's flanks. Despite this planning, it appeared that any deployed deflecting forces were only arriving just as our skirmishers were departing.

The largest deployment of any of Muhammad's forces in one place was the vanguard which consisted of over two hundred scythe wheeled chariots that carried a driver and two archers. It was clear Muhammad intended to use them as shock troops but their effectiveness was limited in the narrow river valley. On a broad plain, they would have been a lethal weapon against our infantry.

The vanguard was about a mile away from our position and slowly making its way towards us when two riders emerged from the lines at the front of our main force and cantered leisurely following a zig-zag path toward the enemy chariots.

'What is this?' demanded the queen. 'I gave no such orders for this. What on Earth are they doing? Who are they?'

It seemed the eyes of our army and those of the enemy were all on these two riders casually gambolling their horses in their zig-zag progress across the narrow river valley and along it.

Ruth, her eyes sharper than mine, turned and signed a 'C' and an 'R' to me. I put my forefinger to my lips in reply. I now had an idea of what was happening, especially as each of them had a saddlebag sitting against each of their horse's flanks. I could just see that the bags were spilling small items across the breadth of the plain. This was unseen by the enemy.

Caspar was fully attired in his Hospitaller armour, surcoat and carried a spear with a pennant of St John's white cross on a black background flying from it – a symbol unknown to either side in the coming conflict. Raymond was dressed only in a *dhoti* but had an enormous turban on his head that had multiple ostrich feathers sticking up from it and ribbons of many colours trailing from around its border. He looked truly comic and equally absurd in this prelude to the coming battle. Added to his attire, he kept appearing to try to provoke Caspar by standing in his stirrups and lowering the back of his *dhoti* to reveal his backside to the knight. Caspar would feign insult and wave his sword in mock attack while Raymond continued to jiggle and wiggle his backside at him as they cavorted around the plain. All this time, the bags were slowly spilling their contents upon the plain.

A silence grew from both sides and the vanguard ground to halt as everyone on the plain and hills surrounding it watched this unheard-of display upon the field of an upcoming battle.

Raymond continued his clowning as the pair slowly moved

closer and closer to the enemy line. He rode across their front, waving and blowing kisses while an inept-appearing Caspar clumsily chased after him, waving his sword and calling out colourful insults. It was their swordfight over again.

'What in Shiva's dhoti are they doing?' asked the queen.

'I believe they are setting a clever trap, Majesty,' I replied. 'Do you see the contents of their saddlebags slowly spilling across the plain?'

The queen turned back to look again. 'Now you mention it. Yes.'

'They are four sharply pointed pieces of iron arranged in such a way that wherever they land on the ground it will rest on three spikes and one spike will always point upwards. Some call them caltrops, the ancient Romans called them *murex ferreus* which means "jagged iron thing".'

'What of it?' she said.

'I think you may shortly find out,' I replied.

It was at this point I noticed a trail of white rocks unobtrusively dotting the plain from where the two were performing their antics back to our lines.

Caspar and Raymond were now within fifty paces of the chariots. Raymond was still blowing kisses and waving and some of the enemy troops were waving and blowing kisses back to him. Many appeared to be laughing at this unexpected entertainment.

On a signal from Caspar, the two reached under some sacking that had been placed across the horn of their saddles and retrieved what was under it. As one, they then threw them high in the sky to land on a chariot larger and more ornamented than the rest before turning their horses and galloping as fast as they could back along the irregular line of white rocks dotting the plain.

The two dead piglets ignited an indignant and righteous furore amongst the chariot corps for the insult to their commander. The line of chariots broke and took off in pursuit of the two infidels who had perpetrated the outrage against their commander, themselves, the Prophet and Allah. By the time they got up to speed, Caspar and Raymond were well ahead when they unexpectedly halted their horses by the last white stone and turned to watch the oncoming spectacle unfold.

'I don't understand,' said the queen.

Just as she said this, the first of the chariots reached the 'seeded' part of the plain. Horses screamed in pain and terror as the 'jagged iron things' pierced their galloping hooves. They went down in droves overturning chariots and spilling their crews amidst the chaos. Those chariots coming from behind were unable to stop in time and the horses either had their hooves pierced or careered into other upturned chariots with fatal results. It was a noisy, bloody and chaotic riot of death and pain.

The queen was laughing and cheering in delight. The little prince upon her lap was doing likewise. Ruth turned and smiled at me as if to say, 'What a pair they are.'

Caspar and Raymond sat on their horses less than fifty paces in front of the melee, watching it unfold. Caspar raised his pennant and waved it as a signal to cavalry units further up our lines and to warriors waiting behind rocks along the edge of the plain. Immediately, there was a resurgence of skirmishing up and down the enemy line and squads of deadly *urumi* whirling warriors ran into the chaos of dying men and horses waving their deadly razor-sharp ribbons of steel with lethal efficiency.

It only took another fifteen minutes before the best part of Muhammed's vanguard lay dead and slaughtered.

63

The defeated and slain vanguard not only represented a setback in the battle to Muhammed but they also served to pen his army in the valley by blocking his advance as did the remaining 'jagged iron things' still seeded on the edges of the plain although most were by now lodged in the hooves of hundreds of dead and pathetically dying horses. Caspar and Raymond's feat had also served to cheer the queen's army and give them more heart and courage for the next stage of the engagement.

From our position at the command post overlooking the valley, we could see squad after squad of the queen's flying cavalry and archers tormenting the enemy who were now crammed into the narrow valley with little room to manoeuvre or turnabout. Ghor's army put up a stout defence that continued all morning but their numbers and will to fight were gradually being whittled away.

Twice Muhammed mustered his cavalry for a charge to go around the vanguard's carnage and into our defensive line and reserves. Twice teams of *chakram* bearing warriors bravely stood their ground in the face of the charge and launched wave after wave of spinning razor-edged discs at the legs of the oncoming horses. The results were just as effective as the 'jagged iron things' as the deadly discs severed the soft tissues of the horses' legs sending their riders spinning and tumbling to the ground where they were finished off by more discs, archers or the lethal ribbons of the *urumi* bearing warriors gathered along the periphery of the charge.

At some stage in the early afternoon, a messenger arrived from down the line and told the queen that Muhammed was mustering his elephants for a charge. I could see the green awning of Muhammed's *howdah* well back down the valley. A long line of elephants was gradually making their way along the flanks of his forces to the front of his lines. This manoeuvre not only hastened the movement of his elephants to the front but also served to maintain a defensive shield for his column. This frustrated our skirmishers and took a larger toll in casualties.

Throughout the morning, except for receiving messages from down the line and sending back orders, our command post had been inactive. Within myself, I was glad of this and I suspect Ruth was as well. We both wanted to be healers, not warriors, and our current positions were at loggerheads with our hopes and dreams. I was quietly hoping that the battle would unfold with our victory as its finale and that we would not have to move from our vantage point above the river plain to play a part in it. As yet, the queen had kept her elephants in reserve behind us and they had played no part in the battle so far due to the limitations of space in the narrow valley. Her army of elephants was arrayed behind and below us beneath the ridgeline and as yet unseen by the enemy although Muhammad would have known they were around from the reports of spies and observers.

'This is good,' said the queen, addressing Ruth and myself. 'Muhammad is mustering his elephants to the front of his column. We may have the opportunity to divide his forces here.'

She turned from us and spoke down to a horsed messenger below us. 'Tell the engineers to wait for the red pennant as my signal. The commanders on the ground will know what to do after that.'

With that, the messenger saluted, turned his horse and sped

away, his place taken by another equally ready to speed the queen's orders to her commanders.

It was another hour before the bulk of Muhammad's elephants were mustered at the front of the column, the remnant acting in defence of the column behind. The green awning of Muhammad's command elephant was much closer now and we could make out the figures in the *howdah* although it was too far to make out any facial features.

'Come closer, Muhammad, come closer,' said the queen, whispering to herself.

As if in response to the queen's wishes, the green awning started moving through the amassed army of elephants.

'Good. Good. Good,' commented the queen, her excitement becoming more palpable. 'Raise the red pennant.'

Halfway down the valley it narrowed and, on both sides where the hills were higher and steeper along its edge, the engineers went to work smashing the barricades that held back the tons of rocks that had been gathered, carried, rolled and carted to their location in the weeks before. Dead trees and shrubs had been put into position to disguise their location and purpose from the enemy.

The timing was near to perfect as an avalanche of rocks poured down both sides of the valley at once in a slowly growing thunder of noise, dust and screams from the soldiers, horses and elephants below unable to get out of the avalanche's way. As the dust settled, we could see that the avalanche had taken a reasonable toll in dead and dying men and animals. The noise of it had also panicked some of the elephants at the front and we could see desperate handlers trying to bring their beasts under control. The most important outcome was that it had essentially divided Muhammad's forces separating his elephant corps from the bulk of his infantry and cavalry.

The queen was correct when she had said her commanders

would know what to do in the wake of the avalanche. In the distance and through the dust, we saw the slaughter of the centre and rear guard of the column begin. Archers and spearmen rained arrows, javelins and spears down on the enemy from their protected positions above the hapless invaders. Cavalry units mounted charges into their panicked ranks slicing and cutting their way through them in a bloody swathe. Other specialist units attacked the elephants that had been left behind. Their principal tactic was the use of the heavy cutting hammer to smash and shatter the tusks of the elephants sending them into a mad rampage of pain and panic that took its toll in any soldier, friend or foe, who got in their way.

All this while Muhammad and his commanders were trying to bring order to his elephant corps in readiness for a charge. It would no longer be an offensive charge but one which would need to break through and break away in a humiliating retreat for Muhammad and his remaining army.

The queen was chuckling to herself in delight and pointing out various features of the battle to young Mularaj, still seated upon her lap. He too was laughing and clapping at the mayhem below.

It was now mid-afternoon. I recalled the queen's briefing about my shields and making use of the late afternoon sun. I began to feel a twitch of anxiety as I sensed our part in the battle growing closer.

64

'Oh, now my little prince, the fun will really begin.' The queen laughed to her son who giggled in an excited response and looked expectantly around him for some of the fun.

Below us, Muhammed's handlers had brought most of their charges back under control and were forming the elephants up again in an offensive arrowhead formation. The *howdah* with the green awning was even closer now and we could see the turbaned figure of Muhammed gesticulating wildly and shouting commands.

On the other side of the valley, I could see puffs and trails of smoke starting to appear from behind the ridgeline overlooking the army. I wondered what new trick the queen was preparing.

'Bring the blue pennant to me,' ordered the queen.

A young horseman carrying a spear with a pale blue pennant attached to its point rode up and passed it to the queen.

'Now, my darling,' said the queen, placing the butt of the spear into her son's hands on her lap, 'we will give the signal for dinner!'

I was perplexed by what on Earth she meant by 'dinner' as the two of them, the queen assisting her little son, raised the pennant high and waved it about.

Muhammad's elephants were nearly all in position below us and officers and handlers were looking to the green awning for the command to commence the charge when loud and panicked squealing took away their attention.

On the other side of the valley, hundreds of pigs with flaming bundles of kindling tied to their backs were charging wildly and without order down the slopes and into the amassed elephants of the Moslem army.

'Look, my darling. See how the fire and smoke spook the elephants and makes them run about,' said the queen to her son.

Mularaj was laughing and enjoying the spectacle he had been brought along to witness. He was clapping his hands and yelling, 'Yah, yah, yah,' with an enthusiasm that seemed out of place in one so young.

'And see, my darling, how the silly soldiers are hesitating to go near and kill the pigs. They fear they will be contaminated and not allowed into heaven should they die this day. Which they will,' she added confidently.

Below us, all was total chaos again. Although quite a few were now dead or dying of their burns, the flaming pigs were now everywhere amongst the elephants. The great beasts charged about in panic. Some careered into other elephants in great thudding collisions that knocked *howdahs,* their crews and *mahouts* to the ground where they were soon trampled by other rampaging beasts. Other elephants fought each other to get out of the way of the fiery little pigs. Muhammad's elephant was obviously highly trained and desensitised to the presence of fire. Even so, we could see that it was skittish with the panic going on all around it as its *mahout* was clearly struggling to keep it under control.

The sun was getting lower in the sky as the afternoon progressed. Most of the pigs were dead and burned and occasional small spot fires burned amongst the chaos of Muhammad's elephant corps.

'Ruth. Get your knives ready. Ippolito. Get your shields ready,' said the queen quietly to both of us and then more loudly, 'Bring the royal pennant.'

I sensed rather than saw Ruth's reaction. I think it was much the same as mine. Cold fear in my stomach, shaking and sweating hands, a dry mouth and a strong urge to use my bowels.

The queen raised the royal pennant and gave the order to the massed elephants standing behind us on the hill in a great voice that defied her sex. 'Move out!'

As one the great grey mass of elephants slowly crested the hill and started to move downhill the queen leading the way. Halfway down the hill, her massive voice gave the command to charge.

Mularaj still sat on the queen's lap where she held him still with one hand against the chaotic motion of the *howdah* bouncing around on the elephant's back. In her other hand she held a javelin. Ruth had gathered her knives in their box beside her and one in each hand ready to throw. I stood behind her, a shield raised in each hand just above and behind her shoulders ready to fend off any projectiles or other weapons.

'Ippolito,' called the queen, 'see your reflections ahead. Point the large one at Muhammad's beast and those in the *howdah*.'

I did so and watched the brilliant white central reflection of my shield-mirror settle on the *howdah*. Immediately, hands went up to shade and cover eyes. Other smaller reflections from the facets scintillated and flashed all around it having a similar effect on other *howdahs* and their crews. It was going to be difficult defending Ruth and pointing the beam at the same time.

As we drew closer to the enemy, Ruth began throwing her knives. As predicted by the queen, her fearsome appearance and the magical effect the thrown knives had of looking as though they were bolts of lightning and blue fire threw the enemy into more chaos. I noticed that Ruth's knives were not killing throws rather ones that she aimed to maim, injure and incapacitate the enemy. They pierced legs, arms, hands, feet, shoulders and any other exposed part that was not fatal. Wounded enemy soldiers are more of a hindrance to the foe on the battlefield than dead ones as they get in the way of their comrades, reaching out and calling for assistance.

I was glad. To me, it meant Ruth did not have the heart to kill.

The queen was urging Ravi to guide *Ganesha* through the melee to where Muhammad's mounted bodyguards were mustering themselves around his elephant. Around me, the two archers were firing their arrows almost at point-blank range at any elephant and its squad foolish enough to challenge the queen's elephant and her crew. The two long-pole spear-women were keeping up a steady up and down motion as they stabbed down at infantry trying to get beneath *Ganesha's* great girth and slit his soft belly open or slice at his testicles.

I somehow kept my shield work up: deflecting arrows, javelins and spears thrown at Ruth and trying to blind and dazzle enemy elephant handlers and their crews. Little Mularaj was screaming, whether in a precocious battle joy or abject terror I could not tell. I was too busy keeping Ruth and myself alive. Arrows and spears flew all around us and I heard the fleshy thunk of one hitting one of the warriors behind me. I did not have time to turn and see which of our crew was down.

The queen got up from her seat and the protection of the iron mesh screen in front of her, pushing Mularaj down to the floor of the *howdah* and grabbing a javelin from the bracket beside her. She started screaming insults at Muhammad whose elephant was now only yards away from us.

'Beaten by a woman, a child and a bunch of squealing pigs. You piece of catamite's dung. Your balls are like chickpeas and your dick is a peanut. You little, little, little man.'

Muhammad must have heard her clearly as he turned to look directly at her just as she launched her javelin. He ducked just in time but not before the javelin had taken his turban off and pierced the man behind him. It was enough for Muhammad.

He jumped from the other side of his *howdah* utilising the protection of his elephant. He must have been gathered up by one of his bodyguard as the next thing we saw was him clinging to the back of a rider and attempting to flee the field closely followed by his other guards.

The queen's opportunity for a personal defeat of Muhammad was gone but the queen's battle rage still boiled and she took the battle to the next elephant coming near us.

Gradually, the realisation that Mohammed had left the field must have filtered through the ranks of the enemy as their soldiers started to throw down their weapons and lie down on the ground in surrender and supplication not to be slaughtered. Some fools chose honour over ignominy and elected to fight on to the bitter end.

Even so, soldiers all around us were raising a great cheer of victory and I was just about to put down my shields and give Ruth a great hug of joy when *Ganesha* stumbled and went down on one knee. It was enough to send me tumbling over the side of the *howdah* and onto the great sweeping tusk-sword *Ganesha* was waving about as he struggled to raise himself on to four legs again. I felt the great sword rip into the flesh of my neck and shoulder and then proceed diagonally down across my chest and abdomen before tearing open the muscles of my leg from groin to foot.

I knew no more.

65

Dreams are funny things. They are an unreal reality. The problem is recognising the reality in the unreality but that is hard when you have become an unreality in a reality. For that is what I was, a dreaming, drifting denizen of a netherworld somewhere between an existence that was only a half existence and one of frightful pain and a non-existence in which neither I, nor pain, existed. It probably does not make much sense to anyone who has never experienced this but there were times when I felt I had crossed a barrier into another existence. I liked it there. No pain – physical, mental, spiritual or emotional – can trouble you there. It feels nice, secure and warm. You don't seem to remember the pain in that other place either.

But it is pain that calls you away from this other place. It comes ripping back into you unexpectedly like the thief in the night. Gone is that sense of peaceful surrender, that feeling of floating and of at last being at one with all that is. Was it a reality or an unreality? I don't know, but instead, reality becomes all that you wish it would not be.

I have glimpses of memories from that time. I'm glad they are only fleeting. For there were times when I thought I must be in the pits of hell. I thought at one stage that little red imps and demons were pinching me with red hot pincers and pulling pieces of my seared flesh from my body and tossing them to strange beasts that scuttled hungrily about their feet. At other times I was hot.

So hot I could feel the flames consuming me despite the rivers of perspiration I could feel running all over me. And, of course, there was the never-ending thirst. Thirst can drive you mad in a different way to pain. I wanted to bite my tongue and make it bleed just for the sensation of having fluid in my mouth and then slowly swallowing it and savouring the feeling of it going down my gullet. This was my madness. This was my pain.

There were moments of respite. Moments when the fires were quenched. Moments when slow drops of cool water found their way into my mouth and body or I became aware of my body being gently bathed in it. There were other times when I knew my body was wracked with tremors and rigors but I seemed to be held and soothed in the arms of a mother I never knew. She smelled of lavender. At other times, I knew by the bitter taste of the poppy in my mouth that the pain would ease and I could drift away again.

Gradually, hell cooled and the pain became a little less and my dreaming took on a fragmented aspect that mixed the reality of the here and now with the unreality of what might have passed, what could be now and what might someday be. Memories and people from the past came back to me along with their voices. These voices mixed with voices from a present I had not yet returned to. They were all disconnected, coming from different times and places as they did, and they were all tossed together like the ingredients of a salad. Dream voices tell you things like where we are at times, what is worrying us, what our demons are, where we are going, who we are loving, who is loving us, what is hurting us.

Some of these voices and their conversations seemed to be real and going on around me. Most of them were not real but they did seem to have a message underlying them. Rudolphus and Godfrey argued with Benedict about lies, fantasy and indoctrination. Ruth listened intently to Maria's tales of my childhood misadventures and the best way to win my heart. My father and Usamah debated whether we could believe Herodotus or not. Saladin and the Sufi, Abubakar, were reproaching Mohammed Sabah, Kali kept apologising for something. Hadar's voice kept asking me questions. Caspar announcing that Baldwin had died. Ruth whispering to me and sounding very tired.

Then there was a real voice, not disconnected from my reality but a part of it.

'Ippolito. Can you hear me?'

It was Hadar's voice.

'Can you open your eyes?' he asked gently.

I wanted to but my eyelids were too heavy. I wanted to make a sound, a noise to say I am in here but my tongue was stuck to the top of my mouth and my lips to each other.

I drifted off.

I came back again sometime later. Someone was holding me close. They smelled of lavender. I liked it. Then I flew away.

Then there was light. Very bright light. It hurt my eyes. So, I closed them again.

The light did not hurt the next time I saw it. It was a soft evening light diffused with the pinks and purples of a setting sun. I liked it.

'Ah, Ippolito. So very good to see you,' came Hadar's voice.

I moved my eyes to look around. Where was I?

Hadar must have understood the movement of my eyes. 'You are in the *Dhanvantari Maristan* back in Anhilwara Patan.'

A flickering memory of the tusk sword ripping me open rushed in on me startling me for a second. It brought on a reflexive jerk that caused whatever was in or on my chest to feel like it was being torn.

'Do not try to move, Ippolito.' Hadar's voice was firm this

time. 'You should be dead. Indeed, you have looked it at times over the last couple of weeks. You are very lucky to be alive. But you must stay still right now. At least until we have you a little more healed. Do you understand me?'

I blinked my affirmation.

I wanted to say something but all that came out was, 'Oooth?'

'She is sleeping right now, Ippolito. I gave her a sleeping draught. I had to. She has barely slept since the battle and has been constantly by your side day and night for all that time.'

Reality was, at last, getting better.

'Know this, Ippolito,' continued Hadar. 'That girl loves you greatly. She saved your life at Gadaraghata. Someone else can tell you that story. She was by your side the entire time we travelled back from there in the queen's *howdah* when your life hung by the most-slender of threads. She has attended to all the changes of dressings on your wound, for it is indeed just one long great big scar. She has dripped water into your mouth tickling your unconscious chin to make you swallow each drop. She did the same with the poppy milk and the feverfew and valerian tisanes we made to keep you comfortable. She bathed you for hours on end when you were burning up with fever. She held you closely and securely when your rigors and tremors threatened to burst your wound all over again. And know this too, Ippolito. It was Ruth, not Kali, who washed and cleaned you each time you soiled or wet yourself.

'If I had not made her take the sleeping draught, and believe me it was a strong brew, she would have stayed on here without further sleep or rest until she dropped. It is amazing how love can fuel the greatest acts of courage and determination.'

This news was healing and I closed my eyes again.

66

Raymond was sitting by my bed the next time my eyes opened. His hand automatically went to cover mine in a gesture of comradeship, concern and care.

He smiled at me. I think my mouth moved in a similar way back to him as his smiled broadened when I did.

'By God,' he said, 'and all the crazy gods of Hind as well. You have given us a scare, Ippolito. It is good to see you awake.'

'Ehya,' I managed.

'Was that a yeah?'

'Ehya.'

He laughed at this. This made me laugh which made the scar along my abdomen feel like it was being torn. I grimaced in pain.

'Don't laugh and I won't either,' he said.

'Howwww... heya?' I asked.

'How did you get here?' he checked.

'Ehya.'

'After our little stunt with the chariots, Caspar and I made it up the hill and found ourselves rides for the elephant charge. We were right behind you when we saw the queen's elephant stumble and go down on one knee. Do you remember flying through the air?'

'Ehya.'

'Well, it looked impressive for a second, that is until you encountered *Ganesha's* tusk-sword. That is some scar, Ippolito. No one will believe you survived such a slash when they see it. You hit the ground like a limp rag doll and lay there on your back not moving. Your blood was moving though. In great pulsing red spurts that matched the paint you were covered in.

'Two enemy polemen were about to finish you off when I saw Ruth hurl two of her blue knives in quick succession at them. One dropped straight away with a knife in his eye. The other staggered a short distance away before falling. Ruth's knife was in his neck.

'I was trying to clamber down the side of the *howdah* I was in to get to you. Ruth jumped over the edge of hers and landed right next to you. She was trying to wash some of the blood and red paint away to see the extent of your wounds when I came running up to help. Ipp, I have never seen so much blood come from one person. Godfrey did not bleed as much as you.

'Ruth pointed to one of the fires still burning nearby on the plain after the queen's little pig ploy and...' Here, Raymond stopped and looked directly at me. 'Then she snapped at me. "Raymond. Red hot embers. Quickly."'

Raymond was looking directly at me to gauge my reaction. In my fuddled state it took me a moment or two to digest the import of what he had just said.

Ruth had spoken.

I had not dreamed her voice before.

I nodded my head as vigorously as I could to indicate go on.

'It was odd, Ipp. I did not realise that she had spoken because of my concern for you and an immediate desire to do something to help.

'I gathered up a helmet lying on the ground and raced to a

nearby fire to scoop as many embers into the helmet as I could and raced back to her side. She still had those protective gloves on her hand the queen had given her before the battle. She deftly picked up a glowing ember and laid it on the worst of your bleeds before picking out another and doing the same. She did this down the length of your wound. Each ember sizzled and popped on your skin and made a foul-smelling smoke. I had to hold you down as each ember's touch made you jerk like a lunatic even though you were unconscious. Eventually, the worst of the bleeding settled under the cautery of the embers and we both breathed a sigh of relief.

'The queen had brought her elephant up to stand guard over us while the last pockets of fighting were still going on about us. She handed down some water canteens from the *howdah*, which we poured over your wound to cleanse it and over the burns to cool them down. The queen set her guards to make a stretcher from one of the royal pennants on the side of the *howdah* and their long-pole spears. It worked well as we were then able to hurry and carry you through the fighting to behind our lines with *Ganesha* leading the way. Ruth had not spoken since telling me to get the embers and I had not yet realised she had. *Ganesha* showed the way to the field hospital where we found Hadar and some of his colleagues from the *Dhanvantari Maristan*.'

Just then Hadar's voice broke into Raymond's story. I had not seen him enter the room.

'Ruth would not let anyone except me near you. When one of my colleagues suggested butter upon the burns, she turned and snapped at him, "Ice water, you fool. Get some! Now!"' Hadar chuckled to himself remembering the incident. 'The funny thing was she said it with such authority that he ran from the room and got some! You know, what is even more peculiar is that even at this stage Ruth had not realised she had spoken. She was totally focused on you, Ippolito. In that time, you were the entire centre of her universe so great was her will to protect and save you. You were, and still are, all that matters to her. I remember saying to you that you would be an important part of Ruth's healing. I just did not expect it would be so hard on you.

'It is as I told you a day ago. Ruth has barely left your side. She has denied herself sleep, barely eaten for worry over you and delivered every bit of care you have needed herself.' And here, he chuckled to himself again. 'If I did not know better, I would say she is madly in love with you. Only you and forever you. I can see your eyelids drooping, Ippolito. Perhaps it is time Raymond and I let you rest again.'

I could feel them getting heavier as well. But, oh, what sweet dreams they augured.

Something was different when I next awoke. There was that smell of lavender again and I turned my head toward it. It was Ruth's hair. She was asleep beside me. I breathed her in for several minutes and then must have fallen back into the restoration of a healing sleep.

67

There was much for me to digest in the next few weeks as I made the long journey back to health and vitality. The first, and most important to us all, was the news that Baldwin had died of his disease, putting an end to our mission to find a cure for his leprosy. Caspar had first heard it in the market of Anhilwara Patan and traced the source back to a Persian caravan. The news was verified a week later with the arrival of another caravan from the west. This put our speculation as to the truth of the news to rest. It meant that our little troupe could return to Jerusalem with our mission incomplete. After all we had been through, collectively and individually, the idea of going home should have been a comforting thought. For some reason, it left me feeling hollow. I put the feeling down to my poor health.

The biggest change was in my relationship with Ruth. Not only was she my personal nurse, physician and closest friend; it was not to be very long before she became my lover and soul partner. After that night when I awoke and found her beside me, her hair scented with lavender, she curled up beside me whenever I slept.

Before all that happened, we had a bridge to cross. It was named Narmala.

'My feelings for you were confused, Ipp,' she told me. 'What Benedict had done closed a door inside me. Narmala was soft, kind and gentle with me. She sensed the damage to my being and gently massaged my soul and spirit so that the closed door to my heart began to open, but just a fraction. She taught me about the secret things being a woman can mean. She taught me about my body and what and how to give it pleasure. I liked it. Actually, I liked that part a lot. It, too, confused my feelings and I wondered which of you I had the strongest feelings for. They were different feelings. To Narmala, I felt a great gratitude and a craving for what we could do with each other. My physical being loved that part. But I was beginning to realise that there had to be much more in a relationship for it to be one blessed by happiness and completeness. For you, my feelings were pure and from the heart but the chain placed around it by Benedict's act had locked them away. It was only when I saw your body slashed wide open and I thought I might lose you that the chain snapped and the door to my heart burst wide open. In my heart, I knew I could never love another in the way I love you. It was what brought me back to you. It was what returned my voice to me.'

In turn, I told Ruth of my confusion during this time and how it had made me reckless for my safety. I told her of Hadar's support and guidance through this time and of the intense pain I had felt. Ruth cried over the hurt she had caused me and begged my forgiveness. I told her there was no need for that as had our paths been different, we may not have arrived at the same destination together.

We had each other and we shared the dream of a free hospital.

I was still bed-bound and had not taken any steps from the bed a few nights later as Ruth curled up beside me. She had a parcel with her. She said it was a present from Narmala to both of us and that we were to open it together. Inside was an illustrated book of great beauty and artistry. It was called the *Kama Sutra*.

But that is another story.

Shawline Publishing Group Pty Ltd
www.shawlinepublishing.com.au

SHAWLINE
PUBLISHING
GROUP

More great Shawline titles can be found by scanning the QR code below.
New titles also available through Books@Home Pty Ltd.
Subscribe today at www.booksathome.com.au or scan the QR code below.